ANDREW MALES

Copyright © 2024 by Andrew Males

The right of Andrew Males to be identified as the author of this work has been asserted by him in accordance with the Copyright, Designs and Patents Act 1988.

All rights reserved.

No part of this book may be reproduced or distributed in any form without prior permission in writing from the author, with the exception of non-commercial uses permitted by copyright law.

First edition

Cover design by Claire Yeo

ISBN 979-8-8794-1246-8

www.andrewmales.com

For every England fan
who has suffered the agony
of an international tournament exit

In memory

Pete Haine
Terry Venables

Contents

You're the Daddy 1
Ice Ice Baby 12
Team Talk 25
Completed It, Mate 35
Unbelievable, Jeff 44
Placenta Circle 55
Back to the Past 64
Ceefax Page 302 68
Do You Want Fries With That? 76
The Dentist Chair 86
Mystic Alex 108
Dutch Courage 121
Alex the Arse 130
The Big Reveal 137
The F-Word 143
The Split 153
Transfer Rumours 164
Luck of the Draw 174
Go Go Go! 185
Wembley Way 195
Déjà Vu 210
End of the Dream Team 215
Lineker's Near Miss 223
Fight or Flight 234
Peter Imperfect 239
Date With a Dead Woman 247
Final Countdown 256
I'll Be Back 264
Sit Down, Shut Up 274
Hospital Pass 291
Getting Stuck In 304
Painful Challenge 314
Game Over 322
Coming Home 327

"Why didn't you just belt it?"
 – Barbara Southgate

You're the Daddy

Monday, 18th July 2016

"I'm pregnant, it's yours, I'm keeping it. Discuss."

Helen dumped her house keys onto the table by the front door and waited for a response from her boyfriend.

Sitting on the floor in the middle of their living room facing a huge TV with a PlayStation controller in his hands, Alex whipped his head round and glared at her. "Pregnant?"

"Yes, pregnant. As in expecting … with child … up the duff … one in the oven."

"But … but … you can't be!" Alex's voice rose two octaves higher.

"I'm pretty sure I can be, and I'm absolutely sure I am." Helen threw a handful of plastic sticks at him. They clattered as they hit the wooden floor. Without pausing the football game he was playing, Alex put down his controller, picked up a stick and studied it. The pregnancy test showed two pink vertical lines in a little window.

"That's not possible! We're always careful."

"Let's just say our safety record has lost one or two stars. I'm not sure precisely when, Alex, but I'm guessing it was on our anniversary, when we went out for tapas. We finished the best part of two bottles of wine and all I can remember of the magical event was waking you up when you fell asleep on me."

With Alex not controlling his team, the opposition scored, causing the TV's speakers to burst into life with the commentator shouting, "Unbelievable!"

Alex dropped the stick and gazed at the screen.

"So," Helen said, "are you going to say anything else?"

Alex turned back towards her. "But ... how? How can we have a baby, Hells?"

She flopped down into a beige armchair and picked up the nearest magazine from a table next to her. "I'm no expert, but I know it involves a great deal of pain for me and not much work for you. Which you've already had plenty of practice doing."

"I meant ... us. You. Me. I'm not ready to have a baby, nowhere near."

"Oh, for goodness' sake, Alex! Not ready?" Helen threw the magazine at him. "Not ready? You're thirty-eight years old. How much longer do you want? Shall I waste another five years of my life with you? Should I come back in another decade?"

He looked down at the floor.

"Well, you're going to have to be ready, because in about seven months' time you're going to be a dad."

"Seven? How the hell can it be seven? I know biology class was a long time ago, but I do remember that pregnancies last nine months."

Helen picked off a few pieces of fluff from her grey skirt. "Yes, but I'm already two months gone."

"Two? How come? Doesn't that mean you've missed two … you know …"

"Periods," Helen replied, with less volume. "You can say the word, Alex. It won't hurt you. And yes, I've missed two. It's just that I didn't realise last month and so put it down as one of those times it doesn't come."

Alex opened his mouth to respond but realised his knowledge of such female matters was unlikely to bring anything constructive to the conversation. Unfortunately, his expression must have portrayed a very judgemental look.

"It can happen, OK? I'm not a Yellowstone geyser – I've been known to miss a month in my life. This is the first time I've missed two, so I thought something might have happened. I was clearly right, and here we are."

Alex tossed the magazine on the sofa. "You found out today?"

"No, it was last night. I waited for you to fall asleep after watching *Escape to Victory* for the umpteenth time and then I did the tests."

"Last night?" Alex shot up from the floor. "You found out we're going to have a baby last night and you didn't think it was important enough to wake me up and tell me that my whole life was about to be ruined?"

"Ruined?" Helen jumped up and put her face within a few inches of Alex's. She was about three inches shorter than him, but pushed up onto her toes to be nearer his level. "Is that what you think? Is that how you'd describe becoming a dad?"

Alex backed away, accidentally treading on the controller before scooping it up.

"No, not ruined ... I mean ... well, that my life was going to change for the—"

"Worse?"

"Not worse exactly." Alex fiddled awkwardly with the buttons on the handset and the game behind continued. "It's just that it wouldn't be a good thing for me at this time."

Helen knocked it out of his hands. "But it's a good thing for me, is it? I know I've said I've always wanted kids, but now I'm wondering do I really want one with a jerk who has all the maturity of a three-year-old chimp?"

"Come on, Hells, that's a bit harsh. I have no idea how to be a dad, that's all."

"Tell you what, I'll carry, grow, and give birth to our bastard child and leave you to play your pathetic little games on that penis extension of a screen!"

As Helen stomped upstairs, Alex could hear the game's crowd softly chant in the background, but it wasn't enough to drown out the sobbing. He was preparing himself to go up and attempt to repair a situation that he had zero clue how to deal with, when his phone rang. A photo of a face with a big cheesy grin appeared on the screen and he reluctantly answered the call from his colleague, Miles.

"Alexander the Great – how're you doing, buddy?"

"Now's not really a good time, Miles. Can I—"

"I just need to know you're ready for tomorrow."

Alex's mind was currently drained of anything else other than babies, so he remained silent.

"You're worrying me, Alex. Our biggest sales pitch of the year is at ten tomorrow morning, so I was kinda hoping you'd all be prepped by now and that we could go over our spiel on the phone."

Alex rushed over to his work bag and pulled out some handwritten notes on A4 paper. He was meant to be the technical expert for ZenNoise, a small company that produced software for the entertainment industry, and the one who could dazzle prospective buyers with the technical benefits of such an amazing system. Alex had demoted the notes to second place behind his desire to get England into the quarter-finals.

"Er, well, I've still got a few things to commit to memory. Sony's a large company, you know, lots to learn."

"I'm sure they are, but we're actually meeting NBC."

Alex looked down at the NBC logo and grimaced. "NBC, yes, that's what I meant, sorry. Got a lot on my mind right now."

"You better get yourself together, Alex. We need to continue our top form. Me and you – the Dream Team – top salespeople of the year. I can almost taste the awards dinner now."

"I'll be on it, don't worry."

"Good man. Let's meet at eight, Starbucks King's Cross. We'll rehearse it then. All good?"

"Yeah, I'll be there, ready for action."

"Great! I know you won't let me down, Alex. You're the daddy!"

Alex switched off the PlayStation and strained his ears to listen for any more crying from upstairs. Everything was quiet, but he hesitated on the bottom step of the stairs. What was he going up to tell her? What could he possibly say right now that would smooth things over? Deciding it was best he left her alone for a while to calm down, he grabbed his keys and headed out. On the way to his car, he sent a text to his best friend, Pravi, that he was coming round and needed help. When he arrived at Pravi's flat, he soon realised help might be in short supply.

"You're totally screwed."

Pravi pushed himself into the kitchen, the wheelchair just narrow enough to fit through the door. Alex slumped onto the sofa and looked around the flat. He couldn't begin to count how many hours they'd spent over the years in this place, playing games, discussing football and talking crap. They'd originally moved in together at the start of university, and while Alex moved out afterwards, Pravi had never left.

"Beer?" Pravi shouted back to Alex.

"No, I better not," Alex replied, head in his hands. "I'm driving and after tonight's news, if I start, I might not stop."

Pravi returned to the living room with a can of Foster's

in one hand and throwing a Diet Coke with the other. It landed on Alex's lap. "Drown your sorrows in sweetener, then." He manoeuvred himself out of his wheelchair and onto a black gaming chair. "Sorry – did you say tonight's news?"

Alex grabbed the can and opened it, white froth spilling over the sides and onto his legs. "Great. Yeah, tonight."

"But it's only eight o'clock now. You mean to say she's just told you this momentous news, and you've run out and come here?"

"You didn't see the state she was in. When she's that upset, I know from experience there's no point in reasoning with her."

"I'm sorry, but you're screwed. Royally."

"Because I've come here?"

"Because you ran away from your pregnant, emotional girlfriend, because you have no idea how to handle responsibility and because you'll be so up to your eyes in nappies that you won't have time to play games and I'll forever wipe the floor with you on *FIFA*."

Although Pravi always denied it, Alex was sure Pravi had kept their head-to-head record on their computer football game rivalry for the last twenty years. He took a big swig of his drink. "No, I'll have time to play it during paternity leave."

"You'll be too tired to play anything," Pravi said, turning on the PlayStation and starting *FIFA*. "Anyway, hopefully soon we'll have a new game to play. I backed a cool

Kickstarter project a while ago. Looks like a cracking retro Euro 96 game."

"So, you promised money to a random bunch of people in the hope they might somehow develop a new game years from now?"

"Hey, they've developed it and it's being released. I'm getting some cool stuff as their top backer."

Alex smirked. "How much did you pledge?"

"Er, let's just say I was a tad enthusiastic."

Alex's smile widened.

"What?" Pravi said. "A client had just paid me heaps of money to illustrate their range of books, so I went a tad wild." He turned back to the TV. "I don't have a pregnant girlfriend to answer to, though."

Alex fiddled with the ring pull on his can as Pravi set up their usual options for the match. "She called me an immature chimp."

"Ha," Pravi said. "I'd say you were more orangutan, though. With less charisma."

"What am I going to do, Prav? Can you see me as a dad? Looking after a baby, pushing a pram around the park? How will I teach him anything?"

Pravi selected to play as Barcelona. "Him? It could be a girl."

"A girl? What do I know about girls?"

"Based on my observations, not much." Pravi passed him a controller.

"I'm serious."

"So am I. You shouldn't be here talking to me, but if you are, then at least have the decency to get your arse whipped at *FIFA* while I listen to your whining."

"Whining? Don't you think I'm allowed to be annoyed at this? I didn't ask for Helen to get pregnant. I don't need the hassle of a baby at this stage of my life."

"Mate, we're nearly forty." He gestured to Alex to confirm his Real Madrid team.

"I mean my career, my friends, everything. You saw how Moobsy changed when he became a dad. We didn't see him out until his thirties."

Pravi took a sip from his beer. "Have you tried to look at it another way?"

"Like what?"

"It could be a good thing. Make a man of you. I doubt it – that would take a considerable amount of work – but have you thought that this might end up as the best thing that's ever happened to you?"

Alex looked at Pravi as if he'd suggested that David Beckham would make a good Mayor of London. "You're joking, right?"

"Why not? Maybe you should settle down, get some responsibility, finally move on to the next stage in your life."

"Says the man who's never been with a girl longer than a month."

"Hey, I'm fine, having fun looking for the right woman. You've been living with Helen for two years, so it's about time something happened. I thought she'd wear you down and get you to pop the question, but this way's even better."

Alex got up and looked out the window. "You don't think she planned this, do you? To trap me into it?"

"Nah, she's smarter than that. Of all the people to trap, judging by the speed you must have fled, you are most certainly the worst. It was an accident, but it's happened. Deal with it. Grow a pair."

"I can't lose out on our regular gaming sessions, though," Alex said. "You could come and live with us. We could sneak downstairs and have a few sessions while the baby sleeps."

Pravi winced. "Yeah, right. I'd have Helen bossing me about from day one and you'd get me changing all the stinky nappies. I'll pass, if you don't mind."

"So what do I do?"

Pravi laughed. "Kiss goodbye to the life you have now, but say hello to a glorious future of reeking bottoms, no sleep and plenty of crying … some of which might come from the baby." He pointed at the screen. "But first, we play."

They played in silence for a while, Alex barely registering a touch as Pravi took control of the game. One of his players went down injured to a dodgy tackle from Pravi which didn't even earn a booking.

"That was a red card all day," Alex said. To make matters worse, he messed up the free kick, giving it straight back to Pravi, who scored with a long-range shot.

"Woah! How do you like that beauty?" Pravi said.

Alex threw down his controller. "Bastard."

"When it's old enough, I'll teach your offspring how to play. They'll be beating you by the time they're out of nappies." Before Alex had time to reply, Pravi grabbed his phone as a message appeared on his screen. "Damn, I thought it was tomorrow." He gulped down some more beer. "Sorry loser, but I've got Jasmine coming round in ten minutes. You've gotta go. Looks like you get off with a 1-0. Sexy brunette stops play."

"Jasmine? You haven't mentioned her before. I've only just got here, can't you cancel?"

"Let me consider. Option A – kick you out and spend the evening with a gorgeous woman. Option B – blow her out and stay here listening to you whinging all night."

Alex stood up. "You're throwing me out in my time of greatest need?"

"You can't hide here forever, Alex," Pravi said, clearing up. "Go home and talk to Helen about the baby, about the future. How hard can it be?"

Ice Ice Baby

The first thing that hit Alex when he opened his front door was silence.

Aside from the distant hum of the American-style fridge freezer in the kitchen, the house was quiet. He peeked into the kitchen to see if there had been any signs of food being made, but it looked like Helen hadn't eaten in the hour since he'd been away. An upset Helen was one thing, a hungry Helen was a different beast altogether.

He figured he could gain a semblance of goodwill if he made her a snack. The idea gained momentum when he remembered that pregnant women had cravings. But what did they crave? Coal? The closest thing he had was a lump of Tesco instant light charcoal. He dismissed that idea and tried to think of anything she might have yearned for in the past. All he could recall was a holiday in Tenerife where every night she ordered fish. With no other ideas coming his way, Alex opened the fridge and saw to his relief a nice bit of salmon still within its use-by date. "Result!" Soon he was well on the way to concocting Alex's fish of the day, complete with ginger rice.

"Hungry?" Helen said, standing in the doorway dressed

in a black nightshirt as Alex almost dropped the frying pan in surprise.

"Oh, hi, Hells. I didn't know you were there."

"I wasn't. I was upstairs. Asleep. Before you bumbled in, decided to cook yourself a snack and stink the entire house out."

"It's not for me, it's for you." Alex held out the pan to her. "See – fish."

"I can smell it's fish. Both sets of neighbours can probably smell it's fish, too."

Alex replaced the pan on the gas stove. "Rina and Tiffany are away in France."

"There's a fair chance my statement is still true," Helen said, sitting down. "So, is there any reason you're cooking fish for me this late, or are you intending to bump me off with extreme food poisoning so you can go back to leading a single, carefree life until you need a nursing home?"

"It's for your cravings."

Helen looked at him blankly. "What cravings?"

"Well, you're pregnant and I thought seeing as you've probably not eaten, you might be craving something now."

"What I crave is a boyfriend who doesn't run away crying to his little pal about how doomed he is."

Alex switched off the hob and slid the salmon onto a plate. "How do you know I went to Pravi's house?"

"Come on, Alex. Where else would you cry off to? Did a nice game of fake football help smooth your pain?"

He narrowed his eyes in response.

"Plus I stalked you with your phone's GPS."

He grabbed the plate and turned to her. "So, would you like this or not?"

The grilled salmon lay on a bed of rice next to half a slice of lime.

Helen sighed. "No, I'm not hungry. You have it, unless you stopped at Kebab 3000 on the way home?"

He looked at the food and for the first time in the evening realised that he hadn't eaten.

"No, I need at least five beers before I get my chicken doner special there." He sat down and began eating his creation.

"Good?" Helen asked.

"Hmm," Alex said. "Not bad at all."

"S'pose I should say thanks," Helen said, looking down at the table. "First time in aeons you've done something for someone other than Alex."

Alex put down his cutlery. "I'm sorry I went out. It's just that …"

"I know, it was a massive shock." She looked into his eyes. "I'm sorry too."

"For what?"

"For dumping it on you as soon as I came in."

"Wow." He picked up the fork again and took a chunk of the meat. "That's the first time in aeons you've apologised for something."

Helen grinned. "That's because I don't screw up as often as you." She reached her hand across the table and Alex took it. "I would have told you the night before, but I know you hate me interrupting that film, and then you looked so peaceful when you were asleep."

"How can you not love a film with Sylvester Stallone, Bobby Moore and Pelé in it?"

"I'll take your word for it." She squeezed his hand. "Look, we need to talk about this, but not tonight. I've been weighed down by this all day and I need to get to sleep. Also, you have a big meeting tomorrow, and knowing you, you'll still have lots to prepare for."

"Crap." Alex started to eat quicker. "I'd forgotten about that. Yeah, Miles has already been on my case. We'll talk tomorrow, OK?"

"Tomorrow's fine. Try not to freak out too much, Al. This should be a wonderful thing for us both."

"You sound like Pravi." He took a forkful of rice. "Hope you don't mind me telling him."

"No, I guessed you'd tell him. I'm surprised he hasn't got one or two kids secretly tucked away, the number of women he entertains these days."

"Tell me about it," Alex said.

"Jealous?" Helen gave him a playful look.

"No, of course not. As I always tell you, I have everything I need right here."

"And more," Helen said, patting her tummy.

Alex breathed a long breath out. "Yes, and more."

"Right, I'll go up. Don't be too late revising."

Alex finished his meal, kissed Helen goodnight, and

cleared up the kitchen. As much as his mind was as far away from work as it could possibly be, he went back to study his notes for tomorrow's presentation. At least that was one hurdle that would be over by lunchtime.

* * *

At ten past eight the next morning, Alex rushed into Starbucks at King's Cross Station and scanned the room for Miles. Several people were perched on stools, huddled over their laptops, and in one corner, a group of Scandinavian tourists chatted excitedly. By the window with a bright orange tall mug was Miles, beckoning Alex to join him.

"Here he is – Alexander the Late," Miles said, laughing so loud that he drowned out the sound from the espresso machines.

"How many coffees did it take to come up with that?" Alex said, as he sat down opposite him.

"Just the one – a tall, skinny latte with hazelnut. You get yourself settled and I'll get you one too. They're awesome." Before Alex could even reply, Miles bounded off to the counter.

Alex got out a folder holding his notes on the proposed sale and tried to re-absorb the information. He was reading the second page when Miles returned.

"Get this down you," Miles said as he plonked a cup in front of him with 'Alex' written on it in black ink from the barista. Before Alex could even pick it up, Miles had grabbed it again and began scribbling something on the side.

Alex tilted his head and examined the scrawl. Miles had added to the name so that it now read 'Alexander the Latte'.

"Have you thought of a career in stand-up?" Alex said.

"All the time. By day, software salesman Miles Morris. By night, renowned comedian Miles Miles! That's the dream."

Alex slurped his latte. "Miles Miles?"

"That would be my stage name. So good they named him twice."

"Don't give up your day job."

Miles beamed. "So, are you ready for today?"

Alex shuffled his notes. "Er, not quite. I had a bombshell land on me last night and got distracted."

"Wow. Helen run off with the milkman?"

"We stopped having them years ago," Alex said. "No, it's not that it's …" He realised it was probably too early to tell everyone his news. Besides, he thought, he wasn't ready for the influx of questions that would surely follow from his colleague. "Just, er, football related."

"Poncy football? All that rolling around feigning injury, two months on the sidelines with a broken eyelash while earning a gazillion pounds per week. Makes me sick. Rugby – that's what you should be into." Miles finished the rest of his coffee and slammed down his empty mug on the table. "Footballers spend more time in the hairdressers than on the pitch."

Alex congratulated himself on his diversion. "Talking of pitches, I need help with this." Alex pointed at his notes.

"I'm having problems committing this lot to memory. I don't understand most of it."

There was always a set pattern to their sales pitches: Miles would lead, his natural charisma and charm soothing the potential buyers. He would go through what they were getting and the costs, usually making them feel by the end that ZenNoise was giving them a magical solution for a price that their accountants would worship them for negotiating. For the inevitable technical queries on the software and hardware they'd be buying, Alex would be on hand to answer anything that came up.

"Just wing it, like you usually do," Miles said. "I met some of them last week and they're cool. Bit of techno-babble, you'll be fine. No one will understand it anyway, aside from geeks."

"I suppose they can't ask anything too deep," Alex said. "Their techies have talked to ours and are happy with the details."

"That's right," Miles said, as he took the notes and flicked through them. "Nope, don't have a clue what all this means, but it looks the usual type of stuff. Don't sweat it." He put on his suit jacket. "Come on, let's go so we can get there early. Psych yourself up and bring your 'A' game – the Dream Team is about to seal the deal!"

Miles opened the meeting in his usual charming manner, whilst Alex scanned the ten faces in the audience to get a feel of who they were presenting to. Miles had said that two women were pregnant, reminding him again of his predicament.

"And finally, I'd like to introduce you to my partner in crime, Alex Cornhill, Technical Sales Executive."

"Hello." Alex broke from his reverie and smiled. "I'm sure you've covered everything in the technical sessions you've previously held with my colleagues, but if there's anything remaining, I'll try to tackle it today."

"Fantastic!" said one woman in an American accent who Alex figured was pregnant. "Hi, I'm Viv, the Chief Technology Officer. I missed the previous session, so I hope you've warmed up your baseball swing as I've got plenty of big ones coming your way."

Outwardly, he held a fixed grin and said, "Bring it on!" Inwardly, Alex was deafened by his own scream.

Miles excelled as he always did, extolling the virtues of the software they were selling, its benefits and sharing the customer case studies, which all made it sound like it had god-like abilities to transform any company. Normally by this stage Alex would have been planning which gadget he would treat himself to with the commission that was surely about to be earned, but he stood there imperceptibly shaking at the thought of Viv launching a volley of questions that would leave him looking both ignorant and incompetent. He reached over in front of him to a small table to check his notes. NBC had also provided a big jug of water filled to the top with a thick layer of ice cubes floating at the surface. Picking up the jug, he went to pour himself a glass but ended up with barely a teaspoon of liquid as large cubes of ice clanked their way out of it, overfilling the glass. A few landed on the table and slid over the edge, but with Miles captivating the audience, Alex only turned a few heads towards him. As Miles was finishing his piece, to Alex's surprise and relief, Viv rose from her seat and strode out of the room.

"But enough of me," Miles said. "I'll now hand you over to a man who knows his bits from his bytes – Alex."

Alex sipped his remaining millilitres of water and stepped forward to his audience, rattling the glass of ice. Turning to his colleague, he said, "Thank you, Miles." He glanced at his watch. "I know we're running out of time and you probably are dying to get away from us and into the canteen, so I'm assuming everything technical has previously been covered?"

Alex listened to murmured conversations between several groups before a man with a goatee announced that they'd got everything from the last meeting. Result, thought Alex. Easiest away performance ever. "In that case, I'd like to thank you for—"

"Woah, hold it, hold it, hold it!" Alex swung round to his left as Viv swept into the room again, waving her arms. "Don't you even think about leaving, mister. We've got ten minutes of your time left. My bladder is now empty and I'm ready to shoot."

Alex wished he'd had a gun. "Terrific! I hate it when I come all the way and get no questions, so I'm very glad you can make my journey worthwhile."

"Excellent." Viv picked up a large tablet and begun tapping the screen. "So, question one: what encryption are you using?"

"Er, that's a very good question." Alex looked down at his glass. "I think we upgraded it recently."

"Surely you must know something as vital as what algorithm you encrypt your customers' data with?"

"Yes of course, it's just that … well …"

Miles spoke up, "Viv, whatever we use – and I'm clearly no expert – it is the bleeding edge in encryption, the best of the best. Houdini and a squadron of hackers with Swiss Army knives couldn't get through our systems."

Viv paused briefly to take in Miles's strange amalgamation of analogies. "OK, that's good, but I would like confirmation from an expert." She cocked her head and looked at Alex.

"Yes, sorry." Alex composed himself. "I have no idea why it's popped out of my head, but … ah, my notes." With the sudden realisation that the answer was written on one of his bits of paper, he strode up to the table. Unfortunately, he failed to see one of the ice cubes on the floor and stepped on it. With a glass still in one hand, he was unable to stop himself from sliding into the table, crashing down onto the floor and knocking over the jug. Water and ice poured onto his head from above. "Damn!"

"I forgot to tell you Alex provides the entertainment!" Miles boomed out to everyone as he rushed to help Alex.

"Been practising that move all week, haven't you?"

Several people came to help Alex and mop up the mess, all waving away Alex's apologies. Down on the floor in a soggy and smeared mess were his notes. He got to his knees and picked them up.

"Hey, don't worry, Alex," Viv said, who was now at his side. "Let's end here and you can email answers to my questions later."

He was soaked through his suit to his shirt, was sure that his lower back was bruised, and was more than a little embarrassed, but somehow he'd got a victory. Viv yanked onto his arm and went to pull him up, but he waved his hands at her. "No, no, please stop. I don't want you straining yourself in your condition."

Viv kept hold of his arm, but stopped pulling. "Condition?"

"You know ..." Alex tilted his head towards her stomach. "Pregnant. You're not supposed to lift heavy objects."

Viv let his arm go, stood up and folded her arms. For a second, he thought she was one of those stubborn, have-a-go types that would happily lift barrels until her waters broke, but the thunderous face that now looked down on him confirmed his calamitous mistake.

"You think I'm still pregnant?"

A drop of water hit the wooden floor.

"Alex," Miles came in and placed a hand on Alex's forehead, "did you bump your head? I told you it's Aleska who's pregnant. This is Viv, remember? She had her baby three months ago. You must be confused." He dragged Alex to his feet, gathered all their stuff, and ushered him out the door. Turning to everyone, Miles said, "Look, I may have to take him to the hospital to get him checked out. Thank you for your time, and once Alex has stopped hallucinating, he'll send over the answers. I look forward to receiving the paperwork on Monday. We'll see ourselves out, goodbye."

Once they were out of the building, Alex ran his fingers through his wet hair, trying to slick it back into something passably presentable. "You could have at least let me stop in the toilets to dry myself."

They started walking towards a busy main road and Miles snapped his head round to face him. "And give you the opportunity to do more damage? You were on such a roll you'd probably short circuit the hand driers and fuse the entire ground floor, or accidentally racially abuse the cleaner."

"It was just a slip. As for Viv, I assumed she was pregnant, especially as she dashed out to the toilet. Don't pregnant women do that a lot?"

"News flash, Alex – *all* women need to go to the toilet." They reached a pedestrian crossing, where Miles stopped and jabbed the button a few times. "Even if you're not sure, you never – and I mean never – say anything that indicates you think a woman's pregnant when you're not certain."

"I was only trying to protect her. If she was, you see."

"You should have been trying to protect the deal I spent

so much effort on. I dazzled them for over an hour, had them practically about to sign, and then I hand over to you and in less than two minutes you turned us into forgetful, incompetent, ignorant fools."

"I'm sorry."

"Absolutely incredible, Alex." The traffic continued going by, so Miles pressed the button another five times.

"It was quick thinking of you to suggest I had banged my head."

Miles turned to face Alex again. "It was, wasn't it? Do you know why? It's because I'm a professional. I think on my feet, I prepare, I execute well and I make damn good lemonade from the lemons I'm given by some people."

Alex fiddled with his tie. "I've got a lot to deal with right now."

"Then deal with it." The traffic stopped and Miles marched off across the road towards the tube station and called back, "Because right now Alex, it looks like you haven't got a clue about anything."

Team Talk

Given that he was wet, cold and would have to survive an afternoon of cutting remarks from Miles, Alex decided that going back to the office was not on the agenda. Instead, he returned home, changed his clothes and typed up the meeting notes, minus his disastrous cameo. It was only one o'clock, but it had already felt like a long day.

Once he'd sent the notes to Miles and devoured a ham and pastrami ciabatta sandwich, he took the plunge and opened the door into the mysterious world of babies. He knew it was as likely to scare the hell out of him as it would educate him, but figured he had to start somewhere to get clued up.

After only two minutes of reading, Alex had to resort to Google five times to look up the definition of some of the terms used. Pregnancy seemed to have its own lexicon, words he never knew existed. He even discovered parts of the body he didn't even know had their own names. It was like an undercover mission behind enemy lines, gathering covert information and cracking codes. Just as he was being astonished by a diagram of a womb, a cryptic text came in from Pravi. *It's come!* Alex sighed and called his friend.

"What's come?" Alex said.

"The Kickstarter game, the retro one I backed," Pravi replied. "Looks cool – dedicated to the Euro 96 tournament with high-res graphics, like you're actually there. Picture of Gazza on the back of the box in the classic '96 kit is friggin' awesome."

"Sweet. Will have to check it out with you."

"Thought you might want to come round and play it after work?"

"Sorry, I can't. Got to talk things through with Helen. We didn't have a chance last night."

"I know what you mean. Me and Jasmine didn't talk much last night, either."

"Bet you didn't, you lucky sod. So did you get a good look at her perineum?"

There was a brief pause before Pravi replied, "Her what?"

"Never mind, look it up. I had to."

He finished up with Pravi, promising to come round the next evening to play his new game. After hearing about Pravi's exploits last night, he decided he couldn't face the womb diagram again and so perused the sports pages for the next half hour until his phone rang.

"Alex, it's Miles. How ya feeling?"

Alex thought about his fall in the meeting and rubbed his lower back. "I'm OK, thanks. What's up?"

"Been trying to message you online but you weren't responding. Figured you were in training."

How did Miles know about his research?

"Training? For what?"

"*Dancing on Ice*, of course! Ice cubes – that's how Jayne Torvill probably started. Judging from your performance at NBC this morning, you've got a long way to go, but you've got potential."

"Ha ha," Alex said. "I thought you weren't talking to me?"

"After you cocked it all up? Yes, well, what did you expect? However, guess what?"

Alex's heart raced. "Please don't say Caroline fired me." Their boss didn't accept failure.

"Fired? And break up the Dream Team? No – I'm calling to say that NBC has said they've provisionally agreed to go ahead with the deal. There's still the paperwork to complete, but I reckon we've bagged this baby."

Alex did a little jig in his seat. "Nice one!"

"Obviously, they had their reservations thanks to your Bambi on ice routine, but I smoothed it over, saying we wouldn't be letting you within a million miles of the project come implementation."

"Oh," Alex said. "Thanks."

"It's for everyone's benefit. I'm sure you'll be back on form for the next sale once you've sorted out whatever's bothering you. Catch you tomorrow. Ciao."

Alex laid back on the bed and breathed out slowly. At least that was one worry off his mind; he couldn't begin to contemplate dealing with getting another job on top of handling everything else. His laptop went into screensaver mode. He closed his eyes and began to make a list of things he could buy with the commission, starting with a new bedroom TV. A short while later, he was asleep.

Waking to a slamming door, Alex opened his eyes wide and bolted upright. He slapped the sides of his face with both hands.

"Al? Are you up there?" Helen's voice came up the stairs, followed by the sound of her footsteps.

He jumped up and smoothed out the bed. Although he rarely did, Helen always suspected him of slacking off when working from home.

"Hi honey. Just, er, finishing off an important report." He went to the desk and pressed a key on his laptop to turn the screen back on.

"Really?" Helen said, lingering in the doorway. "Because you've got that look about you when I've caught you playing a game when you should be doing something else."

"Me?" Alex said, then put up his hands in mock defence. "OK, you got me. I'd finished my report and had a quick five minutes on *Football Manager* before you came in."

"Five? C'mon Alex, I've known you to lose an entire weekend to that game."

"OK, OK, I admit it – ten minutes." He got up and packed the laptop away. "So, what do you fancy for dinner?"

"Don't know, but not fish." Helen went back into the main bedroom to change, so he followed her.

"I decided – lasagne," she said as she unzipped her dress.

"Are you sure? You just said you didn't know. I was thinking spag bol."

"No, I'd like lasagne, please. You asked me and I've made my mind up. I don't dilly dally like you do all day on decisions."

"Fine, but spag bol would be quicker."

"Quicker? Why, are you going somewhere again tonight? Perhaps we can discuss the baby another time, then." She grabbed her phone and hovered a finger over it. "Shall I book you in somewhere around its eighteenth birthday?"

"No, I'm staying in so we can talk."

"I'm honoured."

Alex enjoyed the important talks with women as much as he enjoyed watching Spurs lose to Arsenal. Unfortunately, given enough time, both events were inevitable.

A cheesy smell filled the kitchen as Helen entered it an hour later. Now dressed in black leggings and a blue long-sleeved top, she popped her head round the door. "Hey you."

Alex remained standing at the granite sink with his back to her. "Hey."

"Is today's Italian special ready yet?"

"Perfection will be delivered any moment now." He checked the oven's timer and then turned around.

"Garlic bread?" Helen asked, stepping into the kitchen.

"Madame did not specify garlic bread, but the chef guessed she would require some."

"'Madame' is French. I would prefer 'signorina'."

"As you wish, signorina." Alex peered inside a cupboard, moving around a few items before taking out a bottle. "Wine? I've got the same one we had in Sorrento last year."

Helen stood there, arms folded, head slightly to the side. Alex looked at her and waited. When no answer came, he looked at the bottle to check he wasn't offering up the cleaner's bleach, then back at Helen and said, "It's past midday, we're having red meat … am I missing something?" The oven beeped behind him.

"Did you want our baby coming out with a drink problem?" Helen said.

"Oh crap! Alcohol, right." He put on some oven gloves and got out the bubbling lasagne. "It's just all different. Old habits and all."

Helen sat down at their oak table. "I'm glad one of us knows a thing or two about it, or goodness knows how it will come out."

Putting the wine back in the cupboard, Alex said, "I guess our carefree days of spontaneous weekend breaks to random European cities are numbered."

"Yep. At least for the next eighteen or so years."

Alex sighed. "What did you say to me in Reykjavik? That our love was as beautiful as the northern lights?"

Helen laughed. "Hmm. Two years on, I'd say it's more akin to the Blackpool Illuminations."

Alex served up a generous portion of golden lasagne, the stacked layers of pasta held in a perfect rectangle next to two golden pieces of garlic bread. Handing one plate to Helen, she hummed in approval.

"Thanks, hun. You may know sod all about babies, but you can cook a decent lasagne."

"Don't you start," Alex said, putting two glasses of water onto the table. "Miles called me clueless today."

Helen put down her fork with a clatter. "You told him? Already? Alex …"

"Relax, I haven't told him anything." He explained the debacle of the meeting. After she finished laughing, she said, "Don't suppose you recorded it? I'd kill to have seen your face when you realised she wasn't pregnant."

Alex munched on his bread.

"Well, I'm glad no one knows yet," Helen said.

"Apart from Pravi, who's absolutely loving it."

"So, you still freaking out?"

Alex took a sip of his water. "To be honest, I don't know what I think right now. If we'd been planning it in advance, I would have had time to prepare myself, but there I was, trying to beat Germany to get to the semi-finals, in my own little world, when you burst in and change everything forever."

"It was for your own good," Helen said, smirking. "You'd have only lost on penalties."

"I'm glad you find it funny."

"If I didn't laugh, I'd cry."

Alex continued eating. "OK, hit me with the facts."

"Facts?"

"Like how many weeks you are gone, the expected due date, how long we can put off telling people, that sort of thing."

"You're not prepping for a presentation, Alex." She mopped up some sauce with her bread and sighed. "According to this website, I'm about nine weeks gone, making the due date towards the end of February."

"February," Alex said, staring into space as if a portal was about to open and give him a glimpse of the alien world called Fatherhood.

"I'd like to start telling most people after the first scan," Helen said. "That way, we'll have something to show them."

"Those grainy baby photos freak me out," Alex said, grimacing.

"You might change your mind when you see that it's your daughter."

Alex's mouth dropped. "Daughter? You know it's a girl already? Why didn't you tell me?"

Helen smiled. "I don't *know* it's a girl – it'll take a few weeks before anyone can tell us – but I can feel it. It's a 'she'."

The rest of the conversation was a blur as Alex tried to get his head round the fact that he might be having a girl. Of course, he knew before that he *might* be getting a girl, but Helen was weirdly prophetic at times, like the Brexit referendum and the morning of the Euro 2016 England v

Iceland match when she'd been convinced England would lose 2-1. Maybe she was just attuned to this strange year, but often her hunches were right. After finishing dinner, he began to load the dishwasher.

"I've started a list of things we have to do," Helen said, tapping at her phone.

Alex groaned. "You always have a list."

"I'm a project manager," Helen replied. "That's what we do, make lists and assign resources. So far, I have thirty-six items."

A plate clattered as Alex dropped it in a rack. "Thirty-six? Fuck me, Hells."

"Already done that, hence the need for the list."

He gave her a sarcastic smile. "Is there an item that says for you to improve on your jokes?"

"No, but number five is to get Alex to stop swearing."

"What? I thought this was a list of things to do before the birth?"

"It is. Babies can start hearing by eighteen weeks. I don't want the very first word she hears from her daddy being a swear word."

"And while I remember," continued Helen, looking at the phone's calendar, "I've invited Peter and Becky for dinner next week."

Alex swore in his head. "What did you do that for?"

"To share our news with them early. And because it's a grown-up thing to do, inviting our friends for dinner."

"*Your* friends, Hells. They don't like me."

"Don't be silly. Peter likes you, and I'm sure Becky does, too. She just enjoys giving you a hard time."

Alex wiped down the kitchen worktop. "She called me a little shit the last time I saw her."

"Hey – no swearing, what did I just say? Use a substitute word instead." Helen got up. "Becky was drunk and you wouldn't let her change channel on the TV. Her own TV."

"What did she expect? It was transfer deadline day – Premier League clubs had only thirty minutes left to sign new players. That's like switching off a film right before the climax."

"If you say so." Helen went towards the door. "Anyway, aren't you seeing Pravi again soon? Enjoy your game time because next week they'll be no TV, no football talk, just four adults having dinner, sharing our wonderful news and talking babies."

Alex closed his eyes. "I can't fu … dging wait."

Completed It, Mate

Wednesday, 20th July 2016

Gascoigne had sold Kuntz a dummy and was clean through on goal. The TV screen covering most of the wall in front of Alex and Pravi showed there were two minutes left before the computer referee blew his whistle. Joining forces and playing Pravi's new game together as England versus Germany in Euro 96, at 1-0 down they knew this was their last chance of forcing extra time in this semi-final. England's creative genius was currently being controlled by Alex, while Pravi sprinted behind him as Alan Shearer.

"Shoot!" shouted Pravi as Alex's Gascoigne bore down on the German goalie. "Spank it!"

Alex hesitated, and the keeper came out to claim the ball on the ground. "Dammit!"

"Mate! Why didn't you pull the trigger?" cried Pravi, flopping back into his seat.

"Thought I had more time." Alex remained hunched forward, gripping his controller. "C'mon we can still do it." Teddy Sheringham regained possession, but David Platt soon gave it away and seconds later the game had finished.

Just like in the real thing, England had been knocked out in the semis.

Pravi threw his controller onto the sofa.

"Crappy game anyway," Alex said, picking up Pravi's controller. "What's so special about this, then?"

As the top sponsor of the Kickstarter project, Pravi had received an advanced copy of the retro Euro 96 football game and a modified controller, based on a mini gamepad. It was much smaller and thinner than the standard Sony one, without any handles and features such as vibration feedback. A small, two-digit LED display had been added on the back, which was currently blank.

"Dunno, nothing about it in the instructions," Pravi replied. "The project promised that 'The controller would give a true retro experience', but I thought that's what the game does."

"Did you ask the bloke who sent it to you?"

"Yes, but he never replied to any of my emails. During the whole campaign all he did was confirm my pledge, the target completion date and when it would be shipped."

"He's probably one of those geniuses who codes all day and hasn't communicated with anyone in the last decade," Alex said.

"Whatever he is, he knows how to make a good game."

"It's a bit on the tough side," Alex said. "Gazza in his prime would've buried that."

"Yeah, but he wasn't being controlled by a hesitating gimp." Pravi got into his wheelchair and headed to the kitchen. "So how's the pregnant one?" Pravi had been so eager to play the game with his friend that as soon as Alex had arrived at his flat, he'd shoved a controller in one of his hands, a beer in the other and told him to sit down and play.

When Pravi returned, Alex accepted the bottle offered to him and said, "I'm having a girl, apparently."

"Isn't it too early to tell yet?"

"It's one of her predictions."

"Like when she said Spurs would win the league this year?"

"That was just to wind me up. No, that's what she feels, she says. A girl. I'm going to have a daughter."

Pravi raised his bottle to Alex. "Cheers to your unborn daughter."

Alex clinked his bottle with Pravi's. "I'm still struggling to get my head round this. Helen made a list of things to do before the birth. There's all these things we have to buy and we have to create a nursery room."

"Bang goes your man cave then."

"What? I've got to keep that. She only lets me play games downstairs when she's not in."

"No offence, but you haven't exactly got many other rooms to choose from. Unless you have a watertight business case for keeping the cave, it's toast. Either that, or move to a bigger house."

Alex sighed and banged his bottle down. "We can barely afford our house now, and judging from Helen's list of essential baby items, we might not be able to keep that."

"Not that it matters about the cave anymore. You'll be too tired from the lack of sleep to do anything fun."

Alex stood up and paced around. "Everything's about to get complicated, isn't it? I don't want this, Prav. Man, how easy was it when we were at uni? Go out any night we liked, cheap pints, playing *Tekken* until four in the morning. Those were good days."

"They were." Pravi grinned. "Especially the time I beat you forty-one times in a row."

"You're such a loser for keeping count," Alex said.

The pair settled down again and restarted their tournament, playing once again together as England. The game gave you the chance to play all the Euro 96 matches held in England in 1996 with the real players in stunning, realistic stadia. By ten-thirty, they had reached the semi-final again, another match against the old foe Germany. Pravi had given them the lead after fifteen minutes, but with ten remaining, a shocking attempted pass by Alex led to a German equaliser. The final whistle blew and it was into extra time.

"Don't forget extra time is golden goal," Pravi said.

"I'd forgotten we had that in '96. If anyone scores in the thirty minutes they win, right? Game stops there?"

"Yep. Do you remember how tense the real England–Germany match was? What about that Gazza miss?"

Alex bowed his head. "Don't … just don't. I'm welling up thinking about it. That was our chance. I remember Shearer crossing it and thinking all Gazza had to do was get a touch on it and it was in the back of the net. I swear the ball went through his leg."

They played on, but with no further goals, the match reached penalties. The boys were pleased to be able to select their own penalty takers. "Put anyone ahead of Southgate. Even Seaman if you have to," Pravi said.

"Now what? Do we get to control the goalie as well?" Alex said.

A German player stepped up to the spot, and the view shown to them both was of the goalie from behind. Pravi pressed the left button, and the goalie reacted by shuffling in the same direction. "Looks like it. Here goes nothing – it is Germany after all." Thomas Häßler ran up and although Pravi made Seaman dive the right way, the ball blasted its way into the top corner.

"It's realistic, I'll give it that," Alex said.

The teams went through a further three penalties each, with no misses. Stefan Kuntz was the fifth German to take one against Alex. Alex guessed the right way and parried the shot past the post. "Yes! Have it you German Kuntz!"

"Nice one!" Pravi said, getting ready to take what could be the winning penalty. "And that joke never tires."

Ten seconds later and the pair were celebrating getting England into the final. They toasted their achievement with another beer and set themselves up for the final at the virtual Wembley.

"This is how it should have been," Alex said. "That summer was the best of my life. Britpop, New Labour on the rise and it was all set for an England win."

"Then pick up your pad and let's re-write history."

Just like in real life, the computer had sent the Czech Republic to the final. Whether it was over-confidence or the beer kicking in, they found themselves 2-0 down at half-time.

Alex got to his feet. "Prav, this is it," he said in his best Terry Venables voice. "This is our moment. We have forty-five minutes to make our nation proud. One half of football to unite the country." He paced the small living room with his hands behind his back. "Fans of Oasis and Blur will sing together. This is our comeback. This is our home. This is our trophy. Football. Is. Coming. Home!"

Pravi let out a roar and they started the second half.

"Get the funk in!" Alex said, thirty seconds after the restart when he made Sheringham sweep in a cross to make it 2-1.

"Lovely finish," Pravi said as they watched replays from multiple camera angles. "What's with the 'funk', though?"

"Huh? Oh, I'm practising not swearing – Helen's orders. She thinks the kid's gonna come out effing and blinding with me around otherwise."

"That's a slippery slope. She'll be having you wear one of those empathy bellies next."

"Empathy what?"

Pravi pressed a button to exit the replays and the Czech Republic kicked off again. "Tell you later. Concentrate – we still need an equaliser."

The Czechs came close with Patrik Berger rattling the bar from thirty yards and both Pravi and Alex frustrated each other with long dribbles running into opposition defenders. Undeterred, on seventy minutes, Alex sped past two players with McManaman and was chopped down in the box.

"Ref! Penalty!" they shouted in unison. The camera zoomed in on the ref who blew his whistle and pointed to the spot. Alex guided Shearer to blast low and hard to the keeper's right to make it 2-2 and then leapt round the room with his right hand up in the air, mimicking the striker's classic celebratory move.

"Shearer!" shouted Pravi. "Sheeeeeear-er!"

"C'mon," Alex said, sitting down again. "About time you did something. I'm carrying you here."

"If you weren't such a bloody ball hog, I might get a look in." The game continued and as they pushed for a winner, Karel Poborský went clean through for the Czechs. Pravi had control of Seaman, came rushing out and managed to clear the ball upfield.

"Well done, keeps," Alex said as he gained control of the ball.

Pravi broke right with McManaman and yelled, "Send me! Send me!"

With a precision pass, Alex slid the ball through to Pravi, who took two touches and lashed it goalwards with Shearer. As the ball hit the back of the net, Alex jumped up and Pravi punched the air in delight.

"Have it!" screamed Alex, high-fiving Pravi.

"2-0 down, 3-2 up. Unbelievable," replied Pravi. "See what happens when you pass to me?"

"Whatever. Right, let's see this home."

At ninety minutes, they shouted for the final whistle, which eventually came with a loud roar from both the crowd and the boys. They sat back and waited for an end sequence, perhaps a special video or presentation for winning the tournament.

"You couldn't have done this with Jasmine," Alex said.

Pravi laughed. They watched the extended celebrations as the trophy was passed around the different players. Alex took a few photos of the screen from his phone. "Wow, they've really gone to town with the ending. What's next, a fake Terry Venables interview?"

A message popped up onto the screen:

CONGRATULATIONS ON WINNING EURO 96 WITH ENGLAND

A slight pause followed until another message appeared underneath, flashing in blue:

SPECIAL CONTROLLER ACTIVATED

Finally, a third message said:

FOR A TRUE RETRO EXPERIENCE, PRESS THE SHARE, OPTIONS AND FOUR SHOULDER BUTTONS TOGETHER

"Cool," Pravi said. "Must be some kind of bonus mode."

Alex grabbed the controller from Pravi, noticing the display on the back now showed two green, flashing dashes. Pressing and holding down the shoulder buttons, he said, "Which other buttons?"

Pravi leaned over and said, "These small ones here."

Pravi pressed them ... and Alex was instantly blinded by a brilliant, bright light.

Unbelievable, Jeff

Saturday, 8th June 1996

A strange whooshing sound was gradually disappearing as Alex's ears depressurised. He tentatively reached out his hands ahead of him.

"W-what was that?" a voice said in front. "Where am I?"

It took a few seconds for Alex to respond. "Prav? What just happened?"

"I … I don't know. I can't see a thing," Pravi said. "Are we like, dead?"

Gradually, dark shapes were appearing to Alex as his vision recovered. He could make out the image of something in front of him, until the recognisable outline of Pravi's back came clear. "Prav, I'm behind you. Are you OK?"

He watched as Pravi moved his arms and touched the floor. "Yeah, I'm on some tiled floor or something."

Alex still didn't have perfect vision, but as he looked around, he could see they were in a tiny room with a door in front of them. Looking behind him, he said, "I think we're in a toilet cubicle."

By this time, Pravi had also got his vision back and frantically looked around. "What? How? But we were … weren't we at home?" He peered at the brown-stained toilet seat. "If this is heaven, I ain't loving it so far."

"Try this," Alex said. He turned round, closed the toilet lid and helped Pravi to sit on it. "Got to be better than sitting on this floor."

Before Pravi could thank him, they heard a door open in the room beyond their toilet and someone walk in.

"C'mon England!" a man shouted in a rough southern accent that sounded local to Alex.

By the sound of the gushing stream of water, they realised there must be a urinal just outside their door. They listened as he zipped himself up and then opened the door again to return to what sounded like a crowded place.

Alex waited a short while before saying, "I'm going to see what's out there." He stepped forward and trod on the game controller. Picking it up, he noticed "99" was now displayed in red on the back. "Here," he said, giving it to Pravi, "hold this."

The door was locked, so he slid the catch back and pulled it slightly inwards. His heart raced as he took his first glimpse into the impossible. They were in one of two cubicles and the wall to the left was filled with a single silver urinal trough with little yellow bricks scattered about the bottom. To his right, were two white sinks with a grey bar of soap on each, under a large mirror. The only other item he could see was an old hand dryer mounted on the wall.

He pulled his head back into the cubicle and locked the door to face an expectant Pravi. "It's definitely a toilet."

"Thanks, Sherlock," Pravi said. "A toilet, but where? And how did we get here?"

"Beats me," Alex replied. "It looks like a typical pub toilet. Only a bit ... I dunno ... weird."

"A pub kinda makes sense from the noise we heard when that guy entered the room. But I know that there's no football tonight, so why was he cheering on England? Unless it's rugby?"

"This is messed up," Alex said.

"Go and see what pub we're in, who's out there, which sport is on. Maybe we'll get a clue of what's going on. There's got to be some explanation. Did we really drink that much beer?"

Alex went out of the cubicle, closing the door behind him. "If you can reach, lock it, Prav. When I return, I'll give you three knocks so you'll know it's me."

He walked two steps before Pravi replied, "Or you could just say that it's Alex."

As he approached the toilet's exit, he was breathing heavily. Once he was out, he stood at the edge of a large group of people all fixated on a screen that he couldn't quite see from his angle. There were flags hanging everywhere from black rafters, mostly English but some Scottish, too. The place was packed, proper crowded, with the bar four-deep and staff rushing around to cope with the demand. Fruit machines blinked their lights behind two women smoking in front of them. An even odder sight was that so many of the men here were wearing old England shirts, mostly classic Umbro ones with blue collars. Alex realised he couldn't see any modern ones at all.

The commentary boomed out of speakers all around the pub, and now that Alex was listening, he undoubtedly could tell it was football.

"Neville, you prick!" shouted a man in a grey shirt, thrusting his forefinger towards the screen.

Alex craned his neck towards the TV. Neville? It certainly wasn't Gary or Phil commentating; he'd recognise the Mancunian drones of that pair anywhere. He moved further into the crowd to see what match they were all watching, apologising for bumping into several men holding large jugs of beer and treading on the foot of one man who looked like a proper Millwall fan. Finally, he made his way to a spot behind a gnarled wooden pillar to glimpse the screen. England were playing Switzerland, and with Gascoigne's blond hair bobbing around in midfield behind Shearer and Sheringham, Alex realised the pub was showing a replay of England's first group match of Euro 96.

"Why's Shearer playing?" slurred a man next to him. "Bloody useless for us, don't you think?"

Alex remembered a recent documentary on the tournament, detailing how Shearer had gone twelve England games without scoring before this match.

"He scores the opener in this match though, doesn't he?" Alex shouted back. "About twenty minutes?"

The man gave Alex a strange look and continued drinking.

Alex felt a nudge from behind as people swayed forward as England advanced in a promising attack. He looked around and saw that everyone was massively into this match. Alex remembered the tournament well, especially England's nervy, slow start, and yet everyone was sucking in every second of the game. This wasn't unprecedented – someone once told him of a group of Everton fans who'd celebrated the anniversary of their 1995 FA Cup Final win by running the entire match as if live. As sad as he found that, it was plausible for fans of a club. But for England?

Alex looked at the sea of retro shirts ahead of him, the casual smokers at the bar and the old-fashioned screen showing the football. Every hair on him stood on end before he bulldozed his way back to Pravi in the toilets.

"Prav!" he shouted as he burst into the men's toilets. A man peeing into the trough looked round, startled. "Sorry, mate," Alex said, as he hurried to the cubicle door. "My friend's in there." He heard the lock slide and opened its door. As he went and closed it behind him, he heard the man outside say, "I know what you two are doing in there."

Pravi looked at Alex expectantly. Alex looked to the ceiling. "It's not what you think," he shouted back.

"S'OK man, I do drugs here all the time," the man said. "If you have any spare, then sort a geezer out, will ya?"

"I, er …" Alex stuttered. "We're down to our last two lines of Charlie, sorry."

They listened to him grumble and then leave the room.

"Last two lines of Charlie?" Pravi said. "Is that how a druggie actually talks?"

"Who cares? I wanted to get rid of him. We have bigger problems. Unbelievable problems. Ridiculous, it-can't-be-happening, mind-warping problems."

Pravi shifted a little on the toilet. "What's out there then? What's going on?"

Alex cleared his throat. "We're in a pub. Which is ridiculous, seeing as a few minutes ago we were in your flat, right?"

"Were we drinking absinthe?"

"Even if we were and somehow got here without remembering, being in a pub is not the strangest bit."

"What is then?"

"Everyone outside is watching the football – England versus Switzerland."

"Switzerland?"

"Yes, the very first game of Euro 96."

Pravi thought for a moment. "What, a documentary?"

"No Pravi – live."

"They're replaying the whole game in a pub? That's strange. It wasn't even a great match, either. Now if they'd shown the Holland match, I could understand. When our fourth went in, I—"

"I think it's actually *live* live."

"Huh? Live as in 1996 live?"

"Yes."

Pravi looked around the cubicle as if trying to validate Alex's absurd claims. "As in … we're in 1996 live?"

"Correct."

"But that's impossible."

"So I thought."

"Are you sure?"

"Is there any other explanation? If one minute we were playing your new game at your flat and the next—"

"Wait a minute …" Pravi held up the game controller. "Alex, it can't be a coincidence that we were playing as England in my Euro 96 game."

"What did that last message say?"

"Um, something about a true retro experience."

Alex held his hand out toward the door. "You don't get much more of a retro experience than actually being here."

They stayed in the cubicle for a while in silence, partly due to other people coming in and out of the toilets and partly due to them both trying to process their seemingly impossible situation. When it was again empty, Pravi spoke first. "Putting aside the absurd fact that we're here, you realise that without my wheelchair I'm practically stuffed?"

Before Alex could answer, there was a massive roar which vibrated throughout the entire building. Shouts and screams and cries of jubilation filled the air.

"That'll be Shearer's twenty-something minute goal then," Alex said.

"Twenty-third,"

"Whatever, you geek."

"As much as I'd like to go in and join the celebrations," Pravi said, "I don't fancy crawling out on the floor."

"I could give you a piggyback?"

"Last time you did that was when we celebrated Beckham's free kick against Greece. You had to take a week off work."

"I remember. Told 'em I had done it decorating. OK, forget that."

Pravi took some toilet paper and wiped his brow. "This is so … I can't handle it."

"Shh," Alex said, as someone entered the room and went into the cubicle next to them.

"We can't be in 1996," Pravi whispered. "You can't just invent a pad that takes you back in time. No one's that clever. We must be dreaming, or drunk, or unconscious or it's an elaborate hoax." He slapped the side of his head and said, "Of course it's a trick! Must be a setup – they're all actors outside. You've been duped, we both have."

The man in the cubicle next door let out a massive fart. "Do you two mind? I'm trying to have a crap here."

"Good one, mate," Pravi said. "We know, you know. I've no idea how you guys pulled off this stunt, but we've sussed it."

A loud noise came in reply as the man emptied his bowels. Alex winced and waved the air around his nose. "I don't think—"

"He could be a method actor." Pravi waved the controller at Alex. "Bet if I press the same buttons again nothing happens. Whoever's behind this can't be ready for us now. Watch …"

"No!" Alex got a hand on the pad but couldn't stop Pravi from pressing the same button combination as before … and the cubicle instantly became empty again.

Alex stayed motionless as the shock of the reoccurring blindness and the whooshing noise in his ears subsided. He could now hear his heartbeat racing in his ears. As his vision gradually returned, he could see Pravi sitting on a sofa, controller on his lap with his hands over his ears. Alex looked around and could see they were back at the flat again. With the wheelchair next to Pravi and empty beer cans littered around, it looked as how they'd left it. He glanced at the TV screen as the previous message disappeared. Now, all it said was to press 'X' to return to the main menu.

Pravi looked all around him. "What the …?"

"We're back," Alex said.

"Looks like it. Did you get the blinding light and noise?"

"Yeah, both times. Scarily intense."

Pravi threw his pad onto the sofa beside him and moved into his wheelchair. "I ain't touching that again." He went off towards the kitchen. "I think we both need some water."

While Pravi was gone, Alex found his phone and confirmed the date; it was still the same day that they'd started the game. He checked the phone's time, then looked at his watch and frowned. "Prav," he shouted, "you got a clock in there?"

"Microwave says it's 11:25. Why?"

"My phone says that, too."

Pravi re-entered the living room. "So what?"

"So my watch says it's 11:50."

Pravi handed him a glass. "That's because you paid five dollars for it in New York."

"It's never been wrong until now. That's a difference of twenty-five minutes."

Pravi sipped his water. "What time were we playing to?"

"Dunno." Alex grabbed his phone again and searched the photos. "I took one of Adams lifting the cup. Let me see the time … I took it at 11:20, about a minute before we saw that message and you pressed the buttons."

"How long do you reckon we were … wherever we were?"

"Let's think. We were at least twenty-three minutes into the match, as Shearer had just scored. And we may have arrived right at the start of the game."

"Seems about right," Pravi said. "So, we were away for about twenty-five minutes."

"Then if we – jumped, for want of a better word – at 11:20, spent twenty-five minutes there and have been here for five, then my watch showing 11:50 is about correct."

Pravi flicked the TV over to a news channel. "But it's definitely 11:25 now."

"Exactly," Alex said. "Which means we jumped back around the same time we left, even though we spent twenty-five minutes in 1996."

Pravi considered the facts. "As much as I love sci-fi, I know you can't travel back in time. This game must have done something to our brains. Some weird memory manipulation effect. We must be guinea pigs for some sick experiment. The Kickstarter guy must be governmental."

"That doesn't explain my watch," Alex said. "It's analogue, so it's not a smart watch that can be hacked into."

"Probably zapped it with some sort of electrical field. The controller's been modified – who knows what they've done?"

"I think you're over-analysing it."

Pravi gulped down the rest of his drink. "Well, I haven't got a clue what happened. All I know is that I ended up in a dirty pub toilet without my chair." He turned off the PlayStation. "I'm going to bed. Perhaps this will make sense in the morning."

As Pravi headed off to the bedroom, Alex got up and left, wondering if anything could make sense of the previous half hour.

Placenta Circle

Saturday, 30th July 2016

"Helen, darling, you're looking gorgeous as usual."

Peter stepped through the door and bent down to kiss Helen on each cheek.

"And if I'm not mistaken, that's Chanel No. 5 I'm smelling? Always been my favourite."

Helen blushed as Peter reached past her to extend a hand to Alex. "And Alex – hope you're still taking care of this one?"

Alex shook Peter's hand and felt the bones in his own fingers crush. "She's still alive, so I must be doing something right."

"Excellent, excellent. Your cooking can't be that bad, eh?" Peter slapped Alex on the top of his arm, slightly knocking him off balance. "Looks like we'll be safe tonight. What's the chef got in store for us?"

"Oh, nothing fancy. Beef wellington followed by crème brûlée. Mussels for starters."

"Sounds wonderful, Alex." Peter checked his reflection in the hall mirror, running his fingers backwards through his brown hair. "Still not applied for *MasterChef* yet? Helen always said that's what impressed her the most in your little speed date all those years ago." Before Alex had a chance to answer, Peter turned back to Helen. "Do you remember, H, that time at uni I tried to cook a roast chicken for us? Almost got us burnt out of the halls of residence in our first year!"

Helen laughed. "The only thing we saved was the carrots – all two of them. Worst Sunday roast ever. Sorry Becky, come in. Don't get me and Peter started on old uni stories otherwise we won't even get to dinner."

Becky came into the hall, air-kissed Helen and gave her a bottle of an expensive-looking red wine. "Hi, Helen. We'll leave cracking this open until later in that case."

Alex had made sure he was wearing his best, newest shirt and a decent pair of jeans, but when Becky approached, she still looked at him as if he'd raided his wardrobe blindfolded.

"Hello, Alex," she said, giving him a kiss that was in a different postcode to his cheek. Straightening out his collar, she added, "So, have you made an honest woman out of Helen yet? We were wondering if tonight there was going to be a special announcement."

Alex and Helen looked at each other. Alex began to stutter a reply when Helen moved in. "He should be so lucky. No, we thought it was high time we repaid the favour from January. Come on through and sit down."

The four of them sat in the front room, Alex and Helen on one black leather two-seater at right angles to Peter and Becky on another. As Peter and Becky gave updates on their jobs, not for the first time Alex's mind wandered to a week ago. He'd only spoken to Pravi once since it happened, and even then, only briefly. Pravi hadn't touched the game or the controller since and apparently had no intention of doing so.

Helen prodded Alex's legs and brought him back into the conversation. "Tell them about your sales meeting, honey." She turned to her guests. "He went ice skating and then insulted their Chief Technology Officer!"

"I'd rather not," Alex said. "It wasn't exactly my finest hour." Alex rose and put some music on. "How's the cricket season going, Peter?"

"Could not be better – I'm on course for top run scorer for the third season running." Peter mimed smashing a ball. "Are you doing any sport at the moment?"

"Him?" Helen interjected. "Not unless you call video games a sport."

Alex stuck his tongue out at her.

"So, what about the meeting?" Becky said. "Why were you skating and what did you say?"

Alex told them the story, which had Becky giggling and Peter covering his face. He looked towards Helen, who was now deadpan. She took a deep breath.

"It wasn't all his fault, though. He had babies on his mind that day because …" She looked at Peter and Becky and patted her stomach. Becky ceased laughing and gaped at Helen. Peter was still hiding behind his hands, but as silence descended, he moved them away and was momentarily confused at the scene in front of him.

"H? I don't understand?"

"I'm pregnant. Ta-da!" She waved her hands in the air. "Sorry, didn't know how to announce it."

For a second, looking at the frozen expressions on both their friends' faces, Alex thought that somehow time had gone awry, that a pause button had been activated.

"But you can't be," Becky said.

"Don't you start," Helen said. "That's what Alex said when I told him. I am – just over two months. I was going to wait for the first scan to tell you, but that's soon and so I thought tonight was too good an opportunity to miss."

"I mean … you didn't even say to me you were trying," Becky said.

Helen gave a brief cough. "Er, we weren't. It was a surprise." She held Alex's hand. "A nice surprise, but I admit it was quite a shock."

Becky went silent and looked at Peter to comment. Alex knew from Helen that Becky and Peter had been trying for a baby unsuccessfully for a while. He scrutinised their faces during the long pause.

"I'm not sure what to say, H," Peter finally said, sitting straight up. "Of all the things me and Becky tried to guess why you'd invited us round for, it certainly wasn't that."

"How about 'congratulations'?" Alex said. The horrified look on Peter's face after Alex's remark was worth every penny of Waitrose's finest beef.

"Of course!" Peter said as he shot to his feet. "Where are

our manners? Congratulations to you both!" He went over to Helen, held her hands and kissed her cheek, before shaking Alex's hand like he was trying to get water out of a deep well. "I'm sorry, but it took us by surprise."

Becky and Helen stood up and embraced. Alex didn't know the etiquette for receiving congratulations from someone who didn't really mean it, but he rose to his feet and looked at Becky.

"Didn't think you had it in you, Alex," Becky said. "Though I didn't have you down as a dad type." She gave him a gentle hug before pulling back and looking him up and down. "More like … an irresponsible uncle."

"He's going to have to learn to be responsible," Helen said. "Not only does he need to look after me for the next six-and-a-bit months, but I've got to get him trained on all things baby-related."

"Like nappies," Peter said. "Have you ever put one on a baby, Alex?"

"Er, no, don't think I've had that pleasure," Alex replied.

"And cleaning up poo," Becky said.

"I'm sure I'll have to do lots of that, but—"

"Burping, I hear that's tricky," Helen added.

"Just getting them off to sleep is an acquired skill," Becky said.

Alex watched as the three of them played baby poker while each addressing Alex in turn.

"Projectile vomiting!"

"The moment when their belly button falls off."

"Nipple squirting! I saw this thing on YouTube where the mere sound of a baby set this mother off shooting milk out of her boobs like a machine gun."

"And reflux. Also whooping cough. That's nasty."

"The placenta!" Peter said, pointing at Alex. "Now, surely being a man who's adventurous in the kitchen, you'd want to cook the placenta?"

Alex had gone pale. "What's the placenta? Is that a special meal the dad's meant to cook when the baby comes home?"

The three of them burst out laughing as he sat there waiting to be let in on the joke.

"Dear, dear Alex," Becky said, "you've got so much to learn." She tilted her head and looked at him apologetically. "The placenta is part of the afterbirth. It's rare, but people have been known to eat it for its nutritious content."

Alex hated himself for wanting to ask the next question, but he had to know. "After … birth?"

"Yes, you know – the stuff that comes out of the woman's uterus after the baby comes out."

"That sounds disgusting," Alex said.

"It's perfectly natural, part of the whole birth process," Becky said.

"And you say people cook it? Prepare a meal based on something that's come out of your body? That's gross."

"Fry it up with a pinch of salt and pepper – might be a MasterChef first!" Peter said.

Alex felt a bit of sick come up into his mouth. "Excuse

me while I go and check dinner." He left the others to discuss babies and went into the kitchen. Getting out a frying pan for the mussels, he paused. He couldn't picture what a placenta might look like, but his brain had given him an image of a circle of bloody entrails and mucus sitting there ready to be fried to a crispy brown. Dry-heaving, he rushed to the window to get some fresh air but all he could think of was poo, vomit and, most weirdly, an army of topless women marching over a battlefield squirting milk over their enemy.

"Are you OK, my friend?"

Alex spun round to see Peter in the kitchen. "Yeah, I … it's roasting in here with the oven on, so just getting some cool air in."

"Apologies for going on about the placenta thing. I think it sounds utterly bonkers. Look, I'm popping out to get some champagne. Can't have us celebrate this fantastic news with a cheap bottle of Merlot, can we?" Before Alex could reply, Peter had dashed out the door.

"I'll start on the mussels soon," announced Alex as he sat down next to Helen again. "So, Becky, what's new with you?"

"Me? Never mind me. Tonight's all about you two, or should I say three!" Becky let out a strange, high-pitched giggle and gulped down some water. "I know it wasn't planned, but you're so, so lucky. So when are we going shopping? You'll need to go shopping for clothes – for the baby and for you. You're going to get ridiculously, gorgeously fat, but I know some great places to get maternity dresses."

Helen inhaled loudly. "I'm not going to get fat, I'm going to bloom. And anyway, once we get the scan out of the way, the first things we'll be shopping for are Moses baskets, cots and car seats."

"We are?" Alex said, facing her.

"Yes. You need to look for a new car as well."

He could almost hear his commission floating away and his bank account draining. Having lived a bachelor life for many years before meeting Helen, he'd accumulated a nice heap of savings, a large chunk of which had now been sunk into their house. They'd had five years of holidays, theatre trips and buying nigh on whatever they wanted, whenever they wanted. After years of working hard and saving, the rest of it was about to go, all thanks to a single night of passion.

Alex slipped back into the kitchen while Becky and Helen continued talking. Peter returned a short while later, brandishing a bottle of champagne that looked more at home on an F1 podium. "Not much good for you now, H, but these," he said, bringing out a huge bunch of flowers from behind his back, "are for you."

"Thank you so much," Helen said. "Very thoughtful."

Alex peered round the kitchen door to see Helen dwarfed by a floral display and hugging Peter, cursing himself that he hadn't thought of giving her anything yet. Peter looked back towards him. "Hope you don't mind,

Alex. I'm sure you've got her a much nicer bunch elsewhere, but I couldn't resist."

"Honey, could you put these in water for me?" Helen said to Alex. "That's if you can find a vase that isn't already in use." She passed them to him with a sarcastic look. Alex sighed, slunk back into the kitchen and picked up his phone to text Pravi.

Dinner party from hell. Next Saturday I'm coming round yours. Wanna go back to 96?

Back to the Past

Saturday, 6th August 2016

"So, dinner with Peter Perfect and Bitchy Becky was as fun as you thought it'd be?" Pravi asked, as Alex arrived at the flat.

Alex collapsed onto Pravi's gaming chair and turned up the sports news on the TV.

"On the plus side, my beef wellington was a hit with everyone. On the negative side, I had to suffer nearly four hours of baby talk."

"Ouch," Pravi said, relaxing on the sofa. "Then I guess you don't want to watch a box set of *One Born Every Minute*?"

Alex growled. "Definitely not. I'd prefer to do something more interesting." He gestured to the controller on the sofa that had been left exactly where it had been thrown by Pravi over a week ago.

Pravi looked up but stayed silent.

"So," Alex continued, "any further theories? We can't just pretend it didn't happen."

"I know," Pravi said. "The whole thing was freaky, but for me not having my chair as well … I kinda panicked."

"I don't blame you. So, what do you think really happened?"

Pravi glanced at the pad. "You tell me. The impossible happened, if what you saw and experienced was true."

"I've been thinking about it," Alex said. "I work with techies who, if faced with this problem, would start with the facts. Firstly, the pad has clearly been modified in some way." He picked it up and examined it. "Quite how they could transport us to anywhere or any time I've no idea, but it's not your normal pad." He flipped it over. "What number did it have previously in the digital display?"

"I remember it showing 99 when we were in the toilet," Pravi replied. "Why? What does it say now?"

"98. Strange. Gone down by 1."

"That doesn't really help us."

"True. Second fact: I remember that the game said the retro controller had been activated. We won the final and unlocked something that activated it."

"'Cause that happens all the time, doesn't it? Complete a game and it goes all Harry Potter on you," Pravi said, waving an imaginary wand in the air.

"Regardless, the facts point to that happening. We then pressed the given button combo and experienced blinding lights and what I can only describe as like putting your head inside a vacuum cleaner."

"A secret Dyson project?"

"And then we appeared in a toilet in 1996."

"That's not a fact, though," Pravi said. "Just a theory."

"Again, true. So what facts do we have that might support this theory?" He stood up. "One – the toilet. It was very old school, basic. Not many pubs still have urinal troughs."

"Hardly conclusive proof. Some curry houses around here still have those roller towel dispensers to dry your hands."

"Two – it was definitely England v Switzerland on the TV, the very first match of Euro 96."

"Could easily be showing a replay, as we discussed."

"But it wasn't, Prav, I know it. I saw the passion in the fans, the excitement and expectation. It was absolutely rammed for what turned out to be our worst game of the tournament, with people all in England Euro 96 shirts. However unlikely it was, they were all in the moment … and we were with them."

Alex could see Pravi didn't have an argument against any of what he'd said. They'd been friends long enough to trust each other's judgement, no matter how bizarre it might seem. "I want to go back."

"No way," Pravi said, getting back into his wheelchair. "Whatever voodoo crap is going on with this, I don't want a repeat journey."

"Aren't you curious? We don't even know where we went, even if we know when. We can't leave it like this. Think about it – we may have … well, time travelled."

"Sorry, McFly, but I'm staying in 2016."

"Dude, we may have gone back to Euro 96." Alex

gesticulated towards Pravi. "Euro 96! Until Southgate's penalty miss, that was possibly the greatest few weeks of my life. Before this, if someone had given me the chance to go back to that period, I'd happily have cut off my right arm."

"Really? And curtail your sex life?"

Alex shook the pad at Pravi. "Let's go back tonight. Get to the bottom of it. If you sat in your wheelchair and—"

"No, Alex. If you want to go all *Doctor Who* on me then go ahead, but I don't want to be your glamorous companion."

Alex sighed and spun the controller in his hands. "Do you think I could go back on my own? We jumped together both times."

Pravi thought for a few seconds. "Yeah, but each time we were both holding the pad."

As much as he wanted to go back with Pravi, after last time he could understand the reluctance. With an overwhelming desire to answer some questions, he had only one choice. "Remind me what buttons I have to press?"

"You seriously doing this?" Pravi said.

Alex pointed the controller at Pravi. "Yes. If you're too chicken, I'll go on my own."

Pravi sat up and told him the combination. "Just promise you won't get stuck there, otherwise Helen will think I've killed you."

Alex gave a thumbs-up. "I'll be back before you know it. Laters, loser."

Alex pressed the buttons and was gone.

Ceefax Page 302

Saturday, 8th June 1996

The first thing Alex heard when he recovered his senses again was a long, drawn-out fart.

"What stunt?" said a voice Alex thought he recognised. He stayed silent, gaining his bearings once more. It looked like the same toilet cubicle they were in before.

"What stunt are you saying I've pulled off? I'm just having a clear out here. You guys must be tripping."

Alex thought back to when he was last here over a week ago. In his confusion and paranoia, didn't Pravi say something about a stunt then? That he knew what "they" were up to? Last time, they'd jumped back home and arrived having lost no time. Now, back in the past, it looked like he was resuming a conversation. All of this suggested that he'd arrived exactly at the point of time he left.

"Er, never mind," he replied. "Too many beers." He looked at his watch – twenty past eight. That time was now irrelevant here, but he guessed from his last visit that it was still around twenty-five minutes after kick-off. Deciding it was time to explore again, he stuffed the game controller in his jeans pocket, left the toilets, and went back into the main part of the pub.

Once again, he made his way through the crowd of people, but this time kept back in a corner near the bar. A glance up to a clock on the wall confirmed it was nearly half past three. Everyone was cheering or smiling, buoyed by Shearer's goal a few minutes ago, and the odd song broke out. Before, he'd only noticed the old football shirts, but now looking around at the jeans and footwear of the people around him it appeared very much like the fashion was from another period. It was only then that it occurred to him that he might look out of place. His pair of jeans weren't stonewashed for a start and his t-shirt sported a logo for a company that hadn't been invented yet, but luckily his retro trainers looked like they'd been bought within the last year.

He'd looked up the match on the internet last week and seen that it had been the only match of the tournament that day, 8th June 1996, three o'clock kick-off at Wembley. Although he had a restricted view of the screen, he decided to stay for a while and enjoy watching some of England's finest players of his generation. He was about to go to the bar for a beer until he realised he had no money on him. Standing in a pub, watching England start to toil, it almost felt like a normal Saturday international football afternoon. After a while, he spotted a copy of *The Sun* sat on a table in front of him, half covered by a man's arm. A newspaper – the classic time travel method confirmation of the current date. Alex asked the man if he could take a look. Heart racing, he peeked at the top of the front page: Saturday, 8th June 1996. It wasn't logical, it shouldn't be happening, but Alex was a time traveller.

At half-time, Alex decided that the next course of action would be to find out precisely where he was. The pub looked familiar, perhaps one he'd had a drink in as a teenager, and listening to the accents of the surrounding people, he was confident he was somewhere not too far away from home. With the pub filled wall to wall with people and blinds pulled down over the windows so the projector screen could be seen, Alex realised he'd not even had a glimpse of what was outside. An absurd thought struck him: what if he couldn't get outside? What if this piece of the past was restricted to this single pub, stuck in some weird anomaly? Or perhaps this was an alternate 1996, one where Britain was different, Labour wasn't primed to take power and Switzerland didn't equalise in the eighty-third minute. There was only one way to find out, so he fought his way to the exit.

The first good news Alex experienced was that there at least looked like a world beyond the pub's doors. It also looked reasonably normal, in that there were no dinosaurs roaming around or alien overlords patrolling the streets. The old Ford Escorts in the car park complied with the timelines he now realised he was in. He pushed open the door, stepped outside into the warm afternoon, and began to explore.

The next good news was that he had worked out

precisely where he was. The pub was The Crown, a mere ten minutes' walk away from Pravi's flat. They'd moved there together in 1995 and Alex shared a few great years before moving on and leaving Pravi to reside there until the present day. As this was the start of Euro 96, he remembered that the flat would currently be empty, given that they had both gone off to Birmingham to stay with friends and get drunk for the whole tournament. With nowhere else to go to, he took a few steps in its direction, but then stopped. Kids were knocking about footballs in the street ahead, waiting for the second half to begin, and a group of lads walked past with beer supplies and headed into a house. After all the excitement of being here, he suddenly realised he was on his own.

He had options, though. Most of his family was in Hertfordshire and he had a few other friends around here that he could see. Unfortunately, showing up as 38-year-old Alex would almost certainly freak anyone out, so that was out of the question. The flat was his only real option, he decided, and as the origin of this whole adventure, he was strangely drawn to it. He continued towards it, on a nostalgic walk of his youth. Was McDonald's ever that garish red? Did people really buy those Skodas? Before long, he was at the entrance to the flat he knew so well, wondering how he could get in. Jumping back to Pravi and asking for the key wasn't going to help because he knew that the key had been changed several times over the years. Two were after burglaries and one was after an angry ex-girlfriend of

Pravi ran off with a key, threatening all sorts of revenge. Breaking in was a possibility, but then he didn't want to alert anyone and risk the unthinkable mess that might occur should he get arrested. He sat down outside the door to think when he heard the letterbox of the flat opposite squeak open.

"Who's there?" said a voice from within the flat.

Startled, Alex leapt up, but then he realised he knew the owner of the voice. "Mrs Winston?"

There was a pause and more rattling of the letterbox. "I'm not telling you. You might be the IRA."

It was unmistakably Mrs Winston – the elderly busybody neighbour whose fear of people was high and quality of eyesight low. He hadn't seen her for years, vaguely recalling she'd moved into a home at some point. But he did remember one very important fact that would help him right now – she had a spare key. "Er, it's Alex, Mrs Winston. From number 82."

"Alex?"

He was unsure if he sounded any different to 1996 Alex, so did his best impression of his young, foolish self. "Yeah, Alex, as in me and Praveen opposite. The teenagers who doss around all day, drink beer and watch footy." He cringed at his effort and the absurdity of having to perform such an act.

"How do I know it's you? I can't see so well these days."

He took a moment to think. Having been trapped in a few doorstep conversations with her, he knew a thing or two. "You have a cat called Casper, your husband was Alfie, you put lavender in every clothes drawer you have and you had your hip replaced on your seventieth birthday."

The letterbox shut and there was a wait before he heard several chains slide back and then saw the door open a crack. "Alex, so it is you. I won't come out though, as it's not July yet."

"That's OK, Mrs Winston. Um, I was wondering, do you have our spare key? I've only gone and locked myself out. I'm such an idiot."

He heard faint laughter, followed by a hacking cough. "Give me a minute, I'm sure I know where it is …"

Ten minutes later, she returned to the door and held out a shaky hand with a silver key in it. Alex took it, thanked his old neighbour and resisted the urge to kiss the metal in his hand.

Letting himself into the flat was like opening a time capsule. The layout made things very familiar, particularly as Alex had only just come from the flat in his present time. But everything was different – recognisably different. As he looked around, memories sparked from every sight. His old, green winter coat was hanging up by the door, last seen in a nightclub in Nottingham circa 1997. He bent down to pick up a pair of Nike trainers that he treasured and wore until they fell apart. On the walls were posters stuck with Blu Tack – *Star Wars*, Oasis and his favourite: Ricardo Villa and Ossie Ardiles with the 1981 FA Cup. He peered into the kitchen, remembering the hideous green tiles and the stained brown lino. But it was the living room that provided him with his best and warmest vision from the past: a worn brown sofa, a Sony 29-inch TV, and the original grey PlayStation.

"Woah," he said as he perched on the sofa that Pravi and Alex had spent so much time on over the years. The console looked so dated compared to the current model and yet here it was, perfect in its natural environment. Alex sat there for a while to take it all in, to soak up the nostalgia. It was home – home to a carefree life where he had all the time he wanted and none of the responsibilities he didn't.

Alex was desperate for Pravi to share this experience with him, especially as he felt that it was only right for him to be here, too. However, he wasn't sure if it was possible, even if he convinced him to return. Assuming he could jump again back to the present at the same time he left, if they both jumped back again, Alex didn't know where they'd end up. Back at the pub's toilets again, or back here? And would time reset to the start of the England match or might it resume? The answer would only come from trying it, something that Alex didn't want to do yet in case he could never return here, to this glorious piece of his past he'd only thought he'd experience again in memories and anecdotes. Instead, he got up and examined his old bedroom. Turning on the light, he almost expected to see his past self lying under the Spurs duvet, but to his relief it was empty. The room was a complete mess – clothes everywhere, cans of Carling on the window ledge, copies of *Loaded* and *FHM* magazines littering the floor and a pizza box wedged under the bed. It was the sort of scene that had Helen ever witnessed, she would have surely run screaming for the door. Pravi's room was far neater, as if it had to balance out Alex's room for the sake of the universe. He took the controller out of his pocket and prepared to jump back, noticing the number displayed on it had decreased by 1, now showing 97.

"One more thing to check," he said to himself, grabbing the TV remote and switching on the TV. "Ceefax … how do I activate that? Ah, yes." The BBC teletext service came up and Alex almost hugged the screen. Checking the date and making a note of the time, he scanned his old flat one last time, pressed the controller's buttons and vanished.

Do You Want Fries With That?

"Alex! Alex! You OK? Are you OK? Do you hear me?"

Alex had fallen onto the floor. A dark shape loomed above his head. "Prav?"

"Of course it's me. What happened? You disappeared and then reappeared immediately. Didn't it work?"

Alex staggered to his feet and collapsed onto the cold leather of the gaming chair. "What's the time?"

Pravi looked at his watch. "8:21. Why?"

Alex held out his wrist. "What does that say? I'm still a bit fuzzy."

"9:30. So that means …"

"I had over an hour in good ol' 1996."

"Wow. Really? What did you see? What happened? Is it for real?"

Alex proceeded to take him through his entire journey and how he ended up back at the flat.

"Wow. My flat? I mean – our flat? Man, that's bizarre. You were here, twenty years ago, but also a moment ago at the same time?"

Alex looked at the two-digit display on the controller again and showed it to Pravi. "Yep, and look – it went down to 97 when I was there, but now it says 96."

"So, it goes down by one every time you jump?" Pravi said, thinking. "Maybe it's the number of jumps we have left?"

"Looks like it. So, wanna join me in some time travelling?" Alex said, gesturing with the controller. "There's a PlayStation original waiting to be played."

Pravi stroked his chin. "What if we end up back at the pub with no wheelchair again?"

Alex got up again. "I'll scout ahead then. Give me your wheelchair and I'll jump back now, see where I end up and then return. From your point of view, that should take milliseconds, right?"

"You make it sound like you're going out for milk." Pravi gave Alex his wheelchair. "Try gripping it tightly to see if it goes with you."

Alex hooked his left arm round the arm of the wheelchair. "Let's see if this works. Laters." He pressed the button sequence and both he and the wheelchair vanished.

As fast as he had gone, Alex reappeared in front of Pravi. Although he was getting used to the effects now, he rubbed his ears. "Woah," he said too loudly. "I wouldn't recommend doing two jumps in quick succession."

Pravi helped him out of the wheelchair. "So? Where did you end up? I take it the wheelchair jumped too, as it also disappeared."

"Back at the flat, at the same time I left it a few minutes ago. Wheelchair intact and functional."

"The exact same time?"

"Yep, I checked Ceefax both times. Give or take a few seconds for me to see again after the jump, it was spot on."

"Ceefax? Awesome," Pravi said. "So if I saw you appear and disappear here virtually simultaneously and you don't lose any time there, then …"

"We jump back to '96 to the exact time and place we left it. And when we return home, we go back to the exact time and place we left there." Alex considered this. "Although, we've only jumped from your flat in the present, so I guess we can't be sure we always end up back home where we jumped. But I could test that, too."

"It wouldn't be the end of the world if we always came back here, but would be nice to know."

Alex started to walk towards the door. "OK, I'll go out and try it. This is amazing!"

"Hang on a second, you moron. Where are you going to do this? You can't do a vanishing act in the middle of the street. Don't forget the state that you end up in when you jump back."

Alex stopped. "Good point." He paused then said, "Don't worry, I've got an idea."

The McDonald's he passed earlier in 1996 gave him the inspiration for his next trip. Going into the present day one, he went straight into the toilets, locked the door and jumped back to 1996. At their flat, he walked into Pravi's old bedroom and opened a drawer by his bed. As expected, he found a coffee jar that contained a bunch of banknotes that

Pravi had squirrelled away.

"Result! Knew I could rely on you, Prav," he said to the empty room. He took out a £5 note and examined it, long since invalid in 2016. He was about to leave when he thought of a prank that would have him chuckling all the way home. On the back of an envelope he found in the bin, he scrawled something and put it into Pravi's jar. He then left and went down the road to McDonald's.

"One Big Mac, please," Alex said to the teenager behind the counter.

"Do you want fries with that?" squeaked the boy in reply.

"No, thanks. How about a McFlurry?"

The boy opened his mouth and then looked for help. His manager must have been busy. "Er, I'm not sure, um …" He scoured the till for a clue then looked behind him again for someone to save him. "What was that again?"

"Never mind, just the burger, thanks," Alex said with a smirk.

The boy dropped his shoulders in relief and fetched the food. Alex handed over the fiver, took the change and then headed off to the flat where he jumped back to the present … and found himself back on the McDonald's toilet floor in the present day. Once he had stabilised, he exited the toilets and headed down to the serving counter. The menu above was so much brighter, with a much bigger choice, and there was a similar-looking youth behind the counter.

"Hello, what can I get you?"

"One Big Mac, please," replied Alex.

After receiving his food, he walked back to Pravi's flat.

"There you go," Alex said, presenting Pravi with two containers. "I got you something – choose."

Pravi peered at each of the gifts. "Big Macs?"

"Here," Alex said, wiggling the box in his right hand, "is your up-to-date model, while this," he continued waving the box in his other hand, "is your retro burger."

Pravi snatched the modern one. "You went to McD's in 1996?"

"Thought it would make an interesting comparison. It also gave me somewhere I could jump from without being noticed."

"Did you end up back there after jumping?"

"Yep. It seems you always return back to where you jumped, both past and present."

Pravi took out his burger. "Cool. At least you know where you're going to and what it's like, as you'll find it exactly how you left it and *when* you left it."

Alex opened his box and examined its contents. "Looks good."

Pravi bit into his burger before saying, "Hang on – how did you pay for it? Haven't we changed some of the notes and coins since '96?"

"Your underwear drawer," he said, before taking a nibble of his food. "Mmm, surprisingly tasty, considering it's over twenty years old."

"My what?"

"Your money jar. That's where you hid it, didn't you?

You thought I never knew about that. I took a fiver out, and then as a special treat added an IOU in shaky handwriting."

"But why?"

"Because when past you finds it, he'll have a right go at past me, who won't have a clue about it. They'll end up thinking I must have been drunk when I stole it." Alex laughed.

"That's messed up."

They headed back to the living room and sat down again.

"It brings me on to something else we need to talk about," Pravi said. "Causality."

"What do you mean?" Alex said.

"For us, this world we live in, 1996 has already happened, right? Whatever went on then was part of events that led everyone to be here, in 2016."

"Ah. I think I know where you're going."

"You've now gone back and changed something in the past. No matter how small, that may have ramifications here, for us, for everyone in 2016."

"You're basically saying I may have changed history. Cool."

"It's not cool – it could be catastrophic. That note you left in my jar – what if we have a massive fight over it and you move out sooner than you originally did?"

Alex considered this. "But I didn't. At least, I don't remember doing that. Even if I did, nothing's changed. We're still here. I didn't start World War Three by buying a Big Mac."

"We need to find out what happens when things do change, though. What if you do something back then which means you and Helen aren't together now? Or that you're still together but she's not pregnant anymore? You wouldn't really want that, now that you know you'll be a dad, would you?"

Alex fell silent.

"Precisely," Pravi said.

"Enough with the philosophical crap. Surely there must be an easy way of finding this out? Let's jump back to our flat and figure it out. At least that's a safe haven. I promise I won't leave any more notes. I can even remove that one if you like."

"I'm not jumping until I know the score."

Alex got up and once again walked up and down the lounge. "OK, what are the time travel options?"

"First is the classic change the past, change your future."

"*Back to the Future*-style?"

"Yep. You kill your dad, you're history. You give yourself a betting tip, you go back a millionaire."

Alex mulled this over. "What else?"

"Second scenario is that you can't change the past. The universe somehow prevents you from doing anything that upsets its timelines."

"Sounds feeble to me. So the gun wouldn't fire when I shoot my dad? I don't buy that for a second."

"Fine. Third scenario is when you can change things, but somehow the universe over time puts things right again."

"Can't see how that works," Alex said. "Another cop-out."

"The last one I can think of is that you can go back and do whatever you like without affecting the present, as they are different timelines."

"But what constitutes a timeline? Is that a whole new universe? How many of them are there?"

"Look, I'm not Albert Einstein and this is all just theory," Pravi said. "I don't know how any of this works. All I know from watching numerous time travel films and reading books is that history is invariably under threat and things get messy."

"So what do we do?"

"We do what any scientist would do: run some experiments, prove a hypothesis, and formulate the result. Pick a theory."

"I'm not shooting my dad," Alex said. "He still owes me twenty quid."

"All right, let's take the first scenario. If you do something in the flat in the past, then if this is true, we should see it here."

"Like what?"

"I dunno, put a hole somewhere? You have to do something not obvious but significant enough so that it lasts and we can prove it."

They discussed options and decided that scratching a name in the concrete underneath the loose carpet in a cupboard would do the trick. If it was only one timeline and the past affected their present, the mark would still be there today. If not, then 1996 was on a different path. Pravi watched Alex grab his phone, jump and return.

"That still freaks me out watching you do that," Pravi said as his friend reappeared. "Now go and check the cupboard when you're finished being blind."

Alex got up and inspected the cupboard. "Nothing. It's definitely not there. Look at the photo I took."

They scrutinised the image on Alex's phone. It was the same cupboard and identical floor under the peeled back blue carpet but with "Alex 2016" scrawled in the concrete.

"What do you think?" Alex said. "There's no way that could have been removed, so it must be a different timeline. No effect on us here. It's a different past to what we know."

"Sounds like we can pop back and do whatever we like. Sweet."

Alex started walking around the room. "We could go back, watch the whole tournament there, get drunk, eat crisps until we puke and we'd have no one and nothing to worry about. How awesome would that be?"

"But three weeks living in the 1996 version of this place?" Pravi grimaced. "We had lumpy beds, a mouldy bathroom and a kitchen that bordered on a health hazard. And I still don't trust this time travel wizardry-pokery."

"Fair points," Alex said. "Why don't we try a day at a time? I could come round every Saturday, spend a whole day in '96 and still get to see Helen in the evening."

Pravi laughed. "Sounds like you've got it all worked out."

He exhaled deeply. "OK, I'm in – let's do this!"

Alex sat down again and faced Pravi. "Although …"

"What?"

Alex looked at the grey carpet. "It sounds silly, but we've got our first scan next week, and I don't want to mess anything up. Let's do it after that."

"Ooh, look at you, Mr Responsible Daddy," Pravi said.

"Sod off. We'd have to work out a few things if we were to stay in '96 for a while, but I'll phone you next Friday after the scan to arrange it." He slapped Pravi on the shoulder. "We're going to be time travellers!"

The Dentist Chair

Saturday, 15th June 1996

"Is this awesome or what?" Alex said as he opened a lager.

For the previous six Saturday nights in 2016, Alex and Pravi had been jumping back to 1996 and spending a day watching the whole Euro 96 coverage on TV, playing old PlayStation titles and generally doing whatever they wanted. Today was the second Saturday in the championship, where hosts England were about to play their old rivals, Scotland.

Pravi leaned forward on the sofa, poured his beer into a glass and raised it to Alex. "One of the finest England moments in our lifetime and we're going to watch it live … again!"

The pre-match analysis was in full swing.

"Ah, look at the Scottish fans," Alex said, pointing at the screen showing the Tartan Army's finest in full voice. "So full of hope, so desperate to get one over us in our own backyard. Suckers."

"Wish I was there, knowing what's going to happen," Pravi said.

"Do you reckon we could've got tickets for this?"

"To Wembley? They must have sold out ages ago and we couldn't just turn up at the gate and pay."

"I suppose not. Mind you, when Gazza scores, we might hear the roar from here."

Alex took a swig from his can and then slammed it down on the table, froth bubbling from the top. "What are we doing inside, alone, watching this epic? Let's get out there!"

"Out where?" Pravi said. "Wembley? Haven't we just covered that?"

"No – out there." Alex pointed to the front door. "Let's go to the pub, mingle with the locals, celebrate as if we're really back in '96."

"We *are* back in '96."

"I know, but it's not that much different to watching a replay of the live broadcast, is it? We're *here* here, possibly the only two people in the entire universe to experience this … and we're sat in your flat like two saddos with no other mates in the world."

Pravi muted the TV. "I don't want to push it. Whatever this is, it shouldn't be happening. If we go out into the world, who knows what problems we'll face?" Pravi looked around the room. "This isn't our time, we're not meant to be here."

Alex got up and walked to Pravi's empty wheelchair. "What a load of rubbish. For a start, this isn't seventy million years B.C. where we're sitting in a cave surrounded by dinosaurs that humans never got close to meeting. This was our time – we're simply revisiting it. It's like we're reminiscing, except that we actually go back and experience the past."

"Like that's normal," Pravi said.

"What are you afraid of? We've already proved that we can't do anything here that affects our present, so what could go wrong for us if we venture out?"

"We could get stuck here for a start."

"We'll be careful. Assuming we're correct on what the number represents, we have over seventy jumps to play with, so we'll be fine."

"It's OK for you, but if I recall 1996 wasn't as accepting or as easy to get around for me compared to nowadays. Especially in crowded pubs – I remember one guy kept spinning me round every time we scored against Holland."

"We'll go to one of the less busy pubs round here."

"Everywhere's gonna be rammed for this match."

Alex pushed the wheelchair nearer to Pravi. "Granted, it'll be packed wherever we go, but we don't have to be right in amongst it as we always used to be. We can be on the edges, hang back and observe. When Scotland win the penalty, we can be all smug and confident and tell people big Dave will save it."

"That was a wild few minutes," Pravi said. "Would be kinda fun."

"An hour till kick-off. Let's do it!" Alex patted the wheelchair's armrests.

"Where will we go?" Pravi said. "Don't think I want to go back to the pub we jumped to. That bloke might still be stinking out the toilet."

"The Crown?" Alex said. "But then I never did like it in there. Wait – what are we thinking? The Dog and Duck hasn't been demolished yet. That's where we always used to go."

Pravi chuckled. "Wow, The D and D. It's been a while."

"Then what do you say?"

"Only one problem: it's our local in this time period. We're bound to run into people we know there. Only they won't know us, well, not this version of us."

Alex scratched the back of his head. "Too weird?"

"Definitely," Pravi said. "They may think I'm my own dad."

Alex laughed. "And that your whole family must be in wheelchairs. OK, somewhere else then?"

Pravi watched a silent Gascoigne being interviewed. "No one ever used to go down to The Sailor. Bunch of old men in there."

"We'll fit in fine, then. To The Sailor!"

Despite complaining the whole way there that it wasn't a good idea and expecting to be stared at by the locals like they were aliens, once Pravi had found a spot at the back of the pub, he settled down. The place was very functional, with sparse decoration aside from frames of old *Punch* cartoons. The clientele consisted entirely of men who were facing the two large projector screens at the front of the pub, their own playing days long over. Alex approached the bar, which sat like a mirage under a simmering haze of smoke. In front of him were two men discussing the match, one in an England blazer and the other wearing a checked flat cap.

"We'd better not lose to Scotland," the man in the blazer said. "My father-in-law's Scottish and he'll make Christmas hell for an eternity."

"I wouldn't count it out," the other man said. "Especially the way we played against Switzerland."

"Can you believe it's been thirty years since '66? This bunch of lads aren't even fit to clean their boots."

Alex couldn't resist joining in. "Gazza's something special, though. Reckon he'll have a good game today."

Both men turned round and gave Alex a suspicious look. The one in the flat cap said, "That fool is past his best. 1990 was his year, he's just a disgrace now."

"No, he's going to score, you'll see. He'll pull off a stroke of genius," Alex said.

"Only thing he's likely to pull is a hamstring," the man in the cap said.

"We'll see," Alex replied, as he nudged his way to the bar. After ordering two pints of the least worst draught they had available, Alex headed back towards Pravi. As he got nearer, he could see him in conversation with one of the barmaids who was collecting glasses from tables. She had squatted down to speak to him and was smiling as they talked.

"Excuse me miss," Alex said to her, "is my friend, Pravi, bothering you?"

The barmaid looked up and rose. "No, nothing like that. We were just chatting. I said I could clear a space nearer the screen if he would like to get closer."

"You two looked pretty close already," Alex said, flicking a glance between them.

She grabbed some empty glasses. "I guess I'll leave you both here then," she said, before heading back towards the bar.

"Thanks a lot, mate," Pravi said, staring at Alex.

"You're welcome," Alex replied, thrusting Pravi's pint towards him while still looking at the barmaid.

"I mean thanks for being a complete bellend."

"What?" Alex looked back at Pravi. "Sorry, did you think you're in there?"

Pravi gestured to the bar. "Didn't you recognise her?"

"The barmaid?" Alex shook his head. "Should I? You see I've not been in here for a while."

"It's her," Pravi said. "It's Ruby."

"Ruby?"

"That's probably not her real name, but that's the name I gave her, back in the day."

"We are back in the day." Alex took a seat opposite Pravi.

"You know what I mean," Pravi said.

"Sorry, but who the hell was – is – Ruby?"

"Don't you remember?" Alex continued his blank look, so Pravi said, "She was a barmaid in the Dog and Duck. It must have been a couple of months from now, so she hasn't met me yet, not past me. I was besotted with her, but she was in her late twenties and I never had the courage to utter a single word to her."

Alex looked back towards the bar. "Don't remember her. You sure?"

"Absolutely. She didn't stay there for long and I never saw her again. I can't believe it. It must be fate."

Alex choked on his drink. "Fate, right. I forgot I saw that in a fortune cookie last week: 'The woman you seek is in the past serving warm ale to old men in flat caps'."

Pravi looked away. "OK, not fate maybe, but she was a few years older than me back then and I was such a wuss, but now I've got some balls. I've spoken to her this time, which is progress."

"And now that you're a mature, wiser, more confident man, you think you can pull her?"

"I just wanted to talk to her. See what she's like."

"Forget it. For a start, we're here for the football. Concentrate on that instead of your dick for once."

Pravi gave Alex a few choice swear words. "It's not like that. Unfinished business, correcting a regret I've always had."

"Dream on. Anyway – here come the boys," Alex said, pointing to a TV which was their best bet for a view at this distance. The two teams filed on to the Wembley pitch, England being led out by their captain, Tony Adams. "If I remember correctly, you can forget the first half."

"Yeah, it all happened after half-time. Will be funny to

sit here and watch it all pan out," Pravi said.

"Spoke to a couple of the locals at the bar about Gazza. They don't rate him now. I'll make sure I go over there later and gloat."

"At least they didn't bet you any money."

Alex's mouth opened wide. "A bet! Why aren't we putting bets on this? Talk about a banker! We'd make a killing."

Pravi tutted. "For one, we haven't got much money here to bet. Also, is it ethical?"

"I'm not talking about betting people here." Alex gestured towards the bar. "I mean bookies. A few choice wagers on the Euros."

"And what would we do with the bags of out-of-date bank notes when we got them? We can't take them back to spend."

"It would keep us in beer here. Or we could leave some for our counterparts. Call it a gesture for them unknowingly letting us stay at the flat."

Pravi scratched his chin. "Still doesn't sit right with me."

"But chasing after a woman you shouldn't have met yet is OK?"

Pravi smirked. "That's different. It's not going to alter the future of my past self."

"It's not going to alter the future of your present self, either. Now forget about her and watch the match."

Alex and Pravi sat silent for a minute until the peace was interrupted by a shout from someone who'd just walked in.

"C'mon you Scotland!"

The whole pub turned to see a middle-aged man wearing a kilt with a bushy brown beard and a huge grin make his way into the pub. As brazen entrances went, this was up there, thought Alex.

Although there were many shocked faces around at the clear intrusion into a partisan pub, some of the locals appeared to have been expecting it and started some light-hearted banter with the Scot.

"He's got some cojones," Pravi said.

"He'll have two of the worst minutes of his life in about an hour's time," Alex said.

"Do you think it'll be exactly the same? Not just the score, but every kick of the ball, every run, every chant from the crowd? Will anything change?"

Alex gave it some thought. "None of the games have changed one bit from what I remember, but the very fact that we're here in this pub means that 1996 has changed in some way at least."

"You talking about the butterfly effect?" Pravi said.

"Possibly. I'm sure our existence holed up in the flat did little to disrupt anything, but now we're here, who knows?"

"Or even just random chance. Will every slight decision or action be the same? Perhaps one game will be different and everything else will change."

"Maybe even Scotland can get out of this group."

"We will – and we'll fuck you up!" shouted the Scot, who was now standing next to them.

Alex looked at Pravi, then back at the Scot. "I wouldn't be too sure of that, mate."

"We won't lose to you bunch of drunken pansies," the Scot said. "We've come to Wembley to win and that's what we'll do."

"Do you want to bet on that?" Alex asked.

"Alex, leave it," Pravi said.

"How much you got, you cocky English wanker?" He delved into his jeans pocket, searching for his wallet.

The barmaid appeared and grabbed his arm. "Leave it, Jack. Let's keep it friendly in here today, please."

Pravi gave Alex his best don't-say-another-word stare. Alex held up his hands in front of him.

"Ah, I'm only playing with them, Abigail," Jack said. "You know how much I love you English really."

"However much love or hatred you have, no matter what the result today, you're not going to show it in here, OK?" The barmaid waved a finger at Jack. "Go somewhere else if you feel the need to antagonise anyone." She shooed Jack further into the bar before turning to Pravi and Alex. "Sorry about that, boys. He's been waiting for this day for months."

"That's fine, Abigail. I'm sure he'll be crying later," Alex said.

"My name's Abby. No one calls me that except him ... and my fella, when he's not happy with me." She glanced back at the bar. "Suppose I'd better get back to it."

Abby left them once again. Pravi sat with a smug look. "Abby. So I wasn't far out with 'Ruby', was I?"

"Er, didn't you hear the bit about her having a fella? I think that dream of yours is over."

"Sounded like a temporary arrangement. It's not like I haven't got time on my hands to turn that around."

Alex waved the game controller in the air. "We're not using this just for your pursuit of Abby."

"Put it away!" Pravi said, pointing at it. "I don't want anyone to see that here. It could end up in all sorts of awkward questions."

"Relax. Even if someone does see it, I'll say it's some prototype."

"Even so. I don't want anything to happen to the controller," Pravi said. "It's our only way back, don't forget. How else are you going to return to the reality that is a pregnant, hormonal girlfriend who's spending all your money?"

"Look, can we just watch the match?" Alex said, giving it to Pravi to hide. "No drooling after unavailable barmaids, no getting us stranded here, no messing up the past."

They sat quietly watching the first half, much more relaxed than the England fans around them who had been berating their team. By the time the second half started, judging from the loud clapping, Jack was delighted that Scotland were still in the game.

"We should have gone up to Scotland," Alex said. "Imagine how smug we could be right now in a pub full of them."

"Imagine how dead we would end up," Pravi said.

"That would give the police something to think about. If they traced our identity, they'd puzzle how such a pair of teenagers could look so old."

Alex could see a gap at the bar. "Another pint?"

"You'd need to make it super quick," Pravi said. "The fireworks are about to start."

"Two pints on their way, sir. And if I see Abby up there, I'll blow her a kiss from you."

Pravi threw a beer mat at him, which Alex deftly dodged, the projectile continuing through the air until its flight was abruptly ended by the bridge of Jack's nose.

The beer mat made a flapping sound as it hit the carpet. For a second, Jack stood there with his eyes screwed shut and teeth clenched. Alex opened his mouth to apologise when the Scot spoke.

"Are you fucking kidding me?"

"Sorry mate, it was an accident. You see my friend—"

"How about I have an accident with this pint glass and your face?" Jack raised an empty glass.

"Sorry, it was my fault," Pravi shouted and wheeled his way forward. "I threw it, but I didn't think Alex had such good reactions."

Jack sneered at Pravi. "I guess I can't glass a cripple, can I?"

Alex knew the right thing to do would be to ignore the insult to Pravi, to stay silent and keep the peace. Unfortunately, he didn't want to choose that option. "You want to say that again?"

Jack kept a tight grip on the pint glass and stepped right in front of Alex, pushing his nose millimetres away from Alex's.

"Alex, leave it," Pravi said, manoeuvring himself alongside the pair. "He's not worth it."

"You heard what the cripple said," Jack said.

Alex turned away from him, clenched his fist, and was about to give Jack his reply when mayhem erupted in the pub.

"Yesssss! Get in Shearer!" someone shouted nearby. Everyone turned to look at the screen, Alan Shearer running away, right arm raised high in the air. Alex unclenched his fist, turned back to the Scot and gave him a grin so cheesy it needed its own deli counter.

Jack bellowed some swear words at the screen that even Alex hadn't previously heard.

"1-0, I believe," Alex said.

Jack reacted by grabbing Alex by the throat. "You smug English git. How'd you like to smile with your teeth halfway down your windpipe?"

Alex grappled with Jack's arm while struggling to catch his breath, backing away.

"Hey!" Pravi said, ramming his chair into Jack's legs. The Scot yelped in pain and let go of his grip on Alex.

"Right – let's see how you get around like this …" Jack said, and grabbed Pravi's front wheels. With a swift upward thrust, he flipped Pravi's chair backward.

Alex tried to halt Pravi's descent to the floor but only

succeeded in going down with him. By now, the commotion had attracted the attention of several people in the pub who had calmed down after the goal and had realised that this wasn't part of the celebration. As Alex was about to spring up and launch an assault on Jack, Abby came out of nowhere.

"Get out!" she roared into Jack's face. "What kind of hooligan fights someone in a wheelchair? I don't care if your precious Scotland are losing, you don't do that in here. Now get out!"

Without even waiting for a response, Abby turned her attention to Pravi, who had unceremoniously done a backward roll, revealing his pants to the rest of the pub as a result. "Are you hurt?" she said, kneeling by his side.

Pravi tried to push himself up off the floor, but as he gazed at Abby so close to him, he let himself slide down again. "Yeah," he said as he rubbed the back of his head. "Think I took a whack."

"I caught my eye on a chair," Alex said, rubbing his left eye. "It's stinging like hell."

"Pravi," Abby said, "Can you see all right? Any problem focusing?"

"He's fine," Alex said. "I'm having trouble opening my eye, though."

Abby glanced at Alex. "You'll survive. Worse case, it'll be a black eye. My concern though is with your friend here."

Pravi squinted at Abby. "I … I think I'm OK. Has that hooligan gone yet?"

Abby turned round to see Jack as he was leaving, cursing under his breath. "Don't worry, he won't be coming back anytime soon."

"Have you got any ice for my head?" Pravi asked.

"Sure." Abby pointed at Alex. "You – sorry, don't know your name – help me lift him up first."

Alex and Abby lifted Pravi into his chair until he was sitting up again. "It's Alex."

"What?" Abby said.

"My name. Alex."

"Good for you. I'll get some ice."

They both watched her disappear behind the bar as everyone else resumed watching the match.

"Reckon she might have to stay with me, in case I have concussion," Pravi said.

"You ain't hurt, you faker. I get a sore throat and a black eye and yet you get all the sympathy."

"That's not looking great," Pravi said, staring at Alex's eye. "Hopefully she'll get me a nice armchair in the back to watch the game."

Abby came back with a bag of ice. "Here – put this on your head for a while, but let me know if it's too cold and I'll get something thicker to wrap it up in."

Alex rubbed his eye and addressed Abby. "Have you got any steak?"

"Your friend's injured and you're thinking of your stomach. Classy."

"No, for my eye."

Abby peered at his eye. "Your eye's hungry?"

"No – what? I mean to help with the swelling. You're meant to put steak on a black eye, aren't you?"

Abby giggled. "I know, dummy. I was kidding." She winked at Pravi. "That's an old wives' tale. Regardless, we don't have steak on the menu."

"In that case, how about some beef-flavoured crisps?" Pravi chipped in, causing him and Abby to laugh.

"Very funny," Alex sneered. "Looks like you've made a full recovery."

Before Pravi could reply, a man approached them. "Abby! Have you not noticed that there's a football match going on here? A football match that's being watched by dozens of thirsty customers, ones that need serving."

"I'm sorry," Pravi said. "It's my fault, Abby was helping me and—"

"As for you two, you can sling yer hook."

Alex and Pravi looked at one another, but Abby intervened. "Look, Stan, they weren't doing anything wrong. And I was helping Pravi, this gentleman, who Jack had a go at."

"Jack's one of our best customers. This feller," he jabbed a finger at Pravi, "is getting in the way with that thing."

"What?" Alex said. "You can't throw us out just because he's in a wheelchair."

"This is my pub and I can do what I like. You two caused a fight, so I'm throwing you out for that. Now be gone."

"What about the match?" Pravi said. "We've come all the

way down here to see it again."

Alex shot a glance towards him.

"I mean, we've been waiting for this match for ages."

"Tough. Go wheel yourself somewhere else to watch it." He wafted his hands at Pravi, as if shooing a fly out of the door. "You go, and you, Abby – get back to the bar."

Alex and Pravi made their way out of the pub and stopped in the car park at the rear.

"Can't believe we got thrown out," Alex said, touching his eye. "Don't think I've ever got ejected from a pub."

"What about the time you got that Gooner in a headlock after he'd said Gary Lineker wasn't fit to lace Ian Wright's boots?" Pravi replied. "I seem to remember you caused a semi-riot in the Red Lion."

"Aside from that. So, now what do we do?"

"Go somewhere else? Still got another fifteen minutes before the penalty." Pravi looked around to see which direction might be best to find them a new destination to watch the game.

"Everywhere will be packed. Let's head back to the flat. At least we can watch it without the threat of being glassed."

"Well, this has been a fun outing," Pravi said as he wheeled himself towards the car park exit. Alex followed, but as they were about to rejoin the main road, they heard a window open from the side of the pub.

"Pravi! Are you guys all right?" Abby said, leaning out of the window. "Sorry you had to leave, but Stan's the boss."

Pravi spun round. "We're good thanks, Abby. I'm taking

Alex here to the butchers to get an eight-ounce sirloin for his eye."

Abby laughed. "Look, are you around for the Holland match? Stan won't be about, so you'll be able to watch it here if you want to."

"Tuesday evening? I'll check my diary."

"You do that," Abby said. "Although no fighting next time, OK?"

"Hey," Alex said, "if we do come down, any chance of a free pint as compensation for today?"

Abby gave a sneer to Alex, closed the window and waved to Pravi.

Alex turned to Pravi. "And you like her because …?"

"She's kind, funny and thinks you're a moron. That does it for me."

They continued to the main road. The only person they saw was an old woman laden down by shopping, shuffling towards the gate of her house. The roads were empty. As Saturday afternoons go, you might have thought there had been a national emergency that had led most people to hole up indoors, were it not for the occasional shout echoing around. The silence was broken by a familiar voice.

"You two! Yer come back for more then, I see!" It was Jack, who in the ten minutes since their altercation seemed like he'd somehow acquired a lot more alcohol. He stumbled towards them, about fifty metres away.

"Leave it, Alex," Pravi said, carrying on towards the flat.

Alex paused. While he was happy to taunt the drunken

fool, he didn't want to miss the most exciting point of the match he knew was coming up. Reluctantly, he turned away and caught up with Pravi.

"Running away, are yer?" Jack continued behind them.

Alex continued towards the flat, fists clenched, looking straight ahead.

"Ne'er mind," Jack said, stumbling before leaning against the wall of a house on the high street and staring through the curtains. "This house has the game on – I'll watch it on my own here."

Alex stopped. "Hold on, Prav."

"What?" Pravi replied. "Hurry up, if we don't get back soon, we'll miss it."

"Why don't we join him?"

"Huh?"

"Why don't we join Jack back there? How priceless will it be when he sees the penalty and then the Gazza magic?"

Pravi faced Alex again. "And have him flip me up again? No chance."

"Stay back then. I'm going to have some fun." Alex proceeded back down the road and met up with Jack.

"Look, Jack, how about we watch the match together in peace? It's only 1-0 and Scotland could still get an equaliser and stuff us up."

Jack sneered and looked somewhere vaguely in Alex's direction. "We will! Don't you worry. The boys won't let me down. I can taste it." He produced a large can of beer from a bag and took a swig from it.

Alex peered through the window at an impressively large TV for 1996 standards, which looked like it weighed more than a bus. The owners were sitting down with their backs to the window, transfixed on the action and oblivious to their uninvited guests outside.

In a few moments, Pravi appeared behind Alex, straining his neck to see the picture. It was the seventy-seventh minute, Scotland were on the attack, and in a clip familiar to them both, Tony Adams' outstretched leg brought down Gordon Durie in the box. This action prompted Jack to shout something that had a rough resemblance to a request for a penalty to Scotland – a request that was duly granted by the referee. A collective groan rang out from every house and pub around.

"Yeerss!" Jack danced around on the spot, can in the air.

"Oh no," Alex put his hands on his cheeks and turned to Pravi. "They've got a penalty. What a disaster."

Pravi moved back to watch, straight-faced.

Jack gave Alex a one-armed hug as they watched Gary McAllister put the ball on the penalty spot.

"Bet he misses," Alex said.

"No way," Jack replied.

"Big Dave Seaman will save it."

"Not. A. Chance."

"Keeper's right."

"Dream on, Sassenach."

They watched as McAllister struck the ball straight onto Seaman's left elbow, the ball rebounding out of danger.

The family inside jumped up, arms waving and pumping in the air, cheers surrounding the whole street.

Alex hugged his new best friend back. "Whad'ya know? Big Dave to the rescue!"

Jack proceeded to machine-gun expletives out to the world, before throwing his can to the ground.

"C'mon Jack – keep watching," Alex said, "You never know what might happen."

Two minutes later, Gascoigne started one of the most famous moves in English football history. Picking the ball up, he flicked it over the head of a bemused Colin Hendry and stroked the ball into the net to make it 2-0.

The street that just moments ago was dead was now full of life. Cheering, clapping, whooping, screaming and general chaos spilled out on to the streets.

"Do the dentist chair!" Alex screamed. As if on cue, Gascoigne threw himself down on the grass and beckoned to his teammates. Redknapp and McManaman rushed onto the scene, with Shearer proceeding to squirt water down Gascoigne's throat, emulating the infamous tabloid newspaper reports of last month's drunken preparations and creating one of the most iconic sporting images in Alex's lifetime. Again.

Jack had slumped, head in arms, leaning on the window. A man inside had stopped jumping around and was now scowling at his new window decorations. Banging on the glass, the man closed the curtains, ending the free viewing.

"We'll say goodbye now," Alex said to Jack, whacking

him firmly on the back twice. "See you on Tuesday?"

Jack made a mix of sounds from sobbing to insults as Alex and Pravi left him.

"As much as that was sadistic," Pravi said, "it was most certainly fun."

"Indeed it was. But the best match is still to come …"

Mystic Alex

Tuesday, 18th June 1996

Alex and Pravi mainly spent the Sunday and Monday that followed the Scotland match holed up in the flat, watching TV and playing on their old console.

The last of the cash in Pravi's not-so-secret jar had been used – mostly on food, but with the rest on a precise bet on the forthcoming Holland match. Whilst Pravi still didn't think it was ethical, Alex had had no qualms in placing a tidy sum on a comprehensive but unlikely victory. If the present played out exactly as it had in their past, then the boys were looking at enough money to sustain their ultimate nostalgia trip for the rest of the tournament at the very least.

On Tuesday, the day of the match, Alex and Pravi were discussing the day's plans.

"Let's do it proper today," Alex said to Pravi at breakfast.

Pravi crunched on some Corn Flakes. "Proper? What do you suggest? Drive to Holland in a Mini with a Union Jack on the roof and do doughnuts every time England score?"

"No, I mean a proper session in the pub," Alex said, heaping more jam onto a near-charcoaled piece of toast.

"It's only right we celebrate in style the finest performance in an England shirt we've ever seen."

"What about the Germany game?" Pravi said. "5-1 away? Even Heskey scored in that one."

"Don't get me wrong, that was a top performance, but it was only a qualifier." Alex stuffed a corner of the toast into his mouth. "This was in a tournament in front of a home crowd. We only needed a draw to get to the quarters, too."

"True," Pravi replied. "But I'm sure it can't be as good as we remember. Still, that third goal …"

"When that went in, I swear I thought we were the best in the world. Absolute beauty."

Pravi nodded. "Speaking of beauty, I trust your plans involve The Sailor and a visit to see the wonderful Abby?"

Alex spluttered as he ate his toast. "Do you honestly think you've got a chance?"

"Why not? She invited me back."

"She invited *us* back. To the pub. With lots of other smoking, drinking, farting and noisy men. Not exactly the most romantic setting in my book."

"You're just jealous."

"So might her boyfriend be."

Pravi finished his breakfast and cleared away. "She can't be that into him if she's inviting strangers back to the pub."

Alex sighed. "And what about Jasmine? Don't tell me – it doesn't count if she's not in the same timeline?"

"Actually, I'm not seeing her anymore."

"What happened?"

"I'm not convinced she was really into me. I think she just liked the thrill of something different." Pravi patted the arms of his wheelchair.

"Sorry, mate. Still, fun while it lasted, right? Move on to the next girl to experience Pravi the studmuffin?"

"Anyway – tonight," Pravi said. "What are you thinking? Go down The Sailor around six? Kick-off's at seven-thirty."

Alex threw a foam mini football at Pravi. "Six? I'm talking about a proper session! Let's get there at three to watch the early games. We can grab the best seats and have plenty inside us before the match starts. It'll be epic!"

* * *

"Two pints of your finest please, barkeep." Alex rubbed his hands together and looked down at Pravi, grinning.

"Barkeep? You do realise it's 1996 and not 1896?" Pravi said. Despite his reservations, he had agreed to come down to The Sailor over four hours before the England match. Being a Tuesday afternoon, the pub was quiet, although most of its usual inhabitants had long ago retired.

"Can you see Abby anywhere?" Pravi asked.

As Alex paid the barman for the drinks, he said, "Excuse me, is your barmaid Abby around?"

"Abby?" the barman replied. "No, she's not in until later. Five o'clock, I think. You a friend of hers?"

"Me? Well, not particularly." Alex took his change. "But my friend here seems to be hopelessly in love with her."

Pravi pushed himself hard so that his wheels caught the

back of Alex's legs. "Easy!" Alex said, laughing. "What did I say?"

"I wouldn't joke about that," the barman said. "Abby's got a man, and he's not one for sharing."

Alex collected the pints, and the pair made their way to a table with a great view of the big screen, next to a fruit machine. Blur's "Girls & Boys" softly came out of the tinny speakers as they sat down at the sticky table.

"So, that's that then," Alex said. "I think we can safely say the pursuit of Abby is over."

Pravi scratched his head. "Not necessarily. Regardless, it's not a pursuit – it's not like one of your sales. She's a person, not a contract to be chased after and signed up."

"All I'm saying is that she's not available, you might get into trouble, and you won't be hanging round here to play the long game."

Pravi sipped his pint. "How long do you reckon we could stay?"

Alex stuck out his bottom lip. "Hadn't thought beyond the tournament. We can't stay forever, can we? If our past selves come home after the tournament and catch us in their flat, it would totally freak them out."

"True," Pravi said. "I suppose after the final it's game over."

"When did we come back to the flat after the final? Must have been the Monday after. That still gives us nearly two weeks here. Two weeks of pure, responsibility-free, football-watching, retro-loving life."

"All carried out in a dingy old flat and an old man's pub." Pravi raised his glass. "To living the dream."

Alex clinked glasses. "To living the impossible dream!"

By four o'clock, the pub had a smattering of the continental, as the build-up to the afternoon's matches started. Three men and one woman all adorning the colours of France sat in the corner, waiting for their match against Bulgaria to start at four-thirty, while a single Spaniard draped in a red and yellow flag stood working out whether he'd be able to see his compatriots in their match against Romania at the same time. The music had been turned up, with tracks from a football anthem CD in an attempt to rouse an atmosphere for the hors d'oeuvres to the main England match later.

"Prav, you're the memory man – what were the scores in their matches?"

Pravi looked up momentarily, as if downloading the information from his brain. "France won 3-1, and Spain 2-1. As I remember it, Spain left it late to score the winner, otherwise they wouldn't have qualified."

Alex smiled. "Brilliant. We could have some fun with that knowledge."

Before Pravi could chastise Alex about unethical betting, Alex had surprised him by walking over to the French group. Pravi watched as Alex communicated in a variety of thumbs-up, handshakes and holding up his fingers to indicate his predicted score. He finished with a resounding "Allez les bleus!" before returning to his table.

"Let me guess," Pravi said. "You're going to claim you have mystic powers later."

"We could be legends here." Alex sat down and stretched his arms out as if seeing an imaginary headline. "The men who could predict the future."

"Can't we enjoy it without drawing attention to ourselves?"

"Loosen up." Alex downed the rest of his drink. "What's the point of being here, with our knowledge, and not using it? I didn't come back to watch the games on TV, I came to live 1996 again." He got up and gestured to his empty glass. "Another?"

By the time the matches had started, Alex and Pravi were buzzing. Within twenty minutes, they were enjoying the celebrations as first Spain and then France took the lead in their matches. The pub was getting busy as fans in England shirts and hats staked out their positions for the evening's game. The commentary had been turned up loud and beer glasses littered every table. Pravi was finding it harder to get a clear view of the bar.

"Do you think she'll come?" Pravi asked.

"Who?" Alex said, not taking his eyes off another French attack play out on the big screen.

Pravi sighed.

Alex finally turned his attention to his friend. "Abby? Of course. She works here, remember? A pub on the day of an England match needs all the staff it can get. She'll be here."

"Yeah," Pravi said, finishing his drink.

"Not that it matters," Alex continued. "She'll be way too busy serving to talk to us. Give it up, enjoy the footy and stop being a big arse."

"There's only one big arse around here," Pravi said.

His glass was swept off the table by Abby who had appeared. "I hope you weren't inferring I've got a big arse?"

Pravi was momentarily stunned as Abby looked at him with a quizzical expression.

"On the contrary," Alex said. "In fact, Prav was saying how much he admired your derrière."

A look of sheer horror flashed across Pravi's features. "What? I never said that! I would never comment on your … you know …"

Abby put her hands on her hips, cocked her head to one side and walked off. Pravi started to follow her but was cut off by a crowd of people rushing by. They were reacting to a big cheer, trying to catch a glimpse of the other screen at the back of the pub that was showing Romania's equaliser against Spain. Pravi returned to confront Alex.

"What did you do that for?" Pravi said.

Alex shrugged. "It just came out. Was only a joke. Thought she'd see the funny side of it."

"You can be such a dick."

Alex looked towards the bar. "OK, I'll sort it. Stay here."

"No, just leave it, will you?"

Alex got up.

"I said leave it!" Pravi shouted above the noise of the crowd coming through the speakers.

Alex ignored his friend and reached the bar. He looked down to see her brown curly hair, head bowed as she filled the dishwasher underneath. Alex put on his best old man's voice and said, "Excuse me, dear, two pints when you're ready."

As Abby got up, she said, "Certainly, sir, now—" Realising it was Alex, she scowled.

Alex put his hands out, palms facing her. "Look, I'm sorry about earlier. Pravi didn't say anything about you at all. He was calling *me* a big arse when you came along."

"Which you are." Abby wrung out a cloth and wiped down the pumps in front of her.

"OK, I admit it then."

"Admit what?"

"That I'm an arse."

"A *big* arse."

"OK, OK. I admit I'm a big arse."

Abby put down her cloth. "Agreed. Now what'll it be?"

"Huh? Oh, right, er, two pints of lager." Alex fished out his wallet from his jeans.

"Actually, make it four – saves me from coming up again soon. And do you have any food? Us arses work up an appetite watching all this football."

Abby pointed at Alex's eye, which since the altercation with Jack three days earlier had come up in delightful shades of yellow and black. "Looks like you never got your steak."

Alex instinctively touched his bruised eye socket. "Looks worse than it is."

Abby got out a notepad and pencil. "Right, we've got chicken in a basket, scampi in a basket, and chips. What does the arse with the black eye want?"

Alex ordered and carefully fought his way back to his seat with a tray of four lagers, watched all the way by Pravi.

"Sorted," Alex said, dumping the drinks onto the table.

"What does that mean?"

"Chicken in a basket with chips, twice."

"I meant what happened with Abby? I saw you talking to her. I couldn't see too much, but she didn't look impressed."

"Don't worry, I smoothed it all over. I told her you weren't commenting on her arse and she believed me. She's cool, relax."

Pravi sipped his lager. "Has anyone told you that you make a lousy wingman?"

Alex opened his mouth in mock shock. "Me? I'm the Darren Anderton to your Terry Sheringham."

They watched the remainder of the half with no further goals from either match. Midway through the break, Alex went off to see the Spaniard, who was slumped in a corner and appearing to be arguing with the TV. Just as Alex returned to their table, he spotted Abby approaching with a tray of food.

"Prav, I'll just have a go on the fruity and give you some space," he said, getting up to the fruit machine nearby, still within earshot.

"Who ordered the lobster thermidor and who ordered

the steak tartare?" Abby addressed Pravi with the tray held high.

"I think there's been a mistake," Pravi replied. "I ordered the caviar with the quail egg."

"Here's The Sailor's chicken speciality instead." Abby set the tray down on the table. "So, I managed to get your friend to admit to me that he was an arse." She cocked her head towards Alex, who flicked a glance her way before rapidly poking a button on the fruit machine.

"Sorry about that," Pravi said. "I honestly wasn't—"

Abby laughed. "It's fine. I heard the whole conversation as I was clearing the table behind. Just wanted to make you both squirm. Especially Alan."

"It's Alex," Pravi said. "Alex the Arse."

Alex resisted the temptation to register any acknowledgement and slammed another fifty pence into the machine.

Abby got out her notepad and started writing.

"What's that?" Pravi said, straining to get a look.

"Oh, it's nothing," she said as she tucked it away in the back pocket of her jeans again. "I like to make notes of things I hear, ideas, conversation snippets. Maybe one day I'll write a children's book or something." She moved the food baskets onto the table and whipped the tray underneath her arm. "Silly talk I know."

Pravi grabbed a chip. "Sounds ridiculous to me. I mean, you serve food and beer. And you're a woman. How could *you* possibly write anything?"

He waggled the chip at her. "You might as well give up that dream and stick to what you know."

Abby looked at Pravi, who was doing his best to hold a straight face. "Sir, you are so right! What am I thinking? A gal like me, writing? I best be getting back to my pumps." Abby winked at Pravi and went back to the bar.

Alex slapped the machine's cabinet as it beeped to say he was out of credits. He dumped himself back in the chair opposite Pravi and began to devour the chicken nuggets.

"Jorge – that Spanish fella – is suicidal. Moaning about yet another impending tournament disaster." Alex stuffed down some fries. "No sympathy for him, though. I know they get through today, but I felt like slapping him and telling him about all the stuff they win in the future."

"You didn't though, did you?" Pravi said.

"Nah. Maybe after a few more beers. Did I miss anything?"

"Not really. Just a mix-up with the food. Can't get the staff these days." Pravi smiled and looked towards the bar.

In the second half, the French collective in the pub was even happier when a goal went in, but a few minutes later a simultaneous groan in their corner went up as Stoichkov pulled one back for Bulgaria. Alex went over to the lone Spaniard again after eighty minutes had gone in their match, who had bitten most of his fingernails off during the game. Alex had great fun announcing, "Don't worry … it's coming … I can feel it …" moments before Amor scored to make it 2-1 to Spain, prompting exuberant leaping around from his new best friend. By the time France had wrapped up their game 3-1 and the whistles blown in both matches, the pub's celebratory mood was up a notch. Alex posed for several photos with the French, holding up three fingers in one hand and a single digit in the other.

Alex sat back down with Pravi.

"Have you finished being Mystic Meg?" Pravi asked.

"Nope. Got the England match to come."

As far as comparisons with the past, everything had been exactly the same today – the score, goalscorers, timings – and so their anticipation for the England match grew as it got nearer. Pravi had even got hold of some cheap plastic hats with the St. George's cross on.

"What sane person is going to believe me that we'll beat Holland 4-1?" Alex said. "I'll look a genius, a visionary."

Pravi swilled the dregs of his pint around in his glass. "Just don't spoil it for them."

"What do you mean?"

"Nobody expected us to play that well, to score four goals. Everyone was surprised and delighted, that's what united us afterwards. If you go blabbing before every goal, then it may ruin it. Just let them have what we had, that glorious feeling."

"You talk some bollocks sometimes. This place will erupt no matter what I say. Anyway," Alex said, sweeping his hand towards the room, "I don't care about these people. They're nothing to us. It's a different world, or something like that."

"These are still real people, dummy." Pravi said. "We might end up spending some time here, making some of them our friends."

"You mean like Crabby Abby over there?" He cocked his thumb towards the bar. "You've changed your tune, after never wanting to leave the flat." They both looked towards her before Alex continued, "Judging from the attention that bloke is giving her at the bar, looks like you've got some competition."

Despite the crowd, a tall man in a tight, black t-shirt had seated himself at the bar, leaning over and shouting to get Abby's attention.

"Leave this one to me, Prav. I'll prove what a wingman I can be."

Thirty seconds later, the wingman was in serious trouble.

Dutch Courage

Tuesday, 18th June 1996

"What did you say to me?"

The man in the black t-shirt was standing up within inches of Alex at the bar, head slightly bowed to avoid it hitting the wooden beams above. A sober Alex might have laughed off his own comment as a mistake, a misheard, unfortunate throwaway remark, before quickly mingling back into the crowd. This Alex – five-pints-in-Alex – was ignoring the multitude of warning buzzers going off simultaneously in his brain and instead was going to engage with the man.

"No need to get uptight. I simply enquired if you also had taken a liking to Abby behind the bar." Alex saw the man's eyes narrow. "You know, the barmaid. You seemed intent on getting her att—"

"I know who she is," the man said, slapping his tattooed hands on Alex's shoulders. "I'm her boyfriend."

"Ah." Alex grimaced.

"So, if you're saying that you also fancy her, then we might have a problem, might we?"

Alex felt a vice-like grip dig down into his skin. "Me? No, no, no no no. Of course not, no. Not me. I meant – I mean – not me. Look—"

"Stabber, me old mate!" Another man squeezed in front of Alex and had started mock-boxing the giant's abdomen. "What ya doing in here?"

Alex took this fortuitous meeting of old pals as a chance to yank himself free.

"Came in here to see Abby when this prick appeared," the man said, smoothing down his t-shirt and pointing a finger towards Alex.

Alex walked sideways towards the heart of the pub. "Misunderstanding, that's all. Looks like you two have a lot to catch up on, so I'll leave you to it." He then turned and brushed his way back through the crowd, Oasis drowning out a few choice swear words that were being shot towards him. With the pub packed with England fans, Alex had plenty of cover, so he made a few detours to make sure he couldn't be tracked back to his final destination opposite Pravi.

"Prav, my man. How long left to kick-off?"

"Ten minutes. What did you do, Alex?"

"Do? Nothing really. Everything's cool. Just had a chat with a psycho who happens to be Abby's boyfriend, that's all."

"The tosser at the bar?"

"Yes, the huge, tattooed guy who could crush my bones with one hand and sprinkle them on his Corn Flakes."

Pravi scratched his chin. "Hmm. Looks like a three Shredded Wheat man to me."

"I don't care if he eats quinoa porridge, natural yoghurt and washes it down a cold glass of nut milk – it's game over for you in the Abby affection stakes."

Pravi sipped his beer and looked at the screen as the England players warmed up on the pitch.

"Are you sure he was a genuine psycho? Or was it the natural Alex charm that may have led him to want to kill you after five seconds?"

"His friend called him 'Stabber'," Alex replied.

"Ah. Well, I like a good challenge."

"You and Paul Ince. I suggest you concentrate on the latter in the game and stay away from Abby."

As the referee blew his whistle to start the match, there was a cheer from a handful of fans in the pub, followed by three separate cries of "C'mon England!", each person determined to be the loudest. Although seen as an old man's pub, such was the fever for the tournament that even this establishment was rammed to near illegal capacities, populated by everyone from teenagers to their great-grandads. A layer of smoke had settled under the ceiling and the smell of it mixed with beer and sweat.

After the Scotland match, Alex had noticed an air of confidence in the fans. England and Holland only needed a draw for them to both qualify for the knockout stages, while even a defeat for either might still mean both could go through. It wasn't a classic Dutch side, but he remembered that there had been little sign of what was to come. By the twenty-third minute, it was just the start.

"Penalty!" The entire pub shook with the roar that resulted from the tumble into the penalty box by Ince as he was tripped by Danny Blind. The ref immediately ran into the box and pointed to the penalty spot as both Wembley and the pub celebrated.

Alex was standing up and shouting at the screen, "Go on, Shearer! Slam it to the keeper's right!" As Shearer ran up to take it, Alex was touching the big screen, pointing his finger to the exact place he knew the striker would blast it to one second later. As the ball rippled the net and Shearer ran off with his hands aloft, Alex made it his mission to high-five as many people as he could, boasting at another amazing show of prediction.

Pravi joined in clinking glasses with everyone around him. Old men were clapping and laughing. England hats were being whizzed through the air. Once Holland had kicked off again, the entire pub erupted into a rendition of "Three Lions".

"Just wait until they see the second half!" Alex shouted into Pravi's ear.

"Shearer was like Gary Lineker, wasn't he?" Pravi said. "Never let us down in the big games."

As the first half continued, the Dutch had more possession and were beginning to take control. Although they'd seen the original match and watched the highlights of it many times over the years, it was the first time they'd watched the match again in its full length.

"Wow. I don't remember Holland having so many chances," Alex said, as another attack broke down. "You don't think that it might be different?"

Pravi thought for a while. "No, don't think so. Perhaps we remembered it differently."

"Better be the same – I've got a lot riding on this ending up 4-1!"

Despite England being in a good position to qualify, after another Dutch corner ended in a decent chance, the atmosphere of the pub had turned into a different one.

"C'mon lads! Sort it out!" came a cry from Alex's left.

"Bloody hell, Seaman, catch the thing!"

At forty minutes, Alex took the opportunity to go to the bar again, looping round to the rear of the pub, scoping it out to see if Stabber was still around. When there was no sign of him, Alex fought his way through to the counter, squeezing in between two lads each thrusting out a £5 note, trying to catch the attention of the barman. He looked past the pumps to his right and saw Abby giving someone back their change. Instead of then serving the next customer, she was writing something on her notepad. Alex took this as an opportunity, so shouted, "Four lagers when you've finished doodling, Abby!"

Abby looked up at Alex, shoved the notepad in her back pocket, and grabbed some pint glasses. Two minutes later, she silently delivered four golden pints to the beaming Alex.

"Oi!" shouted the lad next to Alex. "I was here before this twat!"

"I serve who I like," Abby said, sticking out a hand to Alex but looking at the man. "And he's an arse, not a twat."

The second half resumed with Alex and Pravi stocked up with beer, bladders empty and with expectations of one of the best forty-five minutes of an England game. England soon won a corner, Gascoigne putting the ball down to take it.

Pravi reached forward and held onto the glasses as Gascoigne swung in a looping corner that Sheringham, nine yards out, shuffled around his marker to meet with a flicked header. To the bemusement of the goalkeeper, the ball flew past him into the bottom corner of the net.

2-0.

The belief was back. Beer came flying overhead. The roar of the Wembley crowd coming through the sound system was completely obliterated by the raucous noise now filling the pub. Alex hugged many fans before draping himself over Pravi.

"Get off, you big lump," Pravi said, cradling the beers.

Alex sat back down with a deep exhale before picking up a drink and addressing Pravi. "And now, we sit here and prepare ourselves to witness once again the magic that is England's third goal."

Pravi looked around him at the joyous faces. "I kinda envy them."

Approaching the fifty-seventh minute, Adams tidied up a loose ball just inside the Dutch half. Gascoigne took over, exchanged passes with Darren Anderton, before playing a neat one-two with Steve McManaman. As Gascoigne surged into the penalty box, he left one Dutch defender stumbling on the floor before playing it to Sheringham, who had no one around him.

Sheringham had to shoot.

Sheringham shaped to shoot.

But Sheringham did not shoot.

Instead, completely flummoxing the slipping Dutch defender, he side-footed to his right, where Shearer was standing, both arms aloft.

Shearer took a few steps to meet the ball, opened up his body, drew back the hammer that was his right foot and smashed it into the top corner.

3-0.

This time, it wasn't the joy that Alex and Pravi noticed on the faces of everyone around them – and there was enough of that – it was the surprise. Sheer, wide-eyed, can't-believe-it surprise of seeing England score a goal of such quality. Alex didn't shout, didn't claim any prediction, didn't even try to hug anyone. He simply allowed himself to be taken in by many comments coming in from everyone around him.

"I can't bloody believe it!"

"3-0! Against the Dutch!"

"What a beauty!"

No replay in the present matched this moment in time, thought Alex. When he'd watched the game the first time around, he'd been so caught up in his own emotions he hadn't realised how much that goal meant to everyone else. People were still applauding a full minute after the ball had been smashed in, and some had to wipe away tears of joy. There was even a stirring rendition of "Swing Low, Sweet Chariot" joined in by all.

"I forgot we used to sing that," Pravi said. "Nicked it from the rugby boys."

"We're lucky to catch all this again, eh?"

"Luck, magic, bending the laws of physics – I don't care what you call it!"

Pravi and Alex drained their beers, just in time for two more to be put in front of them by an unlikely source.

"We drink to that goal and also to Spain!" Still draped in his giant flag, the Spaniard had bought the pair a drink each and was encouraging them to down them, which didn't take much persuasion.

"España! España!" Alex shouted as everyone cheered.

Soon after, Anderton drove a shot from outside the area. The Dutch keeper went down low to save but could only push it into the oncoming Sheringham, who slotted in for 4-0. Alex jumped up on to the table and danced as the whole place erupted once again. From the countless replays of the match he'd watched online, he picked his favourite commentary quote.

"It gets better … and better … and better!" he yelled.

Pravi had thrown his arms wildly in the air and allowed himself to be pushed around the pub by harmless, over-excited fans, before returning to the table. He looked up at Alex, who was still on top of the table, and shouted, "That was Martin Tyler's line, you thieving git!"

The next fifteen minutes was spent reflecting on an astonishing scoreline that so far also had the added strange side effect of putting Scotland through should both matches remain as they were for the next twelve minutes. England's unexpected margin of success meant that currently England and Scotland would go through to the quarter-finals at the expense of Holland. Despite the intense rivalry between the two home nations, such was the joy of the night that even a few England fans were cheering at the prospect of their Scottish cousins going through. But when Patrick Kluivert pulled one back for Holland, it was Scotland who were going out and the mood changed once again.

"Oh well – unlucky Scotland!" one fan said, laughing.

"Buy that Dutchman a drink!" another said, raising his glass.

"I bet Jack will be inconsolable," Pravi said.

Around twelve minutes later, the final whistle went. England had not only qualified for the quarter-finals, but had produced a performance few had even thought was possible. All that is, except Alex and Pravi, who were now leading the entire pub in a repeated chorus from "Three Lions" as for the second time in their history, they celebrated possibly the finest English scoreline in their lives.

Alex the Arse

"One for the road?"

Abby was finishing wiping up a lake of beer from the table against a background of George Michael's "Fastlove". The majority of the pub's occupants had staggered out to continue their celebrations into the night. Alex and Pravi had sat through all the post-match analysis and while Alex stared vacantly at the screen, Pravi had his eyes shut, head back, a grin still firmly attached to his face.

"Huh?" Pravi snapped open his eyes. "Oh, Abby. Hi." He straightened himself, scratched his stubble and rolled back a few inches. "I'm a bit knackered, but yeah, why not? Got any Baileys?"

"One Baileys coming right up. Or should I make it two?" Abby turned towards Alex, who was swaying in his seat. He made a vague attempt to focus on her before returning his gaze to the TV.

"Nah. He's had enough. Lightweight."

Abby returned a short time later and put two glasses of creamy brown liquid on the table. "On the house. After tonight's takings, I think we can afford it." She picked up a drink and sat down. "I'll even join you."

They clinked glasses. "Oh – nearly forgot. Here." She handed Pravi her notepad, which he took with a puzzled look. Abby sat back and begun dabbing at the table with her cloth.

Pravi sat in silence as he read the contents of four pages. After a short while, he looked up at Abby. "You wrote this?"

"I did indeed. Our last conversation inspired me."

Pravi studied the notepad again.

Abby rose from her chair. "Never mind. It's only a silly something I came up with earlier, in between pulling pints. It's useless, I know. I'm not very good."

Pravi held the notepad out. "Abby, this is sort of—"

"Crap? I know, I know. It's nothing." She grabbed it back.

"No – I was going to say it's sort of ... good." He looked straight at her. "Better than good. You made all that up yourself, here, now? It rhymes and everything."

Abby flipped through the pages. "You like it? I used to write funny poems as a kid, but this is the first time I've written anything in ages."

Pravi raised his drink. "Here's to Alex the Arse being the start of something good for you."

Abby put the notepad on the table again and took her glass. "To Alex the Arse!"

At that moment, Alex jolted in his chair. "W-what? What did someone call me?" He looked down and saw the notepad. Before Abby could reach down and take it, Alex shot out an arm and picked it up. He blinked a few times, and with an unsteady hand he managed to read the first few lines until Pravi snatched it away and threw it to Abby.

"Is that meant to be me?" Alex addressed Abby, who closed the notepad. "It is, isn't it? You wrote a poem about me ... calling me an arse?"

"It's not a poem, more of a short story, that's all," Abby said. "I didn't mean to—"

"Oh, sod off, Abigail." Alex's words had the effect of making Abby take half a step back.

"Easy, mate!" Pravi said, giving his friend a scornful look. "I know you've had a few but—"

"And you can sod off too, Prav. All this fawning over," Alex threw his right arm in Abby's direction, "this stroppy barmaid. She ain't worth it."

Abby thrust the notepad into her back pocket. "Gee, thanks."

Pravi wheeled himself between Alex and Abby. "You're drunk, Alex. Let's go home." He turned to Abby and mouthed, "Sorry."

But Alex wasn't in the mood for leaving it there. "What? Don't you want to ask her to come back with you? It's not like Jasmine is going to come round anytime soon, is it?" He giggled. "And as for her – she has a jealous boyfriend who'd cut your nuts off." He looked at Abby. "What do you see in that lump? Like it rough, do you? Does he bring home his victims to you as trophies?"

"I think you should leave." Abby turned and walked away, before shouting back, "Both of you."

Pravi went after Abby, but she'd disappeared into a room behind the bar. The pub was nearly empty now apart from two lads who were gearing up for a chorus of "Champagne Supernova". He turned and wheeled himself straight into Alex.

"Ow!" Alex said, rubbing his knees. "What did you do that for?"

"Are you kidding? You. Absolute. Bellend."

"Ah, forget about her." Alex gestured towards the screen. "Football. 4-1!"

"4-1 and yet you still managed to ruin it. She's right – you are a complete and utter arse."

Pravi threw his England hat on the floor and headed for the exit, before turning back and saying, "God help your son or daughter having a dad like you."

Alex watched him leave and then downed the rest of the Baileys. "Guess I'll be going home on my own then."

* * *

"Black coffee, two paracetamols and some toast. Get it down you." Alex was slumped on the kitchen table, so Pravi put everything down next to his nose.

Alex let out a long groan. "Where am I?"

"Our old flat, 1996." Pravi checked Ceefax. "Wednesday, June 19th 10:12 a.m., to be precise. The day after the Holland game."

Alex grunted and raised his head. "Shearer. Sheringham. What a game."

"And how much of what happened after the game do you remember?"

Alex rubbed his eyes with his palms. After a short pause he said, "Absolutely nothing."

As Alex drunk his coffee, Pravi told him of the hostility towards Abby that led him to storm off. "But that's not all that happened afterwards, I'm afraid."

"It gets worse?" Alex said, not able to look at his friend.

"Yes. For a start, you ended up singing with Jack in the park on the way home."

"Jack?" A vague spark of a memory flashed in Alex's brain. "Oh my god. How did you know?"

"I'd gone home but returned later to look for you. When I found you and Jack together, I was gobsmacked. You said that you had found him roaming the streets singing Scottish football songs and crying."

Alex groaned. "That's right. I felt bad for him. Must have been as drunk as he was. I offered him money from the bets we'd made, as some sort of England–Scotland peace offering."

"That explains why you two seemed best mates."

"I'm sorry, Prav. So sorry."

"You should be," Pravi replied, passing him a second cup of strong coffee. "Your duet was bloody awful."

Alex mulled it over. "Why did you come back for me, though? I'd have left me in the pub."

Pravi let out a long breath. "I did." He turned back to the TV. "I, er, went back home. To the present day."

"You jumped?"

"Yep. I then zonked out and slept until the next day."

Alex nibbled his toast. "So why does that matter?"

"Well," Pravi said, "remember that you always jump back to the time and date the controller left the timeline. So, if either of us jumps back to 2016 now, we'll go to the time and day I left on my own, not the one we left together. Effectively, you've lost half a day in the present."

"Oh," Alex said, putting down his food.

"Unfortunately," Pravi said, forcing himself to make eye contact, "it seems we – you – missed something important."

Alex looked quizzically at Pravi and waited.

"Becky nearly broke down my door in the morning. She had been trying to phone and message us the night before, but you and your phone were in '96 and I must have been comatose back home. She said she'd even come round just before midnight hammered on the door, but I didn't hear her."

"Becky? What did she want?"

Pravi cleared his throat. "It's Helen – she's in hospital."

"Hospital?" Alex sat bolt upright. "Is she OK? When? What happened?"

"You see, I was—"

"Prav!" Alex lurched towards him. "The baby – tell me it's not the baby! The baby's OK, isn't it? Isn't it, Prav? Nothing's happened, has it? Oh my god, please tell me—"

"Becky said that the baby's fine," Pravi said. "They're monitoring it. Helen is fine too."

Alex started to breathe heavily, and before he knew it, he was sobbing uncontrollably. Pravi turned round to give him some time. Alex eventually wiped his tears and composed himself. "Sorry, I ... damn. Don't know what hit me."

Pravi swung back to face him. "I guess it's not just you and Helen that you have to think about now."

"No," Alex said, rising to his feet. "Right, well, let's get going then." He gave a big sniff, shoved the rest of the toast in his mouth before mumbling, "Where are my shoes?"

"Sit down," Pravi said. "Helen isn't going anywhere, you see? She's frozen in the present, at least to us. We need to stay here, agree a plan and get you ready before you can return."

Alex looked momentarily confused. "But ... I've got to get back, got to see Helen, she'll be—"

"Still waiting for you, no matter how long we spend here."

"But ..."

"Sit!" Pravi banged the table, causing Alex to wince and flop onto his chair again. "We have to get you presentable and work out a plausible story of not only how neither of us could be contacted last night, but also how you got that black eye from the other day."

Alex groaned. "She's gonna kill me."

The Big Reveal

Sunday, 25th September 2016

"Whatever you do, Alex, don't upset her."

It was eleven-thirty in the morning by the time they'd reached the hospital. Alex strode through the corridors with Becky, his stomach getting increasingly more tense the nearer they got to their destination. He'd managed to get away with giving the bare minimum of details to Becky in a thin explanation of last night, diverting her attention by fixating on Helen's condition. Last she heard, everything was fine, but that was several hours ago. As they reached the ward's doors, Alex stopped.

"She'll be OK, won't she?" he asked Becky.

She looked at him and put her hand on his arm. "I hope so. But you better do your best arse-kissing because she really needed you last night."

He straightened up, and they went through. Becky led the way to Helen's bay, and when they rounded the corner, she was there, lying in bed asleep, her hand being held by someone next to her in a chair with their back to them.

"Peter?" Becky said as she swept up to the bed.

Peter swung round and stood up, the chair scraping backwards on the polished floor. "Er, hi, baby," he said, offering his chair to her. "And Alex – you're alive then?"

Alex stayed back, away from the bed. Helen seemed so vulnerable lying there.

Peter placed a hand on Becky's shoulder. "I thought as you were out looking for AWOL boy here that I'd come down and make sure Helen was OK."

Becky was about to reply when Helen stirred.

"Alex? Is that you?"

Alex moved over to the bed and crouched beside her, squeezing her hand tight. "Hells I'm so, so sorry. I didn't know – had no idea, truly. If I'd known, I'd have come straight away, I really would."

Her eyes were fully open now, and Alex could see the hurt within. "Where were you? The one time in my life when I needed you the most and you weren't here."

Alex brushed aside a tear. "I ... I went out, had a few drinks with Pravi. I didn't intend for it to get out of hand, I promise."

"They got wasted," Becky said, sitting down. "Apparently they had an argument with some guy, Alex got punched, and their phones got drenched in beer in the commotion."

Helen slid her hand out of Alex's grip. "Fighting? Well, that explains your black eye."

Alex prodded his bruise. "Yes. Look, I was a mess, but that doesn't matter right now. Are you OK? Is the baby all right? Is it going to be OK?"

"He," Helen said.

Alex blinked. "What do you mean?"

Helen shuffled up on her pillow. "You mean 'is *he* going to be OK?'."

With the emotion of seeing Helen in the hospital and the effort of maintaining his alibi, Alex failed to catch on. "Huh?"

"Our *son* is going to be fine." Helen patted her stomach. "They did a scan and told me the sex."

Alex's mouth opened, and he stood up. "You mean … it's a boy?"

In a not-so-quiet whisper, Becky said to Peter, "Hope he's brighter than his dad."

Alex hugged Helen and sobbed.

Peter coughed and took Becky's arm. "Let's leave them to it."

"Hang on," Becky said, shaking Peter off. "I'm only going if Helen is sure she's OK with Alex."

Alex and Helen broke from their hug. "I'm fine. Really," Helen said.

"But you wanted to murder him last night," Becky said.

Helen looked at Alex. "Yes, but that was last night. He's here now and I'm too tired to fight."

"Are you sure, H?" Peter said.

Helen nodded. Peter and Becky said goodbye and left.

Alex turned to Helen. "Looks like you were wrong, then."

"With what?" Helen replied.

"You said it was a girl." Alex smiled.

"Do you really think you're in a position to be smug at this moment in time?"

Alex went quiet.

"So – fighting. Talk me through it."

Alex was about to start when he had a thought. "Can the baby hear me?"

"No, it's too early for him to hear voices." Helen stroked her stomach. "Don't worry though, I'll make sure I fill him in on the details when he's older."

Alex took her through the fictional version of his night, ashamed of having to tell her a lie but knowing that the truth was even more unimaginable. He pointed to the huge bunch of flowers in a vase on the table next to her bed. "Your parents get you these?"

"No, they're from Peter. He's been very supportive." She touched one of the pink petals. "He somehow sweet-talked his way past the matron to be allowed in to see me this morning."

"Always the charmer," Alex said, pulling off a leaf.

"He gave me a lot of comfort last night, Alex. They both did. I was scared. Really scared."

Alex grabbed her hand. "Tell me what happened." He stroked the back of her hand. "Please."

"It was just after ten. I'd been in bed for an hour, but I couldn't sleep. Something didn't feel right. I got up to go to the toilet and then felt a wave of pain." Helen rubbed her stomach again. "I thought it would pass, but it got worse.

I didn't want to bother you as I knew you were out with Pravi, but the more it went on, the more scared I got, so I phoned you. I kept trying to call you, but you didn't answer."

They stared at each other through a blur. Alex tried to think what he had actually been doing at that time, but he knew technically he hadn't been doing anything, just frozen in time while Pravi had slept through it. "I'm sorry, babes."

"Don't worry. Just unfortunate timing, I suppose." She squeezed his hand. "Although as Becky said, once I was at the hospital and you were still nowhere to be found, I did want to kill you."

"Understandable."

"And cut off your balls."

"A bit harsh, but you were scared, I know."

"And destroy all your Subbuteo teams."

"Hey! There are some things you don't joke about." Alex shook his head solemnly.

Helen told him how she phoned Becky who then rushed round with Peter and took her to hospital. Becky had taken over the search for Alex, but after many further calls, a trip back to their home and almost breaking Pravi's door down, she'd given up, before trying it all again this morning.

"She's tenacious," Alex said. "Part pit bull, part bloodhound."

"Charming description," Helen said, reaching for some water. "Although I do sometimes wonder whether she's right for Peter."

"Who could be right for Peter Perfect?" Alex put his hands on his hips. "Wonder Woman? Captain Marvel? Or would they too be no match for his all-round superpowers?"

Helen gave him a playful punch. "That's rich, coming from 'Alexander the Great'."

Alex thought back to Miles. "That reminds me – I'll phone in tomorrow and take the day off, the week off if I need to. About time I let Miles know about the baby, too."

Helen patted his arm. "I think I'll be all right, but it might be nice to have tomorrow off together. Tell you what – if we get out of here soon, I'll let you watch any football that's on this afternoon."

"I've had my fill of football for the moment. Beer too, for that matter."

Helen looked at him disbelievingly. "Until the next time?"

Alex didn't answer. With everything that had happened – and could have happened – right now he realised he didn't care if there would ever be a next time.

The F-Word

Sunday, 11th December 2016

"Ten minutes – fifteen, max."

Alex stood by the contents of a large box that depicted a toy car of the kind a child could climb into. He knew his estimate to Helen for constructing it was a bit on the optimistic side, but with any luck, she would be too busy cooking dinner to see when he had finished.

"Al, you don't have to build it now," Helen said, stroking her now substantial stomach. It had been over two months since the hospital emergency and everything had been going to plan.

"It's not like Alex Junior is going to play in it anytime soon," she said.

"I know that, but your parents are coming round soon and seeing as they've been so kind to give us this wonderfully relevant present for our foetus, the least I can do is to put it together before they come round."

"You mean you want to prove to Dad that you can put together something that doesn't involve food?"

"No. Well, maybe. A little. But I have to do something,

since you made yourself chef."

"You know how particular my parents are. I didn't want you to feel pressurised into serving up the perfect meal only for it to be pulled apart."

"And also you wanted to prove to your mum that you can put together something that doesn't involve a spreadsheet?" Alex drummed his fingers on the car box.

Helen stuck out her tongue and walked back to the kitchen.

"One-all, I believe," Alex said aloud to himself as he picked up the instructions.

Alex thought that he'd be the one to buy his son's first car. However, Helen's dad had jumped in several years too early to make sure he'd won that particular accolade, albeit with a plastic, leg-powered police vehicle. At this rate, Alex thought, in about ten years' time he would have to make room in the garage for a top of the range Tesla ready for when Junior passed his test. Well, if he couldn't give his son his first car, then at least he could build it for him.

Screwdriver in one hand, he unfolded the instructions, and to his dismay he saw that he also needed a hammer for reasons that weren't immediately clear. He also needed goggles, but as he didn't own a pair, he decided he'd just screw his eyes up tight when he came to that bit. He went back into the kitchen and rummaged around in the cupboard under the sink.

"Decided to do some plumbing now, have we?" Helen said, straining some red cabbage.

"No, I'm trying to find—ow!" Alex said, banging his head on the cupboard. "Stupid fu—"

"Hey, no swearing, remember? Aside from the baby, you need to be on your best behaviour for my parents."

"Ah, here it is." He pulled out a thin, wooden-handled hammer. "In case your beef is on the tough side."

Helen stood over him with the cabbage tipped precariously towards him. "Would sir like to wear this?"

"Joking. Need it for the car."

"Make sure you put it back somewhere else, somewhere safe. Can't have Junior finding it and wrecking the place."

Alex got up. "Don't I have three months to do that, or does he sneak out of you at night to check out his future dining arrangements?"

Helen sneered. "I just want things to be safe. Go away and build your car. They'll be here in an hour."

Alex returned to the living room. Thirty parts in sixty minutes – and some of those were stickers. Easy, thought Alex as he began with the axle, then the back wheels, using the hammer as directed to ram home the centre wheel nuts. These were a little tricky, and with such a weedy hammer, they needed considerable force before he was confident that they were firmly in place. He mopped a slight sweat from his brow and put the front wheels together with similar force.

"Now we're cooking," he said as he slotted them into the car's plastic body, making sure they were pointing in the correct direction. Ten minutes later, the car's shell was finished, and after locating, checking and precision-positioning each sticker, the whole thing was complete. He stood back to admire his handiwork.

"Honey," Alex called through to the kitchen, "come check out my cop car!"

Helen arrived and walked around the car, giving it a push. "Well done, Officer Cornhill. Didn't know you had it in you."

"Wonder if your cooking is going to be as awesome as my car mechanics?"

"It's not a real car now, is it?" Helen replied. "And anyway, one of the wheels is wrong."

With that, she went back to her cooking, leaving Alex bending down inspecting the wheels. In his haste, he'd forgotten to put a washer on one of the front wheels, although he'd hammered the nut in place. He gave the nut a quick tug, but it was firmly stuck on. It probably didn't matter, he considered. But then the thought of Helen's dad wandering in and finding fault with his own present, questioning Alex's abilities, was too much. He tried to prise it off with the screwdriver, but it had been hammered on too tight. Even a few blows from the hammer didn't budge it. He sat down for a while, considering his options, before searching around on the floor amongst a few extra bits. He then realised he had a spare wheel nut, meaning that if it meant ruining it to get it off, it didn't matter.

"Hammer time," he said, as he bashed away. It started to bend around the edges, but didn't seem to be loosening.

Harder and harder he struck, louder and louder came the banging.

"C'mon you little …"

More frantic banging.

"Piece of …"

He sat exhausted. How could one tiny part give him so much grief? It was looking at him defiantly, bent every way possible but still holding firm. It was now ten times more noticeable. Only one thing for it, Alex thought.

In a frenzied attack, Alex rained down blows on to the nut, grunting with every strike.

"C'mon … it's coming … I'll have you … COME ON!"

With one final blow, the nut pinged off, hit the wooden floor, and bounced straight into Alex's left eye socket. Rubbing his eye, he saw the freed wheel and the defeated old nut lying pathetically on the floor. Alex clenched his fists and roared, "Ha! Fuck you, you fucking little bastard! Nothing beats Alex the Fucking Great!" He thrust his arms into the air, looked to the ceiling and danced around in a circle.

When he looked down again, Helen's parents were standing in the doorway.

* * *

"Honey, these potatoes are fantastic," Alex said, nodding to Helen with more vigour than necessary. "Don't think I could have topped them."

The four of them sat round a small dinner table, upon

which sat a perfectly white tablecloth, a thin black vase holding red carnations and an array of dishes full of various vegetables.

"Fantastic," Helen's mother said. "That's a much nicer f-word, don't you think?"

Alex slumped his head and counted to three. Helen's parents were in their sixties, but were so fit and healthy that he could see them being able to remind him of his outburst for at least another three decades.

"Once again, I am so, so sorry, Lynn." He looked at Helen for support, but she was concentrating on cutting her beef and dabbing it into thick gravy. "I was struggling with the wheel and I kind of went primal for a second."

Lynn looked at Alex, fork loaded and poised. "We could hear all this banging, so decided to let ourselves in. Had we known—"

"To be fair, you were early," Alex said.

Lynn ate some food with a thoughtful look. "At least we know how you behave when you think we're not around."

"But that's not me! Not anymore. I've been trying really hard – you can ask Hells, Prav, everyone, I swear." Alex closed his eyes and screamed inside at his choice of words.

"Yes, we're well aware you swear. I pray to God that our grandson's first words aren't going to need censoring."

Seeing as no backup fire for Alex from Helen was coming anytime soon, Alex turned to her dad. "Bob, you're a man of the world, must have worked with some rough-and-ready types. You know how it is when it's man versus machine, physical battles and so on."

Bob put down his cutlery and looked at Alex for the first time since they'd sat down. "Has Helen ever told you about the time we grounded her for a month when she was thirteen?"

Alex glanced at Helen, who was now looking at Bob, wide-eyed.

"Dad, Alex doesn't need to—"

"She'd wanted to go to a Take That concert with her friends, but we felt she was too young. Kicked up an awful fuss, tried everything to convince us."

"Dad …"

"And when we said a final 'no' …"

"I was thirteen!"

"… so much foul language came out of her mouth that Lynn nearly fainted hanging the washing out."

Helen bowed her head.

"So, we grounded her," Bob continued. "And it did the trick, as she's never sworn since, have you, dear?"

"No, Dad," Helen replied, resuming eating but not looking at him.

Alex was about to argue, when he realised that he couldn't remember the last time Helen had sworn, or indeed any time during their relationship.

"Perhaps Alex," Lynn jumped in, "Helen should ground you next time you swear. You need to learn to control yourself, like she eventually did. You'd soon stop if you weren't allowed to go down the pub or see your friends."

Bob stabbed a few peas on his fork and grunted an approval.

"I'm not thirteen, though," Alex said, taking a sip of water. "I accept that I need to improve – and believe me I will – but I don't think a girlfriend can ground a boyfriend, can they?"

Helen shot Alex a challenging look.

"How about a swear jar? I could put in a pound every time Hells caught me swearing."

"That's not much of a preventative measure, is it?" Lynn said. "Besides, with your job, could you even afford it?"

"Mum," Helen said, "there's nothing wrong with Alex's sales job. In fact, you're on the verge of another big deal, aren't you, hun?"

"Exactly. I'm sure the client will sign up after we take them out next week and—" He dropped his fork, which clattered on his plate. "Oh … bother. I've just remembered I need to arrange the event for it."

"That's not very organised of you, is it?" Lynn said.

Alex resisted the urge to say something sarcastic. "I'll sort something, it'll be fine."

"How about the new Thai restaurant?" Helen suggested.

"No, no – I promised them an event, an activity. Something fun."

"How about bowling? That's easy to organise, surely?"

Alex considered it for a moment. "Yeah, bowling, that should work. Thanks, babe!" He picked up his fork and resumed eating.

"Peter goes to the Hollywood Bowl every week," Helen said.

"Peter?" Alex coughed as a potato went down his throat. "I wouldn't have thought bowling was his scene."

"Yes, he's part of a team. Top of their league at the moment, apparently."

I bet they are, thought Alex. Peter didn't do second place.

"How is Peter?" Lynn said. "I haven't seen him in a while. Such a fine young man, impeccable manners." She glanced at Alex.

"He's good," Helen said. "I saw him yesterday. He likes to check up on me, since the hospital."

"Very thoughtful of him, as always." Lynn put down her cutlery and dabbed her mouth with her napkin. "We always thought you'd end up with him after university."

Helen let out a strange giggle. "Me and Peter? No, we were good friends, but he was always too … predictable. Safe. When you're twenty-one with the world ahead of you, safe isn't what you look for."

"I understand," Lynn said. "But you're not twenty-one anymore, are you? I'd say they sound like the qualities you need right now."

Alex instinctively folded his arms. "And what makes *me* so unpredictable and unsafe?"

"Hun," Helen said, "that's not what Mum meant, I'm sure."

"Well …" Lynn looked at Bob, who returned his best don't-get-me-involved stare.

"See?" Alex gestured towards Lynn.

"With all due respect, Alex, a job in sales is hardly the most predictable career in the world."

Alex clenched a fist under the table. He'd always felt even if he'd brought home a different Ferrari every weekend, his sales job would never have been good enough for her.

"That's my *job*, not me," Alex said.

"And as for being safe, Mum," Helen added, "when have you ever seen Alex not wear oven gloves in the kitchen?" She forced a smile and begun to clear up the plates.

"Yes, but we've seen what he's like with a hammer when he thinks no one's looking," Lynn replied.

"I'm going to call the bowling alley," Alex said, leaping up and leaving the table before he did something he regretted that involved a fork and a lifetime of repercussions. "You can't go too wrong with sport, a few beers and a large dollop of competitive spirit, can you?"

The Split

Thursday, 15th December 2016

"Streeeeeeeeeeeeeiiiiiiiike!"

It was fair to say that the American prospective clients had embraced Alex's idea of ten-pin bowling. After a hard day cooped up in a meeting room discussing the potential contract, the parties from both companies were eager to relax in the evening before they returned the next day to sign it off. Alex had hired a lane in the brightly lit Hollywood Bowl for him, Miles and two of the sales team from NBC. Although originally pitched as a casual wind-down exercise, by the time they'd exchanged their shiny business shoes for the house red and blue bowling atrocities, they'd agreed on an NBC versus ZenNoise, two versus two format, with the loser buying all the beers for the rest of the night.

Alex and Miles were under the usual strict, unwritten instructions from management to make any sporting activity they engaged in with the clients as competitive as possible without actually winning. Judging by the start made by Cameron and Ruth, their American opponents, the not winning part was going to be easy.

"Wow, Cam – two strikes in a row!" Miles said, looking up at the scoreboard. "Any chance that you've played this game before?"

Cameron shone a perfect set of teeth and flexed his biceps as if he'd knocked down the heavyweight champion instead of just ten pins. With his six-foot-seven frame and thick arms, he might well have done. "I was state champion when I was twenty, my man."

Miles raised his bottle of Bud to Cameron. "Alex – looks like they didn't need that head start we agreed then. What say we start playing?"

Alex wasn't looking at Miles; instead, he concentrated on drying his right hand with the air vent whilst he watched as the machine dropped the pins down ready for his turn. He grabbed a blue ball and lifted it to his chest, staring intently at the point to the right of the central front pin. With a seven and eight in his first two frames, he hadn't made the best of starts, even if he had not been giving it his all.

He drew a deep breath, stepped forward and launched the ball.

"That's my boy!" Miles said as the ball sped its way towards the pins, just off-centre. A second later, with an almighty crash, the pins blasted over, spinning and bouncing off the side and back of the alley. All, that is, except one.

"Aw, come on!" Alex said, gesticulating at the defiant pin wobbling at the edge of the lane.

"Never mind," Miles said. "Clear up it, take the spare and move on. The Dream Team is warming up!"

Alex took a lighter ball, strolled to the throw line and rolled it towards the lone survivor. It was on target for ninety percent of its journey until deciding to glide gracefully into the gutter just before it reached the pin. Alex slumped his head.

"It's OK," Miles said as he stood up for his go. "If I have to step up and get a two hundred to carry my partner, then I will."

Alex watched on as Miles backed up his bold statement by smashing down all ten pins. Looking up at the scoreboard, Alex could see that his twenty-four after three frames was by far the lowest score out of everyone.

Cameron's playing partner, Ruth, picked up a blue ball and glided it down the alley for another strike for Team NBC. She was slim, nearly two foot shorter than Cameron and had an effortless bowling style that scarcely disturbed her blonde ponytail.

Two frames later, halfway through the game, Miles was leading with 101 to Alex's meek 47. A hopeless shank of the ball when hunting down the remaining pin of the previous frame led to Alex collapsing into his seat.

"Looks like someone needs some strike action to make a respectable score, my friend," Cameron said, giving Alex a gentle punch on his arm.

"I'm, er, a slow starter," he replied. "Ever heard of the rabbit and the hare?"

Ruth laughed. "I think you mean the *tortoise* and the hare."

Alex put his head in his hands.

Miles handed Alex a bottle of beer. "Don't crack up on me, you hear? C'mon – what is it that you say in football? Game of two halves and all that."

Alex's next attempt wasn't much better, as the ball veered to the left and knocked down three pins, two of which fell down in near slow motion, as if in sympathy.

As Alex stood up and surveyed the remaining seven pins, he was faintly aware of a new group of bowlers that had come onto the lane to his right. He cradled his ball under his chin, stepped forward, swung his arm back … and was interrupted by a voice he knew well.

"Alex! What the devil are you doing here?"

In his surprise, Alex dropped the ball behind him. He hastily picked up as it started to roll away, much to the amusement of the others, and addressed the man to his right. "Peter."

Peter stood there in a golden bowling shirt, a polishing rag in his hand. "I'm not sure if you're new at this, but the pins are that way." He pointed down the alley before holding up a hand. "Sorry, poor form. A man shouldn't interrupt a fellow mid-action. It's just that I was so surprised to see you down here. I thought kicking balls was more your thing?"

Before Alex could reply, Peter began introducing himself to Miles, their colleagues and the others from NBC, shaking hands with each. "I'll leave you all to it. Big league game tonight." He gestured towards an embroidered logo of a bull with a bowling bowl on his shirt. "Bulls versus Bears, top versus second. Alex – if you're any good, give me a call. We have a Bulls third team that could do with an extra tomorrow."

Alex tried to compose himself again, staring down the beige lane. In his peripheral vision, he could see Peter doing his best impression of looking like he wasn't watching Alex.

"Knock those babies down, big man," Miles said behind him.

As Alex went to walk to the throw line, his feet did a stutter on the spot. Aware of everyone watching, his face went flush, and his legs joined in with a judder of their own. For one second – approximately a year to Alex – he looked like he was stuck in a loop, before he finally broke free and launched his ball. Three quarters of the way down, it careered into the left-hand gutter.

"Hey, Peter," shouted Cameron, "I think Alex might need you to step in and help him out."

Peter gave Alex a sympathetic look as he stepped up in his own lane and delivered a near perfect, slightly off-centre ball which obliterated the pins. "I'd love to help, but I need to focus on the Bulls."

Alex's seventh frame was another disappointing score of eight, accompanied by yet more leg stutter, which did not go unnoticed.

After Ruth had produced another smooth spare to go into second place behind Miles, she sat down on the padded seats next to Alex. "You're thinking too much. Forget about the previous frames, they're history. You can't change the past, so focus on the three frames that are left and relax."

Alex stopped staring at his shoes and looked at her. "It's all right for you, with your perfect action. Your body's like a machine."

Ruth sat up straight. "My body's been called many things, but never a machine."

Alex went wide-eyed with panic. "No, I didn't mean—"

She laughed. "Jees, you're even more wound up than I realised."

Alex shifted uneasily in his seat.

"Turn around," Ruth said, gesticulating with a spinning motion.

"Why?"

"Trust me. This will help."

Alex narrowed his eyes, but turned around. A moment later, he felt her fingers softly massaging his shoulders.

"I go to this guy twice a week and he does this to me for fifteen minutes," she said. "I walk out like a new woman."

Alex closed his eyes. His body had done a jolt when he'd first felt her touch, but now he was torn between pulling away and saying something about inappropriateness and personal space issues, or letting her do this for as long as she wanted. Or at least until the bowling alley closed. It was only when he felt his pocket vibrate that he snapped out of his internal conflict and opened his eyes.

"Sorry, I, er, better check this," Alex said, fumbling for his phone.

Alex felt Ruth tap him on the arm. "Was that good?"

He swivelled round to see Ruth smiling at him. "What? Yes, that was very ... nice. Thank you." He took out his vibrating mobile and saw that it was Helen. A sudden rush of panic and guilt swept over him and for a second he looked around, half expecting to see her rampaging towards him. Peter was looking in his direction. Alex answered the phone and walked a few metres away.

"How's the bowling going?" Helen said.

"Don't ask," Alex replied. "I'm having a mare. I couldn't knock down ten pins in one go tonight even if I had a bazooka."

"Ah hun, it's been a while since you've bowled. Just say to Miles and Peter later that you were playing rubbish on purpose, to ensure that NBC were in a good mood to sign the deal tomorrow."

"I suppose." Alex frowned. "Wait, how do you know Peter's here?"

"He sent me a text saying he'd seen you. Bet that was a surprise."

Alex looked towards Peter, who had his arms aloft, presumably celebrating another strike. "Er, what did he say in his text?"

"Just that he was playing next to you, and that you seemed to be getting on well with the NBC lot."

Alex watched as Peter waved to him, giving his blue marbled bowling ball another polish. Probably so that he could see his own smug face in it, Alex thought. "Yes, well, I guess they're OK. Loud and competitive, as expected."

"Peter could show you some tips. I'm not surprised his team is top of his league. He was always brilliant when we played together in our uni days."

Alex pictured a young Helen applauding sycophantically at another Peter Perfect strike. He examined some spare balls in a rack nearby. "I was good in my day, Hells. I've still got it – I just need to focus." He picked a ball and tested it for weight. "Peter's not the only one here who can play. See you later. I've got a strike to get."

He put his phone back in his pocket, and with his new ball marched up to the lane, eyes focused on the ten targets ahead. He was only vaguely aware of encouragement from Miles and Ruth. His legs started to stutter as if he was walking on the spot, but instead of worrying about it, he treated it as if he was charging up his body for the assault. Those pins weren't just going to all fall down – they were going to get annihilated to the point of retirement. Alex stepped forward and let his ball fly down the centre of the alley. It gave a short bounce, and a fraction of a second later there was a deafening sound as the entire lane cleared and every single pin bounced away into the back of the alley.

"Yes!" Alex punched the air in delight.

"You beauty, Alex!" shouted Miles.

Alex turned round to see his partner whooping and Ruth applauding. Sitting down, beaming, he said, "Guess I needed to get angry to play well."

Peter leant across from the lane beside them and addressed Alex. "Not sure about the leg action, but looks like you channelled your inner Hulk with that strike. Or should I say Thor? I've heard you like getting angry with a hammer."

Alex's smile froze as Peter laughed and told the others about Alex's encounter with the Little Tikes car and Helen's parents.

As Miles got up to take his turn, Alex moved closer to Peter. "I suppose Helen told you about that?"

"H? No, it was her parents."

Alex crossed his arms.

"They phoned me out of the blue and happened to mention it."

Peter gave a grin that went off the smug-ometer scale and took his next turn bowling. Alex grabbed his beer. He didn't know what was worse: Helen fawning over Peter's skills or her parents deciding to reacquaint themselves with him. A vein in his neck throbbed.

"It's all down to you, Alex!" said a voice, interrupting his thoughts.

"What?"

"Last frame of the night," Miles said. "I've done all I can to carry the Dream Team to the finish line. Now it's your job to get us across."

Alex took a swig of his drink and looked up at the individual scores, but was too preoccupied to do the maths for which pair was in the lead.

"Not enough fingers for you to add it up?" laughed Cameron, clinking bottles with Ruth. "Hope you're not doing the figures for the deal!"

Ruth leaned into Alex and said, "The facts are that you need twenty to win, nineteen to tie."

"Alex – two strikes and we're home and dry," Miles said, giving him a slight wink.

Alex stood up and took his ball.

"You do know that if you get a strike in the last frame, you get another two goes?" Peter shouted across from his lane, again laughing.

Alex put the ball close to his mouth and whispered an insult to Peter. Four seconds later, the ball was bouncing off the back of the lane and on a victorious journey back to Alex.

"Yeah, baby!" a wide-eyed Miles shouted.

Alex ignored everyone. He waited for the ball to return, picked it up and closed his eyes. One strike for a victory that he shouldn't take. He pictured Shearer through on goal, leg pulled back, ready to blast the ball into the net. Stepping back a couple of paces, he chucked his ball as hard as he could towards the pins. It was going straight ... too straight. A crash and pins scattered everywhere except the furthest one on each side. The leftmost pin wobbled but stayed up, leaving two to get, sticking up like goalposts with a big gap in the middle. Only one ball left to bowl.

"Oh, come on!" Alex said, gesturing at the pins.

"Ooh – a classic 7-10 split," Cameron said. "Unlucky, so close."

Miles put his arm round Alex. "Guess that's it, then. You might as well try and knock one of them down for the draw, and if you don't," Miles squeezed him tighter, "NBC will just have to take the win."

"But there's a slight chance ..." Alex said.

"Do you want me to give it a shot, Alex?" Peter shouted across. "I've never made that split before. Damn near impossible."

Alex watched Peter step forwards with his ball, gesturing to have a go, amazed that there was something that Peter hadn't achieved.

"Make sure you don't go down the middle, otherwise you're buying the beers!" Cameron said.

"And don't shuffle to a foot fault," Ruth added.

He stared at the white pins standing to attention. "If I could just ..." he stood up and motioned a throw as if he might find an angle that would work.

"Alex – forget about getting both – it can't be done!" Miles said from behind.

His phone buzzed as a text came through from Helen. *How much did you lose by in the end?*

"Leave the magic to the kitchen, Mr Chef," Peter said. "The chances of making this shot are less than one percent."

Alex looked round at everyone before facing Peter and snatching his ball off him. "Oh, fuck off, Peter Perfect. Watch this ..."

Transfer Rumours

As he turned the key in the lock of the front door, Alex knew he was about to face one of three scenarios.

Scenario 1: Helen was asleep, and any explanation of the night's activities could wait. Right now, Alex would have given his entire game collection to enter the house and greet that scene.

Scenario 2: Helen was awake but blissfully unaware. Alex could then delicately unfurl his careful explanation that he'd been practising all the way home, hopefully with adequate damage limitation. As he stepped through the door and turned on the light to see Helen sitting in an armchair with her arms crossed, he guessed that Peter must have called ahead and thus put him in the nightmare Scenario 3.

Alex put a hand against the wall and steadied himself.

"Good game?" Helen asked, expressionless.

A tiny, naïve part of him still clung on to the thought that Helen was just angry at him getting in after midnight. "It was all right," he muttered before holding his breath.

"You didn't let me know how it ended." Helen leaned forward. "I'm dying to hear your account."

Alex could see that the rest of her features were playing

the game, but he knew from years of experience that her eyes were saying I-know-everything-and-don't-even-think-of-lying-if-you-want-to-live.

"Did Peter phone you, by any chance?"

"He told me everything."

Of course he did, thought Alex.

"Look, I was wound up, frustrated and—"

"Frustrated? So frustrated that you decided to get yourself the sack?"

"I won't get the sack. I just snapped for an instant, that's all. I'm sure they'll understand."

Helen stood up. "I'm sure NBC are ecstatic dealing with someone who handles pressure by chucking a bowling bowl like he's Gordon flippin' Banksy throwing it to Shearer halfway up the pitch."

In a normal conversation, Alex would have laughed and gently corrected her on the name and anachronism of such a sentence, but some primal defence mechanism kicked in and he let it go. The image of the ball flying wildly through the air played through his mind. "I thought—"

"I know what you thought!" Helen leaned forward and mimicked Alex's voice. "'Peter's never made this shot!' 'I'll show him how to do it!' 'I'll prove what a man I am by recklessly throwing the ball as hard as I can, even though I haven't played for years and can't do a single bowl without performing my weird foot shuffle thing for five minutes beforehand like I'm a hypnotised cat settling down for an afternoon nap!'"

He sensed Helen was clicking into second gear for her insults. "I thought some extra power might help with the split," he muttered, looking away.

"Exactly *whose* split were you aiming at? The ball ended up bouncing and landing three lanes away."

It seemed Peter hadn't left out anything.

"Are you having to pay for the damage to the lane?" Helen said.

"I can hardly expense that, can I?"

"No you can't, especially if you don't have a job."

"They're not going to—"

"Alex, you swore at Peter in front of your clients, flipped out with the ball and then told them that you didn't care that you'd lost because," Helen made air quote marks, "unless they were as thick as their president, they should have known you and Miles were always going to let them win."

Alex sat down and rubbed his face. "Not my finest client interaction, I admit. But I don't think we'll lose the deal just because of my ... misguided frustration in light of extreme pressure."

"Extreme pressure?" Helen picked up an unfortunate cushion and begun stretching it. "You were bowling, not fighting insurgents in Iraq. No, you might not lose the deal, but with this fiasco and the presentation mishap, I would not be remotely surprised if ZenNoise don't want you around as a liability anymore. Lord knows I wouldn't want a loose cannon like you around any deal worth more than a packet of crisps."

The way Miles had glared at him afterwards, Alex was sure he'd be thinking that perhaps the Dream Team was no more. "I did apologise profusely to NBC."

"Only once Miles had smoothed things over. Again."

"And Peter didn't help. All he was worried about was whether his poncy ball had been damaged."

"What did you expect him to do?"

"I didn't expect him to be there at all. I didn't expect him to be such a smarmy, perfect git." Alex looked at Helen. "I didn't expect him to grass me up to you like a tell-tale weasel, seedless prick that he is."

The cushion landed with full force in Alex's face.

"Maybe he'll never be a dad, but he's a million times more of a man than you!"

Alex leapt up. "I should've known you'd take his side. Have your parents been brainwashing you? God forbid their grandchild is raised by me when there is the supreme specimen that is Peter around. I bet you've always fancied him, too, haven't you?"

Helen stepped back and glowered at Alex. "You are ridiculous."

"Ha! See? Not even denying it!"

"Oh, grow up, for once in your sad life." Helen walked towards the kitchen.

"And still there's no denial! Unbelievable!"

Helen spun round. "What do you want me to say, Alex? That I always regretted not hooking up with him at uni? That not a day passes without me wondering how I ended up with the thoughtless, unreliable wreck that is you compared to someone as considerate and solid as Peter? That I owe it to my unborn child to give it the best father I can and that maybe I should ditch the current pathetic choice and upgrade to the better model?" She stood there, panting. "You choose how much of that you want to believe is true. I simply don't care."

Alex watched speechlessly as Helen stomped upstairs, knowing that they might never be the same again.

***

"You should have ripped Peter's head off and thrown that down the alley."

Pravi sipped a thick green liquid from a tall glass. Two days after the argument, Alex was updating Pravi on the latest at his flat.

"Wish I had," Alex replied, sitting on the couch. "At least that would have stopped him from grassing me up."

"You don't really think he's gonna make a move for Helen, do you?"

"I'm more worried Helen will make a move for him."

Pravi put down his glass. "But she hasn't put in a formal transfer request, has she?"

Alex sighed. "Not everything's about football."

"No? She's the in-demand striker who can either sign a new contract with a club that could be in dire financial difficulties and heading towards relegation, or jump ship to a new club vying for a Champions League spot, providing they offload their current number nine."

"I don't know whether I should congratulate you on the analogy or worry how football-obsessed you are."

"You know how to solve both of our problems," Pravi said as he waved the game controller at him.

Alex took in a long breath. "I'm not sure I want to go back, after what happened last time. Too risky."

"Listen, I promise I won't leave you alone again." He chucked the controller to Alex. "If we jump together, we return together – no matter what. Even in the likely event that you become a complete knob. Plus I'm putting together a survival kit."

"A what?"

"Things we can leave in '96 that will help us if we ever get stuck there," Pravi said as he opened a drawer and pulled out a paper folder. "I got some fake ID for me, but I'm still working on yours."

Alex examined the folder's contents: a passport that gave Pravi a birth year of 1957, printouts of various sports results, some old bank notes, and a list of the winning lottery numbers in 1996 and 1997. "Always the thinker, Prav."

"One of us has to be," Pravi said. "I'd rather not have to escape from the flat when our past selves eventually return, and have no money, job or identification. We'd be totally screwed."

"True, but at least we'd be multi-millionaires."

"So," Pravi said, pointing at the folder, "would you still be up for another trip?"

Alex flicked through Pravi's passport. "I don't know, it's not great timing for me at the moment."

"What's timing got to do with it? We jump, have fun for a few days and then return back right here, right now. You know how it works."

The thought of leaving it all behind for a while certainly appealed to Alex. To have a break from Helen's cutting glares and the dread of every work email that came in would be welcome. But he knew that all his problems would still be here, ready to be dealt with when he returned.

"I've got too much going on in here," Alex said, tapping his head. "I wouldn't enjoy it."

"How could you not enjoy Euro 96?" Pravi said. "It's Russia versus the Czech Republic coming up. 3-3 classic."

"What's next for England? The Spain match? That was tense enough the first time around. Nil-nil and penalties."

Pravi drunk some more juice. "Yes, but it's only tense if you don't know the result. C'mon, we can jump, talk over your issues and decide your best plan of action whilst we relax in our alternative universe."

Alex gestured towards Pravi's drink. "Talking of alternative universes – what's that you're drinking?"

"This?" Pravi held up his glass to the light. "It's a broccoli, spinach and mint smoothie."

Alex made a retching sound. "Are you doing it for a bet?"

"It's healthy. I decided to turn over a new leaf."

"And blend it, apparently. So what's with the health kick? Why start now?"

Pravi took another sip. "Trying to lose weight, that's all. More veg and exercise. You should try it sometime."

Alex's face fell. "Me? I cook healthily, thank you. OK, so I don't exercise enough, too much of this." He shook the game controller. "Wait a sec, I know why you're doing it – it's for her, isn't it?"

Pravi finished the rest of his drink and looked away. "I have no idea what you're talking about."

"Yes you do! I'm right, aren't I? You want to impress Abby, don't you?" He pointed the controller at Pravi.

"I'm doing it for my health. It'll also be easier to push my arse around if it's lighter."

Alex laughed. "No wonder you're keen to go back. Don't leave it too late – she'll think you've been on a wonder diet."

"Obviously. I can't spend two months here losing weight and turn up again in '96 looking like a new man, when it's still the day after the Holland match there."

Alex studied Pravi. As much as he thought this was a great new opportunity for banter, a thought struck him.

"You should go back for the Spain match on your own." He offered the controller back to Pravi.

Pravi frowned. "Alone? Why?"

Alex sat down again and sighed. "Look at us. I'm a mess right now, on my way down, head all over the place. But you … you're trying to sort yourself out. You have a goal – Abby – albeit a complicated and unattainable one." He looked down at the carpet. "Maybe I should let you enjoy yourself for a couple of days and stop dragging you down."

Pravi mulled it over for a few seconds. "You do seem to have a habit of messing things up."

They discussed logistics, what Pravi might need, where he would go and how long he intended to jump back for.

The plan was to let Pravi go back, spend the days until the Spain match and then return after watching it. To Alex, though, Pravi would disappear and appear instantly, returning with three days' worth of 1996 experience.

"Sure you don't want to join me?" Pravi said, checking himself in the mirror.

Alex paused. "No, but go ahead. Just don't skip past the Germany match – I definitely want to see that again."

"Don't worry, I won't let you miss out on the joy of losing on penalties to the Germans."

Pravi put the survival kit folder under one arm, held the controller and faced Alex. "Here goes, then …"

Before Pravi had a chance to press any buttons, Alex embraced him, patting him on the back a few times. As they broke, Alex looked away sheepishly.

"Er, since when do we hug?" Pravi said, frozen in shock.

"You never know when this might break or something." Alex gestured towards the controller. "I'm either going to see you again in a few seconds … or never again."

Pravi thought about this for a moment before saying, "If I get stuck, promise me one thing."

"What's that?"

"That you won't do anything soppy like name your kid after me."

"After you? No chance. I'm still working out which Spurs players I can sneak in the name without Hells noticing."

Pravi chuckled.

Alex stepped back. "Good luck with Abby. It'll end in tears, but you've gotta do what you've gotta do."

"Time to go solo," Pravi said before pressing the button sequence. There was a blinding flash and he vanished.

A second later there was another flash and Pravi appeared again, obviously drunk, mumbling and dropping a large bag containing something heavy.

"I take it we won on penalties?" Alex said.

"Never mind that," Pravi said, grabbing Alex's arms. "Let's do it."

"Do what?"

"Change it," Pravi slurred. "It must be possible. We have to find a way."

"Find a way to do what?"

"To change the match, to change history." Pravi shook Alex's arms like a madman. "We've got to get England into the final of Euro 96!"

Luck of the Draw

Whenever Alex had been watching his mates get drunk on a night out as he remained the sober driver, he'd had at least a few hours to see them gradually slip into a drunken mess. With Pravi here now though, it was as if Harry Potter had come in and hit Pravi with an *Inebriatus* spell. He watched as Pravi wheeled himself to a cupboard in the corner of the room, at one point almost falling out of his chair. After yanking open the door and practically pulling it off its hinges, he started rummaging around inside.

"I know it's in here somewhere." Pravi said.

"The only thing you should be looking for is a coffee pot. Or your bed," Alex replied. He went over to help before Pravi ended up as the new contents of the cupboard. "What are you trying to find?"

Pravi threw some DVDs onto the floor before thrusting something towards Alex in celebration. "Got it! This is what we need if we are going to change it."

Alex looked at the old Maxell VHS tape being waved in front of his face. The black cardboard case was well worn and had a white label with careful writing on that said, 'ENGLAND v GERMANY EURO 96 SEMI-FINAL'.

Alex took it. "You kept the original TV recording?"

"Of course I did. Don't you see? Don't you get it? We can watch it and work out what we need to do to change history!"

Alex took out the cassette which was the size and thickness of a hardback book. He could see from the reels that the three-hour tape had been stopped somewhere near the end. "A couple of things, Prav. One – I'm sure you can get the footage from the internet. Two – have you even got something that still plays these?"

Pravi pointed to the bag he had been holding when he had jumped back. "Brought our old JVC player back with me. Can't beat the original recording, pre- and post-match analysis and all. There could be vital clues in it."

"Are you serious?" Alex said, sitting down with the tape.

"I'm seriously serious," Pravi said, collapsing on the sofa again with a big grin on his face. "It's gotta be possible, right? For us to change the outcome of the Germany match?"

"Us? How? It's not a console game. It's not like we can press reset and keep playing until we win."

"True. We've possibly only got one shot, but maybe we can influence the game somehow."

"But how?"

"Ain't got a Scooby my friend, but we've got forever to work it out!" Pravi leaned back on the sofa, arms behind his head. Seconds later, he closed his eyes and fell asleep.

"Keep dreaming, Prav."

Alex had previously considered the possibility of the results changing when they had gone back in time, but in every single occurrence, everything had panned out exactly as it had always done. Whilst they could influence their own path back in the past, it seemed nothing they did affected much else, least of all any of the Euro 96 games. They had been happy to watch history unfold once again, even if it was on course to conclude with ultimate heartache.

Alex looked at Pravi, who was now snoring. It had only just gone nine o'clock, but it looked like Pravi was done for the night. The thought of going back to the house right now and resume the cold war with Helen wasn't the most inviting prospect to Alex, so he picked up the bag and took out the old video player. A few black leads tumbled out onto the floor, and memories came flooding back of Friday night Blockbuster visits and Arnold Schwarzenegger marathons. He wasn't sure if Pravi's TV could even still be connected to such old technology, but if there was a lead to make it work, then Alex knew Pravi would have what was needed somewhere in the flat. Ten minutes later, everything was connected, the tape was in and Des Lynam's face was filling the screen; the TV embarrassed by the appalling quality of the source. The tape had started when the coverage had returned to the studio, lamenting the fact that we had lost to the Germans again on penalties after being so, so close. Watching Des try to come to terms with the defeat almost wiped over twenty years of accepting it for Alex, as if it had just happened all over again.

He remembered how numb he'd felt when the Germans had banged in the decisive penalty, celebrating in front of everyone at Wembley, in England's home. To Alex, it had seemed like England's destiny had somehow been derailed and re-routed to Loserville, a place they were becoming all too familiar with, and would continue to do so for many years. But in 1996, he always felt it wasn't right. It shouldn't have happened. England had lost in the World Cup semi-finals to Germany in Italia 90 on penalties. This was the time for revenge. This was where it was going to be put right. Hadn't Stuart Pearce's successful penalty in the quarter-finals here proved that? Euro 96 was England's. Only it hadn't been. Alex rewound the tape to the beginning. "Let's see where it went wrong, Prav," he said to his unconscious friend as he pressed play.

Alex didn't quite know what he was looking for, but he got out his phone to take notes. It was as if the match was a re-enactment of a crime, which, thought Alex, in many ways it was. It was his job to analyse it, to see where England had gone wrong. The pundits had done that afterwards, but one thing was for sure: they wouldn't have been looking for ways that time travellers decades later might be able to come back and change the match.

After three hours of scouring the tape, listening to the analysis and making copious amounts of notes, Alex left the flat with a head full of ideas.

***

It was the next morning and Pravi had let an eager Alex into his flat and setup a PowerPoint presentation on the big screen. Alex had gone into partly corporate mode, partly Kevin Costner in *JFK*.

"The key question is: how do vee prevent zee Germans from winning?" Alex used a laser pointer to highlight a photo of Kuntz and co celebrating in front of a downhearted section of the Wembley crowd.

"Can we get through this without using terrible German accents and stereotypes?" Pravi said, rubbing his temple.

"OK, OK," Alex replied, and went to the next slide. "The key facts are these." Alex let each point fade in. "Firstly, despite Shearer's magnificent goal after two minutes, Germany equalised on thirteen minutes. It ended 1-1 after full time." A photo of the scoreboard at ninety minutes displayed.

"Yeah, yeah, cut to the chase." Pravi said.

Alex ignored him and continued. "Secondly, no goals were scored during extra time. Remember though – Euro 96 had the Golden Goal rule, meaning that any goal scored within the thirty minutes of extra time would have meant that the match would have finished there and then, with the scorer's team announced as the winner, thus sending that team into the final.

"Finally, England lost on penalties. Germany scored all six of theirs, whilst the only player to miss was England's Gareth Southgate."

"OK, Sherlock – now what?" Pravi said.

Alex continued the presentation. "Key moments in England's downfall. Number one – we concede the equaliser. Two – Darren Anderton hits the post. Three – Gazza almost scores a golden goal. Four – Southgate misses his penalty. Five – every bloody penalty Germany score." Alex drew in a long breath before going to the next slide, which had a graphic fading in. "If any one of those moments went England's way, the result would have been reversed, and this is what could have happened …"

Pravi looked at a dodgy Photoshopped image of England players celebrating and holding up the European Championship trophy. "Your foetus of a child could have done a better job with that. You can still see it's Kuntz's arm holding the trophy."

"I think you're missing the point," Alex said.

"No, I think you're skipping ahead," Pravi replied. "Even if we did miraculously make it to the final, doesn't mean we'd beat the Czechs and win the cup. It was only the semi."

Alex glanced back at his effort. "But come on – we get through that, banish the demons of failures gone by and no one would stop us!"

"So, Einstein, what do you propose two time travellers with absolutely no access to anyone in either team, no tickets to the match and no voodoo dolls or magic wands do to change history? Kidnap Uri Geller and spoon bend us into the final?"

Alex sat down. "Frankly, my dear Prav, I haven't a clue."

Pravi smacked the table in resignation, before Alex continued. "But that's why we're going to have a brainstorming session." He got out some A4 paper and started folding a piece. "We're going to play Crazy 8's."

"You what?"

"It's the name of a technique we use at my work to rapidly come up with ideas. You divide one page of paper into eight and take five minutes to sketch out one idea into each of the eight segments."

"Sketch out?" Pravi said. "I remember when we used to play Pictionary. You once drew a horse we thought was a bus."

"Quality doesn't matter here, just the idea. Blast out the ideas and we'll discuss and decide what's best. You'll be amazed at what you can come up with in a short space of time."

Pravi took the piece of paper and sighed. "Do you play this game in your swanky office sitting on beanbags in a themed room that you entered via a slide?"

"No, we don't have slides at our place." Alex grabbed a pen and set a timer on his phone. "But we have a sliding pole we sometimes use." Before Pravi could reply, Alex pressed a button on his phone and shouted, "Go!"

Five minutes later, Alex shouted, "Stop!" and proudly held up his sheet with eight perfectly unintelligible scribbles on it.

Pravi duly showed his sheet, which compared to Alex's, looked like detailed plans of the Death Star.

"Right, now I look at yours and see if I can understand them," Alex said, taking Pravi's sheet. One by one, he reeled off what he thought was meant. "Tell Southgate where to stick his penalty ... Tell Seaman where Germany will put all their penalties ... Tell Gazza he will have a golden chance ..." Alex paused. "I like that one. What else? Change the list of penalty takers ... Convince Venables to only pick Southgate if it goes to eleven penalties ... Rush onto the pitch and tell Seaman which way to dive ... Rush onto the pitch and put the German penalty taker off ... What's this last one?"

"Tell the England team the truth. That we're time travellers and know what's going to happen."

Alex looked at Pravi.

"I know," Pravi said. "I was struggling for an eighth."

Alex looked down again at the sheet. "They're all beautifully drawn, but apart from the last one and the Gazza idea, they're a bit focused on the penalties, aren't they?"

"Other than getting someone to score a golden goal, how else might we make a change without upsetting the entire match?"

Alex thrust his paper at Pravi. "Think big, man! Take a look at these gems."

Pravi inspected Alex's handiwork. After a minute of peering, moving the paper at different angles and frowning, he said, "I'm sorry, but I can't make out any of these." He pointed to number two. "Isn't this a scene from *Reservoir Dogs*?"

"No, that's my special combination option. Couldn't decide between injuring, kidnapping or killing a German player before the match."

"I thought we were coming up with serious options?"

"These are serious! All right, killing a player is harsh, but we could jump back if we got into trouble. No harm done."

"No harm done?" Pravi dropped the piece of paper. "Not for us, but it's still another timeline. Our other selves' timeline. Abby's timeline."

Alex had been so preoccupied with thinking about the Germany game and his own love life, that he realised he hadn't asked Pravi about the three days he'd had in 1996.

"And how was the crabby one?" Alex said.

"Nice of you to finally ask. Without you, I secured a date. We had dinner on the Thursday."

"Fair play. No football that night either," Alex said. "I take it the age gap didn't put her off?"

"No. She's about to turn thirty, so it's not too big."

"Surprised you didn't round yourself down. It's not like she'd find out."

"I didn't want to lie about that," Pravi said. "I've already had to bend a few truths, due to being out of our timeline."

"Fair enough," Alex said. "So, did you and her …"

"What? She's a classy girl. We talked for ages afterwards. She's amazing."

"She's also unobtainable."

"I've got more chance with her than you have with your stupid ideas."

"Whatever," Alex said, going back to his piece of paper. "How about one of my other ones? Poison them so they'll miss a game?"

"You mean like West Ham v Spurs in 2006?" Pravi said. "Lasagne-gate cost us a Champions League spot."

"Yeah. We could nobble half the German squad with some special sauerkraut or something."

"Have you got anything less severe?"

Alex looked again at his sheet. "Laser pen as the Germans run in for their penalties?" He picked up a Sharpie and pointed it towards Pravi.

"How about something ethical?" Pravi said.

Alex looked aghast. "Ethical? Whatever we do, this whole thing is cheating. We're planning to do something to divert the natural flow of events based on certain knowledge of the future that only we alone have."

"Well yeah, but …"

"You're the one who came back and said we had to get England into the final," Alex said. "Aside from pulling on our boots and convincing Terry Venables to give us a game, I'm not sure we can achieve it without something unethical."

"Surely there must be some other way," Pravi said.

"OK," Alex said, "how about I run onto the pitch, grab Kuntz, whisk him off to the present, change into his kit, go back in his place and miss the penalty? Then do another switcheroo and get back to normal. If we do it fast enough, he won't have a clue what's happened."

Pravi downed the last of his beer. "That has to be the single most idiotic idea anyone has come up with. Ever."

"I know it won't be easy to pull off, however—"

"The only bit of that completely flawed plan that might come off is you shanking a penalty."

Alex helped Pravi clear up the empty cans. "Yeah, forget that. Bonkers idea."

"We're getting nowhere," Pravi said. "Every option is either unfeasible, unethical or wouldn't even guarantee we'd win anyway."

"Except the Gazza one, maybe. If he somehow knew where the ball was going to end up and start his run sooner, that would do it."

Pravi gasped. "Why didn't I think of it sooner?" He grabbed his phone and shortly later said, "Got it. Take a look at this – he's already done it."

Pravi showed Alex an old 2012 video of an advert by ITV, showing a what-if scenario where they had doctored the Gascoigne miss so that he scored instead. "I'd forgotten all about this."

Alex stared. "Wow. I vaguely recall that now. But how does that help us?"

Pravi beamed. "I've just thought of a plan that's as outrageous as Gazza."

"Will it work?"

"Probably not. But what we have got to lose?"

Go Go Go!

Monday, 24th June 1996

"Do you know where you're going, Prav?"

Against his better judgement, Alex had allowed himself to be swept up in the enthusiasm of potentially changing the one game that had haunted him for twenty years. Yesterday, he had watched Germany beat Croatia in their quarter-final to set up the semi-final once again against England. He had abandoned his troubles with Helen and jumped back to 1996, which had now led to him and Pravi going down a country lane for the last ten minutes.

"Sort of," replied Pravi. "But all we have to do is follow those blokes down there." He pointed to two men in England shirts some two hundred metres up ahead. The narrow road was lined with tall, leafy trees, a thin layer of cloud overhead.

They were on their way to Burnham Beeches, the hotel that the whole of the England squad stayed in for the duration of Euro 96. Thanks to various articles they'd read, they had found out that once the tournament had been in full swing, the fans had flocked to the hotel to see if they could see the players. Alex was under no illusion that the English FA would just open the gates and let them in, but apparently there were a few opportunities to get close to the players. And, according to Pravi's plan, that's all they needed.

Pravi had done his research and found out that the hype of the tournament and demand to see the England heroes had led to a rota being established for the players to descend the hotel drive and sign autographs. To save them from having to go every day, he'd been in a few chat rooms in 2016 and talked to someone who'd been there on the day Gascoigne had come down and signed. That day was today.

"We must be mad," Alex said. "This is never going to happen."

"Why not? We'll never know unless we try."

Alex had initially dismissed the feasibility of Pravi's idea, preferring the more hard-hitting but admittedly elaborate options on the table. Doing anything with penalties would still leave it a lottery. Anderton hitting the post seemed unfixable. But they kept coming back to the moment that every England fan watching would never forget. As Pravi had put it, they had a chance of correcting that 'what if?'. Somehow, they had to turn Gazza's miss in extra time into a goal.

The plan wasn't difficult on their side – all they were going to do was to say a few words to Gascoigne when he came out to greet the fans in the daily organised autograph sessions at the hotel entrance. They could hardly tell him the truth – that they knew the future – but perhaps they could influence his decision-making. So, they had concocted a plan to make a strange but strong suggestion to Gascoigne that would ultimately lead to him changing a split-second decision and therefore being able to connect his left foot to the ball and sending it into the net for the golden goal.

"What if he doesn't listen? What if he doesn't understand?" Alex said, as they continued down the road.

"I'm absolutely sure he won't understand," Pravi replied. "All we need to do is make sure he hears it. He won't know that he understands, but hopefully it sinks in on a subconscious level."

Alex looked sideways at Pravi. "Does he have a subconscious? Apparently he was completely unpredictable off the pitch in this tournament, always clowning around."

"And that's going to help us, I'm sure. It's going to sound bizarre. He's bizarre. It might just sink in."

It was early in the morning and they didn't know precisely when Gascoigne would appear, but they'd brought enough supplies to last the whole day if need be.

"You remember the phrase?" Pravi asked.

Alex got out a piece of paper and read from it. "Don't hesitate – the keeper will miss it."

"Perfect."

Alex walked on quietly for a while before saying, "I'm sorry, but on second thoughts, I think it's crap."

"What? You thought it was OK last night."

"I wanted to get to bed. It sounded OK then, but now

that we're here, I can't imagine shouting it. It won't work."

"Why not?"

Alex recalled a pep talk Miles once gave him. "Because it's not positive. It's got 'hesitate' and 'miss' in it. As subliminal messages go, it's not good. It'll confuse Gazza more than it will help."

He gave Pravi some time for it to sink in.

"Since when did you become the psychoanalyst?" Pravi said. "OK, wise guy, what do you suggest?"

"I'm not sure," Alex said. "How about something like, 'When Shearer crosses, go, go, go!'?"

Pravi snorted.

"What?" Alex asked.

"I guess it's positive, but it's not exactly specific."

"How many crosses does Shearer put in? Bet it's not many. But with an extra-time period with golden goal and heightened emotion, might Gazza be more receptive?"

As they approached the hotel gates, they could see a small crowd had gathered there to see their heroes. Alex noticed a group of teenagers by the gate and had an idea.

"We need more firepower," he said, pointing to the group of lads. "How much money do you have?"

Pravi reached into a pocket and pulled out a few notes, which he took. "Cheers. Leave this to me."

Alex got chatting with the teenagers, three of whom he found out were fifteen and the other two were fourteen. Together, they all took the mickey out of the lads who had climbed the trees and were using binoculars to get a good view of the hotel, betting which one might fall out first. As time went on, more and more fans arrived behind them, but Alex, Pravi and the boys had ideal positions at the front. After an hour of waiting, Alex decided to broach the subject he had been gearing up to. But before that, he whispered to Pravi, "Just go with me on this."

He addressed the group, who were killing time by seeing who could take a punch on their upper arm without flinching.

"Do you guys remember Chris Waddle missing that penalty in Italia 90?"

The largest boy, who had introduced himself to Alex as John, replied, "Yeah, course. Gutted. I was only nine, but Dad let me stay up to see it."

"You cried like a baby afterwards, I heard!" one of the others added, as he deftly ducked a slap.

Alex waited for the laughter to die down.

"You see," Alex started, "the night before that game, I had a dream. In my dream, it finished one-all and went to penalties. Just like it did in real life."

Alex looked around their faces to make sure he'd captured their attention. "And in my dream, I saw Chris Waddle run up and balloon it over the bar."

"No way!" two of them said.

"True story, I swear."

Alex looked to Pravi, hoping he'd realise what he was doing.

"That's right," Pravi said. "He told me about it before

the game. It was precisely as it happened. Waddle missed, we lost."

A few murmurs of interest. Time to go in for the kill.

"The thing is," Alex said, "last night, I had another dream – this time about Wednesday's game."

They were all looking at him, mouths open.

"Go on," John said.

"The score is 1-1 and it goes to extra time. Golden goal period, right? Well, there's this one chance. The ball is crossed in from the right and Gazza's running in. It's right along the six-yard line, but the keeper stretches for it. Gazza thinks the keeper's gonna touch it, so he hangs back for a split second. But there is no touch and the ball shoots across the empty goal. It's there for the taking … Gazza's running … he flings a leg at it … but misses it by inches."

"So, what happens?" asked one of the younger lads.

"We lose on penalties. Again."

A few obscenities filled the air.

"That better not happen on Wednesday," John said.

"That's why we're here," Alex said.

A look of confusion came over their faces.

"He predicted Waddle in 1990," Pravi reminded them. "If his dream last night is also a prediction …"

"We can't let that happen," John said. "I couldn't take losing to the Germans again."

Alex smiled. "Perhaps you can help us."

Alex told them of what they had planned to say to Gascoigne, going with his new version of the chant. The idea was that they, Alex and Pravi would all say the phrase over and over to Gascoigne as he went past to ensure he heard it. They were all dubious, ridiculing how anything they could say would make a difference, some even suggesting that his dream was all a load of rubbish.

"I can't take the chance. This is the semi-final – what would you do if you'd had that dream in 1990 and you thought it was going to happen all over again?" Alex channelled his inner Eminem. "What would you do if you had one shot, one opportunity to change it? Would you seize it? Would you do anything you could to make it happen? Or would you just let it slip? It may be a load of bollocks but we owe it to our country, the Queen, Terry Venables, Tony Adams and Gazza to try everything we can to beat the Germans!"

Alex could tell the lads were on the edge of belief.

"Look, there's a tenner each if you go through with it," Alex added, showing them a wad of cash.

"Wahey!" they shouted as a collective.

"Sorted," John said. "You're mad, but I'll take that!"

Alex glanced at Pravi and gave him a discreet nod. As the boys excitedly discussed their forthcoming reward and started singing "Three Lions" for the hundredth time, Alex said to Pravi, "We're going to change history."

Pravi looked over to the lawn. "Better get the boys practising – here they come."

Alex squinted at the men strolling over the grass, the unmistakable figures of David Seaman and a blond-cropped

Gascoigne. Pravi hadn't been the first to spot the pair, and a second after being pointed out, the crowd gathered at the gates erupted. There was a clamour to get as near as possible to their heroes, and Alex did well to hold his position as everyone from six to seventy-six rushed forward to get a better look.

Gascoigne and Seaman got to the gates and chatted to a few of the fans, humouring them and signing a few autographs. There were many cameras, but due to the lack of camera phones, the players were at least spared the million selfies they would have been subjected to in modern times. The fans around Alex were all shouting at them, mainly Gascoigne, as they got nearer.

"We loved your goal against Scotland!"

"You can beat those Germans!"

"We love you Gazza!"

Alex and Pravi were either going to look mad or be ignored. Gascoigne was coming along the line, signing autographs a few metres away.

"This is it, lads!" Alex shouted to the group as Gascoigne neared. Somehow, through the shouts of encouragement, random declarations of love and the obligatory Baddiel and Skinner cover from the surrounding throng, they had to make themselves heard. "Here we go!"

Alex started them off.

"When Shearer crosses, go, go, go!"

Pravi joined in and the pair of them repeated it three times on their own. Gascoigne was only a few metres away now, signing anything that was being thrust towards him, grinning inanely.

Alex and Pravi weren't making much of a vocal impact. Alex flashed the money again at John and his friends, who were busy being star struck. Just when Alex thought they would bail on him, John began his chant, pointing out the money to the others.

"When Shearer crosses, go, go, go!"

This time, with seven of them joining in together, the chant was much louder.

Gascoigne was surely in earshot now.

Alex geed them all up by waving his hands, increasing the volume further. The Geordie was about to be in front of them.

"When Shearer crosses, go, go, go!"

At first, Gascoigne just carried on signing and smirking. One of the boys stopped singing to thank him for the autograph, but everyone else continued repeating the same chant. Gascoigne looked up at the group and momentarily had a flicker of a frown, as if taking in the strange words. For a split second, Alex held Gascoigne's gaze.

"It's for extra time," Alex shouted.

And then Gascoigne was gone, moving across to other fans, laughing and waving.

Alex moved back slightly and someone else took his place by the gate. Within seconds, he had been forced back, before being surrounded by his singing partners.

"That good enough?" John said. "Don't think it'll work,

but we did it, so fair's fair." He held out his hand. Alex slapped a £10 note in it, and then was quickly surrounded by the others like baby birds demanding their meal.

Alex thanked them, found Pravi and the two of them made their way back up the road.

"So, what do you think?" Alex asked as he strolled alongside Pravi.

"Dunno," Pravi said. "Either we invoked the magic spell that will lead us to the next level, or we made absolutely no difference at all and will be forced to watch history repeat itself."

Alex kicked a stone in front of him, caught it up and booted it again. "I was hoping for more of a reaction from Gazza. Like something had clicked inside, a coil sprung for the match."

"If you wanted a reaction, we should have thrust a phone in his face and shown him our replay of his missed chance. But that would have created more questions than answers on several levels."

Another prod of the stone. "So, that's it now? We glue ourselves to the TV and pray that in the ninety-ninth minute Gazza sees Shearer on the right and some cog inside him thinks 'Aha! This is what those strange blokes were talking about! I shall now fling myself towards the goal'?"

"Why watch it on TV?" Pravi said. "We might not have tickets, but there's no reason we can't sample one of the greatest atmospheres the old stadium ever produced …"

Wembley Way

Wednesday, 26th June 1996

"What a magnificent sight," Alex said, pointing to the twin towers of the old Wembley stadium.

They'd headed towards the stadium way ahead of the seven-thirty kick-off to soak up the atmosphere. They had watched several original clips of the pre-match crowd descending on Wembley like a mass migration to a desert watering hole. Nothing had ever come close to this in the last twenty years and they wanted to immerse themselves in the optimism and celebration of a country united once again. By five o'clock, they were surrounded by fans and police officers as they strolled down Wembley Way.

"Still can't believe they tore them down," Pravi replied. "They were sacred. Better than that fancy new arch."

The pair were talking loudly, not that they could be overheard given the vast numbers of other fans around them.

"What a waste. Gone forever," Alex said.

"Not quite – there's still a flagpole base in London. I went to see it once – it's in Tokyngton Recreation Ground."

"You're such a football geek."

The afternoon was overcast, but there was no shortage of colour. Although Union Jacks could still be seen, the St. George's cross was much more prevalent, possibly due to the presence of Scotland in the tournament. Every other face seemed to be painted red and white, some bare stomachs, too. *The Sun* had obviously been giving away plastic hats advertising itself and Snickers, as many children and adults were sporting them. There were pockets of dense crowds where TV crews were capturing the mood. The few Germans who had come down this early were subject to a barrage of banter but were taking it well and joining in.

Pravi jerked to a halt and said, "We haven't done enough."

"What?" Alex said.

"With Gazza. I don't think it's enough to change it. It doesn't feel right."

Alex sighed. "Is this your spider-sense telling you this?"

"I just have this feeling," Pravi said. "If I'm right and nothing changes, then we'll lose on penalties all over again."

Alex glanced at the joyful England fans. "That would suck, but it can't be as devastating as last time."

"But that's not the point, don't you see? It's not just for us – it's for everyone else here. Millions of our fans are going to wake up tomorrow absolutely gutted like we were. We have to do whatever we can to stop that."

"We went through the options. That was the only one worth doing."

"What if," Pravi said, waving his hand in the air, "we use a drone to fly the message to Gazza as he comes off the bus? Moobsy's got a great one that we could go back and get and dangle a note from it. The police wouldn't be expecting that."

"That has disaster written all over it. Do you remember your nephew's quadcopter at Christmas? You totalled it within seven seconds of getting your hands on it."

"How about when the bus arrives, I roll myself in front of it while you hold up the message on a big bit of cardboard to the coach's windows?"

"I can see the headlines," Alex said. "'England team coach in fatal wheelchair accident'."

"There's only one thing left then – you have to invade the pitch."

Alex kicked the wheelchair. "No, no, and no. Just give it a rest, right? Are you obsessed? I'm not getting you killed, or me arrested. We've done all we can without risking everything going completely off track. All we can do is hope."

Alex and Pravi hung around and watched as the crowds poured in and the atmosphere grew.

Half an hour before kick-off, Alex said, "Do you remember what we were doing now in the original 1996?"

"In Moobsy's postage stamp of a garden in Birmingham," Pravi replied. "I remember him dashing off to get more beers because he spectacularly underestimated the amount we'd drink by that time."

Alex laughed. "I'd forgotten about that. To be fair to him, we started at eleven in the morning. Do you remember the sweepstake for the first goalscorer?"

"Didn't you get Shearer?"

"Two minutes and twelve seconds into the match, I was sixty quid richer." Alex put up his arm in a Shearer-like celebration. "At that moment in time, I honestly thought it was going to be the best day of my life."

They were getting close to a group of fans up ahead who looked like they'd had a pre-match tipple or two.

"Do you ever think of us?" Pravi said. "The other us, I mean. The you that you just described is about to experience that memory in Moobsy's garden in thirty minutes' time."

Alex thought for a while as they caught up with the group ahead. "And maybe he'll end up here doing this with you. It's enough to do your head in!"

"Oi, mate," said one of the group as they drew alongside them. "Don't suppose you have any spare tickets, do you?"

The man looked to be in his early twenties, although it was hard to tell with his face painted, wearing a red and white wig, an England flag draped around his shoulders and a giant red cross adorning his bare chest.

"England fan, by any chance?" Alex joked, prompting sarcastic remarks from the others. "Sorry, we can't even get in either. Just here for the atmosphere."

"Us too," said the only woman of the pack, who also wore face paint, a wig and a flag. "I know – let's have a party outside together!"

Alex, Pravi and their four new friends spent the next half hour on Wembley Way getting to know each other, sharing their match predictions, singing and trying the patience of the police in the surrounding area. Alex discovered they were all childhood friends, and this was the start of a summer together before they all went off in different directions and started careers.

A few hundred yards away inside the stadium, the national anthems were being played.

"If we win the whole thing," said the bare-chested man who'd introduced himself as Clive, "I'm gonna stay drunk the whole summer. What about you, Sarah?"

Sarah stumbled as she considered her answer. "Marry Alan Shearer!" she said to a chorus of "Shearer! Shearer! Shearer!" from the others.

"What's the time?" Alex asked, before looking at his watch. "He's gonna score in a few minutes. I can feel it."

Pravi kicked him in the shins. Alex knew it would be the last prediction of an England goal he could definitely make and get right, so he thought he might as well say it. The game kicked off to an almighty roar inside Wembley. And two minutes and twelve seconds later, Alex was proved right.

The noise was like a whirlwind, sweeping around them from all sides. The stadium erupted first, the sound shooting up to the blue MasterCard blimp that hovered overhead. Pockets of local echoes could be heard everywhere – pubs, streets, groups nearby, car horns blaring from drivers listening to radios. Sarah was hugging everyone and Pravi was spinning round cheering, doing his best to look surprised.

"Who scored?" Clive asked, although no one had any radio or TV on them to know.

"Shearer!" One of the policemen was shouting close by. "It's only Alan Shearer again!"

Alex gave an exaggerated shrug to the group. "What did I say?"

Clive put an arm round him. "Wow – you called it! So tell us, what else is going to happen?"

"Not a clue, but I doubt we'll keep Germany at bay for long. What do you think, Prav?"

"Let's hope for a miracle," Pravi replied.

Everyone joined in with "Three Lions" whenever the Wembley crowd struck up the chorus, and there was no doubt from the buzz that was coming from Wembley that England had made a good start to the game. Alex looked at his watch and realised that a quarter of an hour of the game had gone.

He knew that this was when Germany scored. His heart raced at the possibility that this time – somehow – things might be different, that perhaps they wouldn't equalise. That thought was crushed a second later by a muted cheer from the stadium. Initially, Clive, Sarah and co jumped up in excitement, thinking it must be England again, before a long "Nooooo!" was heard behind them, confirming it was the outnumbered Germans that had been cheering.

"What happened?" one of Clive's friends asked, looking

around for confirmation. The air was filled with distant swearing and moaning mixed in with a few cheers from either Germans or, more likely to Alex, Scots.

"One-all, Kuntz," the policeman said.

In the original game, the equaliser had burst Alex's best-day-ever bubble. This time, it seemed to confirm the slide towards the inevitable.

Once everyone had established that Germany had definitely equalised and England had it all to do again, the mood of the group descended into what Alex recognised after years of experience as one of quiet pessimism. The crowd inside Wembley hadn't given up to though, as repeated cries of "En-ger-lund" could be heard followed by "Swing Low, Sweet Chariot".

"We'd beat them at rugby, that's for sure," Clive said.

After a short time of saying nothing and pacing around, Sarah said, "This is ridiculous. We're out here, so close to the stadium and yet we don't know was going on inside."

Even though Alex knew how it was playing out, he wanted to at least see the match somehow. He looked around and could see various gatherings of people milling around, all in the same predicament. But coming down Wembley Way was someone Alex recognised who might provide a solution.

He sprinted off towards a teenager carrying a miniature screen with a long aerial.

"Hey! John! It's Alex. Remember me? Have you got the game on?"

John looked up from his portable TV, squinted, before acknowledging the strange man that had paid him money to shout a mystical chant to Gascoigne at the England hotel.

"Of course I've got the game on," John said, staring at the screen again. "I had tickets with my mates but one of them stiffed me and took his brother instead. Bastard. Anyways, I thought I'd at least come down here and meet them afterwards."

Alex stood beside John so that he could also see the screen. "Reckon we're going to win?" Alex said.

"Deffo. No thanks to your foolish Gazza chant, though."

In about an hour and a half we'll find out, thought Alex. "Look, I've got some friends over there who'd love to watch the game." He pointed to Pravi, Clive and Sarah who were watching him. "Fancy sharing?"

Although John wasn't entirely forthcoming with a positive response, by the time Alex had waved for everyone to join him, he had no choice. For the remainder of the first half, the seven of them jostled for position in getting a glimpse of their heroes in grey doing their best to at least keep parity with Germany.

On the pitch, things were getting physical.

"Show 'im who's boss!" Sarah said as Shearer challenged Andreas Köpke, the goalkeeper, leading with his elbow before shouting at him to get up. Gascoigne did one of his trademark over-enthusiastic tackles that miraculously went unpunished. Everyone winced at the replay and agreed that he was lucky. Stuart Pearce, one of the heroes of the penalty shoot-out against Spain, added to the rising tension by winding up the Germans after a foul.

"Taking on Psycho? Are they mad?" Clive's friend, Abdul, said. "He's well up for this."

The crowd was pushing the team on with waves of "Come on England!". With three minutes to half-time, it almost worked as Shearer narrowly headed wide from an Anderton cross. A close-up of the striker revealed a foul-mouthed yell of frustration.

Shortly after a rendition of "Rule, Britannia!" from the crowd, the Hungarian referee blew for half-time.

"Not a bad half," Clive said.

"I don't want penalties," Sarah said. "Please God, don't let it be pens."

"Nah, don't worry. We've got Seaman this time," John said. "Ace keeper, top penalty saver. I want it to go to penalties – we'll get our revenge for 1990!"

That was what Alex had thought the first time round. He exchanged looks with Pravi.

John blew out a deep breath. "Man, this is close. Good half from us, though."

"I'm going to stretch my legs," Alex said. "You coming, Prav?"

Pravi gave him a quizzical look, then agreed. Together, they wandered off until they were out of earshot of the others.

"The game is exactly the same, isn't it? Identical. The

goals, the reactions, the crowd. Identical," Alex said.

"Yeah," Pravi said. "But isn't that what we expected?"

"I guess, but I had hoped something might be different, like Gazza's behaviour or moves."

"But we don't see him every second, and even if we did, it's so hard to see on such a tiny screen."

"I want to jump home if Gazza misses again," Alex blurted out.

Pravi gazed at Alex and waited for more.

"If it doesn't work," Alex continued, "then I don't want to see the end. I can't watch us lose on penalties again. It would be like watching a video of yourself being kicked in the nuts."

"I can see your point, but unfortunately it would still be waiting at the same point when we jump back."

"But that's it," Alex began gesticulating, "I'm saying we don't come back. Game over. Euro 96 Reloaded finished. It was fun, but time to bow out."

Alex hoped and expected Pravi to agree with him. Watching replays of the penalties was hard enough, without being in the epicentre of the depression when tens of thousands of devastated fans flood out of Wembley and the country starts mourning.

"There's nothing left here for us, otherwise," Alex said, still waiting for a response.

"Maybe not for you," Pravi finally said.

It took Alex a few seconds. "Abby?"

Pravi fidgeted in his chair. "I'd stick around for a while

for her. But it would be easier if you were here, too."

"So that you can both make fun of me all the time?"

"Of course. We'll always have that in common."

"Cheers, mate," Alex said. "OK, I'll stay in '96 to help you in your futile pursuit of Miss Stroppy Knickers, but as soon as Gazza misses, I'm going back to the flat, with or without you."

They shook hands on the deal and headed back to the rest of the group when a cameraman and a reporter approached them.

The reporter, an attractive woman with a bob of orange hair, thrust a microphone at Alex.

"Hi! Are you here to soak up the atmosphere even though you don't have a ticket?"

"Oh no, we have tickets," Alex replied, "but we didn't fancy going in."

The reporter was momentarily stunned. Alex could virtually hear the creation of a story in her mind about eccentric English fans who didn't want to watch their team in their biggest game for decades.

"Joking! Yes, we're here for the craic, for the atmosphere."

A flash of disappointment mixed with anger went across her face before resuming an eager, cheerful look.

"So it's one-all at half-time. What's your prediction?"

Alex smirked, pretended to look upwards for inspiration, and then confidently said, "Finishes one-all ninety minutes. Goes to extra time where Gazza slides in the golden goal in the … I dunno … ninety-ninth minute."

The reporter looked pleased and impressed with such a precise prediction.

"Let's hope you're right!" She bent down to Pravi, and said in a slow way, sounding out each word, "Do you have any predictions for us?"

Pravi looked her straight in the eyes. "I predict that people will be less condescending to wheelchair users in the future."

The reporter blushed, mumbled a vague apology and then rushed off to her next victim, ushering the cameraman to follow.

"Nice one. Though I don't reckon she'll use that, Prav."

"No, doubt it," Pravi said. "So, what happened to your prediction? I thought we're still doomed?"

Alex sighed as they returned to their friends. "I'm an England fan. I'm a sucker for hope, even when there is none."

It looked like the competition to see the second half on John's small screen was going to be intense, given that about another six people had come over and joined him whilst Alex and Pravi had been away. Fortunately, someone else had appeared, a friend of one of the new bunch, who also had a portable TV, and so the group were split. Being not only the biggest match around but also the biggest TV event in the UK that day and indeed that year, both the big channels – BBC and ITV – were showing the game live simultaneously. Although the picture feeds were the same,

Alex and Pravi had a choice of commentator and studio combination, choosing the football purist's choice of the BBC's Des Lynam and Barry Davies.

The shrill blast of the whistle indicated the start of the second half.

"Come on England!"

The rallying cry that often accompanied the start of halves bounced around the area as various groups tried to outdo each other in their support. Alex looked around at the fans around them, safe in the knowledge that he wouldn't be missing anything new. The black, red and gold flag of Germany was well represented, and it seemed that their fans were more relaxed and optimistic than the proud-and-hopeful-but-neurotic English equivalents. Even a booking for Stefan Reuter, ruling him out of the final, didn't seem to faze them. For England fans, every German attack was treated as a potential disaster, everyone yelling at the tiny screens for someone to make an intervention.

Ince shot over the bar after a fine run on fifty-four minutes, causing a mix of applause and frustration.

A few minutes later, there was a big outlet of relief as Thomas Helmer shot over with the goal gaping to Seaman's left.

From the sixty-fourth minute, Alex and Pravi jostled for prime position to see the TV. This was the "forgotten Gazza ten minutes" as they called it – a period where they had seen the best and worst of him. He had been like one of those old toy cars that you wind up as tight as possible and let go, resulting in a short-lived burst of incredible stunts and possible destruction. If Gascoigne had been affected in any way, it might show now.

England's mercurial number eight mesmerised the crowd as he wriggled and tricked his way past three German defenders, sprinted to catch the ball on the by-line and swung in a cross that was headed away.

"He's magic," Sarah said to the sound of general clapping around them.

Seven minutes later, to a crescendo of "Go on!" Gascoigne stole the ball on the halfway line, strode forward, linked up with Anderton and was in on goal until a German toe poked the ball out of reach and to safety. More screams of frustration.

"He's on it today," John said. "He's going to beat them single-handedly."

Pravi looked at Alex. So far, identical. Now for the third act, thought Alex.

The ball was deep in England territory on the right-hand side, Kuntz striving forward. Gascoigne had spotted him and decided that he was launching his whole body at the ball, regardless of whether it would get there or not.

Everyone winced and held their breath as Kuntz flew into the air. His resulting landing and quadruple tumble drew a barrage of swearing from everyone watching, but there was no complaint at the immediate yellow card brandished by the referee, exactly as before.

"Jesus H. Christ," Clive said, looking at the replay. "He

could have gone for that. This is Italia 90 all over again."

"Calm down. Gazza wasn't on a yellow. He'll be still good for the final," Sarah said.

Whether it was tiredness as the clock went on towards ninety minutes, or the increased desire to win, but Gascoigne's wild lunge set the mood for the next fifteen minutes. First, Pearce wound up Andreas Möller to such an extent that the mere helping the German up by the hand provoked an angry, wild response from him. To the delight of the England fans, the referee showed him a yellow card.

"Wow! That's Möller out of the final, too!" Clive said. "If he gets there," he hastily added.

"That's your Italia 90 moment right there," Sarah said.

In the eighty-fifth minute, David Platt somehow survived a booking for a knee-high challenge which looked awful in the action replay. With everyone else getting frantic with worry of a German goal or an English red card, Alex and Pravi stood back and let the clock run to ninety-one minutes before the whistle blew for full time. Thirty minutes of extra time beckoned and then penalties, unless history changed and a golden goal was scored to instantly end the match. In just over ten minutes from now, they would know if their plan had worked or whether everyone around them and every fan in the stadium would be subjected to the same fate that they'd suffered all those years ago.

Déjà Vu

As the players took a break to regroup, stretch and listen to their managers, everyone else watching recovered from the stress of the ninety minutes and prepared for extra time. Alex and Pravi moved away from the group.

"How are you feeling?" asked Alex.

Pravi shifted in his chair. "Like the world is about to change."

Alex stared wide-eyed at him. "Really?"

Pravi sighed. "No. It feels exactly the same."

Alex scuffed his trainers on the ground. "Make sure you have your key when you come back to the flat later. I may have broken out the vodka by then and passed out."

Like a boxer being fixed up and told to get back on their feet to resume the fight, everyone returned to their viewing positions as the first period of extra time began.

"Where's John?" Sarah asked, entrusted with holding his TV as the game kicked off without him.

"Having a slash somewhere," Clive replied. "He won't miss much. Golden goal extra times seem to be cagey."

Alex suppressed a smirk. "Oh, I don't know. Reckon we should go for it."

Two minutes later, England played the ball forward to McManaman down the right. Full of confidence in one of his best games for his country, the Liverpudlian drove for the line and passed to a completely unmarked Anderton who had drifted into the box. The keeper rushed out to claim the ball, but was beaten to it by Anderton's outstretched leg.

The ball travelled towards the goal.

An open goal.

"Yes!" shouted Clive and many around Alex.

The ball rebounded squarely off the post and, as if a dog seeking its master, shot back into the keeper's hands.

"Nooooo!" came a roar from every England fan in the entire world. The second most famous chance was gone.

On the other TV, Kevin Keegan summed it up perfectly by saying, "How unlucky can you be?"

"That was it! That was our chance!" Clive said, head in hands. "I can't believe it. Flippin' post!"

Those still cursing their luck to the skies a minute later missed a German cross flash into the box, evading a lunging Kuntz. Then followed a good bit of pressure from England before Möller steamed through from inside his own half and forced Seaman to push over a fierce shot.

"That sounded intense," John said as he returned, puffing. "Only five minutes gone."

Alex stepped back to watch everyone around him as Germany lined up for the corner. He hoped to God that if anything was to change, it wasn't this.

Amongst a chorus of whistling, the corner was swung in. Kuntz headed into the top corner of the England net.

Germany had scored.

The faces of everyone Alex could see had either frozen in disbelief or were imploding in grief.

Then the cheers came.

"It's a foul!" Clive shouted.

The referee, as he'd done before, had disallowed it for a push by Kuntz before his header.

Wild cheers from the group were drowned out by the stadium crowd. "Three Lions" soon rang out, belting out louder than ever.

"They can't beat us!" Sarah said. "We're not going to lose this now, no way."

Everyone was smiling, mock brow-mopping, high-fiving and generally being relieved over the most significant goal in a generation never scored against England. Everyone, that is, except Alex and Pravi, who knew that Gascoigne's moment – their possible history-changing moment – was about to happen.

Alex's mouth went dry as he grabbed the TV. He could no longer hear anything or anyone around him. Total focus on the two inches of poor-quality TV screen which he was now gripping vice-like.

In the ninety-ninth minute, Germany had the ball deep in their own half, near the touchline on their right as England pressed. Gascoigne buzzed around and eventually Häßler lost possession, with the ball falling to Sheringham.

He was about to look up and send a pass to Shearer on the right, but Alex was concentrating on only one person.

"The box, Gazza!" he yelled.

The ball was floated perfectly to an on-rushing Shearer as Gascoigne briefly went out of the camera angle.

"Get in there!" Alex shouted, causing some confusion for the other watchers.

His heart was pounding.

Just as before, Shearer crossed first time.

Alex stopped breathing.

Gascoigne was back in the picture. Just as before, he was in the middle of the goal.

The ball zipped along parallel to the goal, two yards out.

Just as before, the keeper dived but missed it.

"Slide!" Pravi shouted.

Gascoigne slid.

Early.

Unlike before.

His left boot made only the slightest of touches with the ball, but it was enough to change its direction.

Its last act of the Euro 96 semi-final was to cross the white line and nestle into the German net.

Ignited by decades of hurt, Alex exploded.

"Yeaaaaaaahhhhhhhhhhhhhhhhhhhssssssssssssssss!" Alex screamed, fists clenched and pumping, eyes bulging out of their sockets. When he'd finished, the shockwave from the crowd reached his ears – a screaming, high-pitched wall of sound that seemed to engulf the whole of London.

Surrounding him was a scene of pure ecstasy – people crashing down from huge leaps into the air, men bear hugging each other and not letting go, a boy sprinting down the road and not stopping, women dancing, flags being thrust high into the air. And amongst all that was Pravi, looking to the heavens, tears streaming down his face.

Alex bounded over to him and gave him a hug. "We did it! We did it, Prav! Can you believe it?"

Pravi was shaking his head, but no words were coming out.

John bounded over, leaping up and down like a kid on a sugar rush at a wedding. "Just like your dream, man! But when Shearer crossed, Gazza was there! Incredible!"

The others then mobbed them, now all bouncing up and down in unison. Sarah was giving everyone a kiss on the cheek as she was jumping, and even Clive was doing the same. There was only one song for this moment. Wembley Stadium was singing it. The eclectic group of mini-TV watchers was singing it. The police officers were singing it. Millions up and down the country were singing it.

No cup had been won yet. England had gone through by the tightest of margins. But for Alex and Pravi, in that very moment, football had come home.

"So what happens now, Prav?" yelled Alex.

Pravi was spinning himself round and round, cheering. "We're still here, so let's party like it's 1996!"

End of the Dream Team

Thursday, 27th June 1996

Back at the flat, still hungover from the celebrations last night, Alex and Pravi reflected on the result.

"England in a final – can you believe it?" Alex said.

"And we made it happen," Pravi said. "Us. No one else. Without our intervention, everything would have happened as before." He laid out today's newspaper, which had devoted approximately ninety percent of its coverage to England's success. "This is so surreal – look at this." Pravi laid out another newspaper next to it, this time from the original timeline that he'd kept for the last twenty years and brought back here, covering England's agonising defeat.

"That defines surreal. Same paper, same date, but opposite results," Alex said.

"I hope it doesn't lead to war."

"I don't think the Germans will take it *that* bad."

"No, I mean that we changed history. Who knows what this might trigger?"

Alex considered the question. "It might make things better. If England go on to win, the feel-good factor could create a generation of English heroes who'll cure cancer and solve global warming."

"You may be right. The happiness could create a new generation – nine months from now."

Alex thought for a while. "Do you think we cheated?"

"Who's to say someone didn't cheat us before?" Pravi replied.

"Huh?"

"Perhaps we were always meant to go through, but someone in our original timeline changed it so that we didn't. We don't know. All we know is that there was one match where we didn't make it and now we have."

"Nah. I'm not buying that. You can't second guess every event on the off chance someone went back in time and changed history."

"Might explain a few things though," Pravi said, stroking his chin like a wise man. "Liverpool in 2005, Arsenal in '89, Aguerooooo."

"Rubbish," Alex said. "Whatever this is – however it's happening – I believe we're the first. And frankly I don't care how it's happened or whether there's a whole load of people time travelling, because we're in the final."

Pravi poured himself a drink. "A final that we need to get tickets for."

It was an obvious conclusion that they would see the final. Unfortunately, it wasn't one they'd considered until now, such was the focus on the Germany game. They both knew that every England football fan in the entire world would kill just to be in that stadium, so they would be up against it to obtain tickets.

"The good news is that we have the money from the bets we placed on the matches," Alex said. "Whether it'll be enough for someone to part with their tickets is another matter."

"There's no way we're going to miss this. Not after all we've been through to get here. We'll find a way – we have to."

"How about Abby?" Alex said.

"Why Abby?"

"She's a barmaid. She might know someone who's got some."

"But who in their right mind would give them up if they did?" Pravi said. "And even if they were willing to part with them, it would be for an astronomical amount, I'm sure."

"Can't argue with that, but what options do we have? It's not like we have friends here that we can approach, and no one we knew back then would have had tickets. Worth a shot, plus she is your 1996 girlfriend and you want another date."

Pravi picked up the triumphant copy of the newspaper again. "As it happens, I've got another date."

"Ooh, sneaky," Alex said. "Didn't mention that before."

"Didn't think it mattered if England were going to lose and you were jumping back. But now we ought to jump back as soon as we can to give us more time to think about how to get tickets."

Alex groaned. "Do I have to go back? I'd rather stay here and bask in our glory than return and face Helen."

"We've got barely three days here to sort something, so we need to go back," Pravi said. "Also, I need some new clothes if I want to impress Abby."

"You should jump alone and go shopping with Helen then. She'd pick you out something sharp."

"Is she talking to you again yet?"

Alex's shoulders slumped. "Nope. She thinks I'm a complete loser right now."

"So, what are you doing about it?" Pravi asked. "What's your plan? Cross your fingers and hope that it all works out in the end?"

Alex began to protest vehemently when he realised he didn't have any plan to resolve either his job problems or his relationship with Helen.

"So you have no plan. Lucky that I'm here then," Pravi said. "First, call Miles. He has always backed you up and is the only one who can help. Grovel, commit to self-improvement courses, offer to clean the office toilets for a month, anything. Bottom line – you have to save your job. Helen is weeks away from dropping and is getting more and more stressed. You lose your job and you're history."

"OK, I'll speak to him when we get back."

"And say what?"

Alex looked blank.

"Work out what you're going to say, what commitments you're going to make. Don't just wing it. Write it down now, well, straight after I tell you the second thing you must do."

"Which is?"

"Prove to Helen that you're committed to becoming a father, that somehow you know what you're getting yourself into."

"But I don't."

Pravi flicked a glance to the ceiling. "Yes, we both know that. You need to keep your head down. It's nearly Christmas back home, and I'm sure Helen will have plenty of stress around that. Get through that, help out as much as you can, cook the best Christmas dinner in the world ever and get clued up about babies and how to take care of them."

"I can do that," Alex said. "I've got time off over Christmas, so I can do research then. Any other suggestions?"

"Yes – get some practice. Lofty was on about a get together in the New Year at Sven's house – Lofty, Sven, us and Moobsy. Talked about getting out the old Subbuteo for a laugh. You could have a go taking care of Lofty's Edward. He must be six months old now. Helen's tight with Lofty's missus, so let Helen get the word that you've been getting in some practice and she'll be impressed."

It wasn't much of a plan and the thought of even holding a baby made Alex sweat, but he agreed for Pravi to set it up with Lofty.

After breakfast, they jumped back to 2016 and Alex made some notes about how he intended to put himself on a fast-track plan of improvement, enough to show their boss, Caroline, that he was committed to turning it around. If anyone could convince her, it was Miles.

* * *

Monday, 19th December 2016

It was eight in the morning and Alex was sitting in a small seating area near the office coffee bar, waiting for Miles. Alex had been about to set up a meeting with him later in the day when he'd seen a request via email from Miles to meet early. Alex fiddled with the lid of his coffee cup until Miles strode in and sat down opposite.

"Sorry about the early meeting, Alex, but I needed to talk to you."

Alex inhaled deeply. "I need to talk to you, too. I need to clear up the mess I've made. I need your help in convincing Caroline not to fire me."

Miles was briefly silent. "Ah," Miles finally said. "I'm afraid there's some news that you need to know."

Alex's breath caught in his mouth.

"The Dream Team has been broken up," Miles said.

"You mean …"

"I'm sorry, Alex, but you're no longer working with me."

Alex crumpled the cup lid. "But I can change, I can turn it around, I can—"

Miles broke into a smile. "Alex – you're going to be working *for* me."

Alex paused to process this information. "Huh? You're going to be my boss?"

"Exactamundo, my friend!" Miles changed gears. "Caroline's moving up the chain and has been so impressed by me single-handedly saving the NBC deal, she has promoted me."

"Oh," Alex said. "Er, congratulations."

"Caroline wanted to fire you, of course."

"What?"

"Don't worry, I smoothed it over. Told her you were stressed about the baby and were in a tough place right now but getting help."

"Thanks, Miles. I owe you one, mate – I mean – boss."

"That's more like it. So, tell me what help you're going to get."

Alex put the coffee cup to one side. "I want to take action, to show you I can turn it around, become a better person and therefore a better asset to you, to deliver more value to the company."

"Not bad," Miles said. "Totally rehearsed, but go on."

"I want to go on an anger management course," Alex said. "To ensure I never, ever have a repetition of the bowling incident."

"It's a start."

"And one on software security. To ensure I can give the most accurate answers to customers to improve my presentation experiences."

"Sounds like torture, but that will help."

"And sign me up for the Dignity in the Workplace seminar next week." Alex didn't know if the woman in the presentation he'd called pregnant had ever complained, but he wanted to cover himself. "I want to be sure I treat everyone with respect and know how best to conduct myself in a multi-cultural, inclusive environment."

"Spoken like a man who has memorised the meeting blurb."

Alex sipped some of his coffee.

"What I shall do," Miles said, "is to take you off any major accounts for the time being, sign off these courses with the promise that you shall come back and do a presentation to us on how each one has changed you. You can call it 'Alexander the Greater'."

Alex groaned. "Thank you, Miles, I'll take that."

They finished up talking about Christmas plans before Alex headed back up to his office floor. With phase one in Operation Save Alex setup, he called Pravi.

"Still got a job. Just," Alex said. "Are we on for Subbuteo?"

"Week after New Year's," Pravi said. "Five men and a baby. What could possibly go wrong?"

Lineker's Near Miss

Saturday, 7th January 2017

"The game of kings," Alex said, walking around an immaculately laid, green Subbuteo pitch that sat on a table in a large living room. He and Pravi were at Sven's house, together with their other old school friends, Moobsy and Lofty.

"So, exactly which king had a table football set?" Moobsy said, stuffing himself with peanuts. "In my degree studies, I never read that Henry VIII liked to have a quick match with Anne Boleyn in Hampton Court on a wet Sunday afternoon."

Alex looked at his team of eleven footballers, each about an inch high standing on rounded stands. "They say history is written by the winners. Maybe Anne won, and that's why he cut her head off."

Alex carefully positioned the index finger of his right hand behind one of the players in white. "I must say, Lofty, I love the number transfers you added to each player. Feels like I'm actually playing with David Platt in Italia 90." He crouched down. "Nice touch, although I prefer Euro 96."

He pushed his finger down, ready to strike. As he was about to flick his player towards the oversized ball, a piercing cry filled the room.

"Nice one, Teddy," Moobsy said to the baby cradled in the arms of their friend, Lofty, who was standing nearby watching. "Keep putting Alex off like that and I'll win."

"His name is Edward, twat face, as well you know," Lofty said. "It's a family name, nothing to do with the Spurs scum who was Teddy Sheringham."

"Edward Twat Face? You never told us his full name before," Pravi said, watching *Football Focus* on a humongous TV.

"From a long line of Twat Faces, no doubt," Moobsy said.

Alex stood up from the table. He'd always felt sorry for Lofty, being the only Arsenal fan amongst the group of Spurs fans. He was also the father of the six-month-old baby he was holding. Looking at Lofty was a glimpse into Alex's own future, he realised with more than a hint of dread. "So, Lofty, you sorted out this fatherhood thing yet? Is it easy to pick up?"

Lofty was bouncing Edward up and down, who was still screaming his head off. "I'm doing all right, although to be honest, with my job, I'm not around much, so Leanne does most of it. This is only the second time I've ever had him on my own."

Moobsy nudged Sven. "Can you imagine what Alex will be like as a dad? God help the poor sod!"

Sven laughed as Moobsy said, "Lofty, give him to me. I know a thing or two about keeping them happy."

A reluctant Lofty handed Edward over to Moobsy, who then jogged round the room with him, whilst making aeroplane noises. Sure enough, Edward was transformed into a laughing child who was now looking at Moobsy as if he were the most fascinating person in the universe.

"You've either got it or you ain't," Moobsy said.

Alex went back to the Subbuteo table. "To be fair, you've had three kids. My one is still in the oven."

Moobsy came over to Alex, holding out Edward towards him. "How about some practice?" He looked towards Lofty. "You OK if safe-hands Alex here looks after Teddy for two minutes?"

Lofty and Alex exchanged looks as if to say that they were as comfortable with that suggestion as they would be lying on a bed of red-hot nails.

Alex waved his hands to indicate no, but that just led Moobsy to shove the poor, unsuspecting Edward into his arms. For the first time in his life that he could remember, Alex was holding a tiny child whose care was now completely under him. He looked at Edward. Whether Edward could smell the fear or could see it in Alex's wide eyes, one thing was for sure: this wasn't a happy arrangement for either. A trembling lip and then proper tears preceded the resumption of crying.

"No, no, it's, er, it's OK, don't cry – don't cry!" Alex didn't know whether to bounce him or hug him, so instead tried to do both, which only resulted in upping the volume. He stepped towards Moobsy. "Look, he obviously doesn't like me and I have no clue what to do, so you'd better take him back."

Given his large stature, Moobsy moved impressively swiftly to put the sofa between him and Alex. "No way! If you want to learn, you have to do it the hard way."

Alex dangled Edward with outstretched arms above the sofa, pleading with Moobsy to take him back, to no avail. The others looked on, intrigued by the stand-off. Alex thought about invoking the parent reflexes by rugby-passing the infant towards him, but reconsidered. Still screaming, Alex took him up close to the Subbuteo table.

"Look at the little men!" Alex said, in his best baby voice. "Football. England. Goal."

Alex had to yank Edward away before he destroyed the fencing and knocked down half of the Cameroon team.

Lofty marched over and put Alex out of his misery. "Brilliant, Alex." He took his son back, settled him and put him on the carpet. "Perhaps we should start you on something simpler, like a cactus."

Moobsy joined Alex at the table. "C'mon, Mary Poppins, might as well resume the game."

Alex looked at Edward, who was sitting on the floor a few feet away from the table, seemingly content in chewing a large rubber cube, having got over his ordeal with the scary man. Alex went back to the safety of the game and the far more manageable world of David Platt and co. "Bet Bobby

Robson didn't have to put up with all these baby distractions."

"Gazza cried like a baby in Italia 90," Moobsy said. "Just like you will when I whip your ass with Cameroon here."

Alex flicked the ball to number 8, Chris Waddle. "Why Cameroon?"

Moobsy made a blocking flick, sending his player within a few centimetres of Waddle, blocking his path to goal.

"I always liked Roger Milla, and they lost to us in the quarters. Seeing as you picked England, I thought I might have a go at changing history with Cameroon."

Alex gave a wry smile. "Change history? Impossible, eh, Prav?"

Pravi muttered an insult and continued to watch TV.

Alex flicked the ball sideways to his number 11, and before Moobsy could react, passed it across to a man in space. As he lined up a shot, Moobsy grabbed the long stick behind his goalie to control it. Alex pinged the player as hard as he could towards the ball, which rocketed into the net.

"Yes! Get in! 1-0!" Alex said, arms aloft.

Moobsy swore, and in retaliation flicked the England goalscorer clean off the table and onto the floor.

"Stupid game," Moobsy said, walking over to the coat stand. "I need some half-time sustenance. I'm going to the chippy. Anyone want anything?"

"Depends," Lofty replied. "You buying?"

Moobsy returned a hand signal that implied that the likelihood of that was approximately zero.

"Thought as much, you tight-fisted git," Lofty said, heading towards the kitchen. "Hang on, I'll get some cash."

The sound of a phone vibrating on the sofa interrupted Alex's extended goal celebrations.

"Lofty – it's the wife," shouted Pravi, who was nearest to the phone. Lofty replied for him to answer it, so Pravi took the video call while Lofty sorted out the cash and Moobsy exited for the chip shop. "Hi, Leanne. How's things?"

"Hiya Praveen. Has my husband got you on secretary duty whilst he's looking after Edward?"

"Something like that," replied Pravi. "Although Lofty is about to lose him in a poker game to Moobsy, so we'd better sort out your visiting rights."

"Ha ha. Can I see him?"

"Sorry, he's gone out for chips."

Leanne stuck out her tongue. "You're unusually chirpy today. I meant Edward."

"Gimme a sec." Pravi switched the phone's camera round and pointed it at the baby, who was sitting up about six feet away, hands in mouth with his back to him. Leanne shouted for him to turn round and see his mummy, but he didn't. Instead, he made a funny noise and rocked back and forth.

"Edward?" Leanne's voice went higher. "Praveen, is he OK? What's he doing?"

Pravi shuffled round on the sofa to get another view. "Lofty!" he shouted. "Teddy's got something in his mouth!"

Alex was busy resetting the Subbuteo table as Lofty rushed past him to see what his son was doing. By the time he'd reached him, Edward was going blue in the face. Lofty knelt and examined him. "Eddie? What have you got in your mouth?"

Pravi went to help, but Leanne screamed down the phone, "Show me! Keep the bloody phone still and show me what's going on! Lofty?"

Lofty was now frantically putting his fingers in the baby's mouth. "He's not breathing, babe! Something's stuck! Shit – what do I do?"

"Get it out! Whatever it is, get it out of his mouth!" Leanne's face had tears streaming down it as she watched on, helpless.

By now, Alex was squatting under the table to watch the emergency unfold, swaying one side and then the other behind Lofty to see what was happening. Lofty was moving Edward's head in different ways, trying to get the obstruction out in increasingly desperate manoeuvres. "Fuck! It won't come out! It won't come out!" He whacked him on the back as he sat up to avail. He looked up in desperation at Pravi who was holding the phone with the piercing shrieks of Leanne coming out of it.

"Don't you choke on me, son!" Lofty said as he continued to poke around in his mouth, the baby going limp.

"He's going to die!" Leanne screeched. "Oh my God, he's going to die!"

Something triggered in Alex's mind. He lunged past Lofty, grabbed the baby with both hands and slung him across his left arm, facing the floor. He banged the middle of Edward's back hard – once, twice and then a third time. Upon the third blow, something flew out of the baby's mouth and onto the carpet. Alex lifted his arm up and as he did, Edward's chest heaved in and out and he began a scream like no other.

Lofty grabbed him back, checked his mouth which – from the volume – was now unblocked. Leanne was sobbing uncontrollably on the phone while a stunned Pravi continued to act as cameraman.

"He's OK! He's OK! You're OK, aren't you?" Lofty said, hugging him, trying to settle him.

Pravi looked at Alex with no more wonder than if he'd completed a Rubik's Cube blindfolded, underwater in ten seconds. "Mate, where did you learn that manoeuvre?"

Alex was dumbfounded.

"I don't care where," Lofty said, standing up. "You saved his life."

Alex sat there and looked at his right hand that was throbbing from whacking Edward's back. "I ... I read about it a couple of weeks back. Swotting up on becoming a dad. Came across all these scary things that can happen to a baby. Freaked me out. But I guess some of it stuck."

Lofty spent the next fifteen minutes continually checking Edward and unsuccessfully trying to persuade Leanne not to quit her trip and come back home. He also had strict instructions to take him to the hospital to check there were no other aftereffects.

"What did he choke on?" Lofty asked, gazing at the floor.

As Alex searched, Moobsy returned, coming in the back door. "All right, losers. What did I miss?" He dumped a few packages wrapped in white greasy paper on the table.

"Nothing much," Pravi said. "Apart from Edward nearly choking to death and Alex saving his life."

Moobsy looked to everyone in turn. "You what?"

"Aha! Here it is," Alex said, holding up the offending object. "This is what shot out of his mouth – one Subbuteo figure."

Lofty snatched it up and inspected it. "Woah. Number ten. Lineker."

"Gary Lineker almost killed Edward? That's impossible," Pravi said, shaking his head. "He never even got a booking in his whole career."

Alex sat down, his hands still trembling while Sven filled Moobsy in on the drama.

"Alex saved him?" Moobsy asked, looking at him in disbelief. "Either you were possessed by the ghost of Florence Nightingale or you've been faking incompetence all this time."

"Hey – don't mock the hero," Lofty said. "Alex, I owe you big time." He came over and gave Alex a big hug. "And anyway, Moobsy, I seem to recall it was your petulance that led to Mr Lineker ending up on the floor in the first place."

Before Moobsy could reply, the doorbell rang several times in succession. Sven answered the door, and to Alex's surprise, he could hear Becky loudly asking if he was here, before she barged into the kitchen.

"Alex, we need to talk."

The adrenaline that had been gradually decreasing in Alex's body since the baby incident spiked once again as he stood up and strode towards Becky. Only it wasn't Becky like she usually presented herself. Her shoes and clothes were immaculate as always, but her makeup and hair looked like she'd had a severe electric shock whilst trying to convert to a goth.

"Becky? How did you know I was here? What's wrong?" Alex said, looking into a pair of wild eyes. "Is Helen—"

"Helen, Helen, Helen! Oh, yes, Helen is fine, isn't she?" Becky barged into Alex and sat down on a kitchen stool before spinning around and facing Alex again. "Helen is sooooo wonderful, isn't she? What with the baby and her sense of humour. Fantastic!"

Either she was drunk, thought Alex, or she was in the middle of an episode that he didn't want to subscribe to. "Um, Becky, I don't know—"

"No you don't, do you? You have no idea, not a clue. Poor Alex." She leaned forward and caressed his cheek, with all the tenderness of a Disney witch. "Of course," she continued, her voice harshening and eyes narrowing, "this is all your fault. I shouldn't have any sympathy for you, you pathetic failure."

Sven made a quiet excuse and left the kitchen, but Pravi peered round the door.

"My fault?" Alex said. "What? Why? What have I done now? What's Helen got to do with it?"

Becky's eyes now turned to full beam and she rose onto her toes. "She's going off with Peter, isn't she? He's dumping me to go off with your pregnant girlfriend and all because you're a complete loser."

Fight or Flight

Alex stood and watched Becky pace around the kitchen. "I don't understand," he said. "Helen isn't going off with Peter ... is she?"

Whilst Alex had survived Christmas with Helen, not even the best gourmet turkey dinner had managed to thaw his relationship with her. She had completely frozen him out in the lead up to it, and although she'd given him some thoughtful presents, he could tell they had been bought months ago, before their troubles. He had hoped, however, that they were at least on the road to recovery.

"Don't you guys have any alcohol in this place?" Becky was opening each cupboard and then slamming the doors shut.

"Becky, just tell me what the hell is going on," Alex said.

She yanked open the fridge, grabbed a can of lager and opened it. "Peter and I did tests – fertility tests. I'm sure your precious Helen told you that we'd been trying for ages for a baby and had got nowhere. I'm fine though, everything is working OK down here." Becky pointed to her crotch and chugged back some beer while Alex and Pravi exchanged awkward looks.

"But Peter, as it turns out, does not have fully functioning gonads."

Not so Peter Perfect, thought Alex. "And you think he wants to get together with Helen?"

Becky slammed down the beer. "I know he does! In his deranged mind, he can't have his own kids, but guess who's already knocked up? Only the girl he's been in love with since university. All he has to do is get rid of her boyfriend and he's got himself a ready-made family." She walked to Alex. "But guess what? Here's the kicker – her boyfriend is an idiot and has alienated himself enough so that Helen will gladly open the door and let him in."

"Woah, woah, woah – hang on," Alex said. "You're saying now that Peter knows he can't have a baby, he thinks he can just sweep in and take mine? I'm not going to let that happen!" He looked to Pravi for backup, but he stayed silent in the doorway.

Becky flicked at the ring pull. "Alex, do you honestly think that if Helen weighs up all the pros and cons of raising her child with you or with Peter, you will even score a point? It's a done deal."

Visions flashed through his mind of Peter tenderly hugging a smiling Helen as Alex's son took his first steps.

"You know what?" Becky said, coming close to Alex, "We should leave them to it."

Alex stepped back. "Are you drunk? Why would I do that?"

"I didn't know whether to tell you," Becky said. "I waited

outside your house, but then I saw you come out and followed you here. I had a few drinks in the pub down the road and thought, sod it – he needs to know, so I came back here." Becky gripped his arms. "You see, it solves both our problems, doesn't it?"

Alex looked blankly.

"As much as I love Peter, we're obviously not going to have kids together, so now I can move on and find someone who can give me that. And as for you, you can go back to playing your childish computer games and hanging out with Pravi until you both die in that crappy little flat of his. Everyone's a winner!"

Alex shook himself free of Becky's grip. "But that's not what I want. I'm the father of that baby. My baby. My son."

"I know you're the biological father. But it's not a new toy, a new game that you play with and complete within a few weeks. It'll take over your life – you won't even have a life for years." She looked at Pravi. "You've known Alex a long time – can you see him as a dad? Honestly?"

Pravi stuck out his bottom lip. "He might yet man up, who knows? But he's still the father."

"He may lose that title if Peter gets his way," Becky said.

Alex walked round the kitchen island. "So, what's happened? Has he made a move? Has Helen said anything?"

Becky leant against the fridge, spilling beer onto the floor. "After we got the results of the test, he took it badly. I was being supportive, but he insisted he wanted to let me go so I could find someone else to have babies with."

"How chivalrous of him," Pravi said.

"I was devastated," Becky continued, "but I just thought it was a knee jerk reaction and that he'd come round. But that was before I saw the texts."

Alex's stomach flipped. "What texts?"

Becky drew in a long breath. "Ones to Helen that said he was never going to become a daddy unless he found someone wonderful who he could love who already had kids ... someone like her."

Alex wanted to punch the scumbag. He wanted to strap him down to the bowling alley and fire ball after ball down the lane until he begged him to stop. "And what did she say back?" he spat.

"I don't know. She hadn't replied last time I looked, but he's taken the phone since."

Alex begun pacing.

"OK," Pravi said. "Let me get this straight. Peter's dumped you and has sent a classic not-so-subtle cryptic text to see if she might be interested. We don't know the answer, but you're throwing the towel in."

"If Peter wants something, he can be very persuasive," Becky said.

"So," Pravi said to Alex. "What do you want to do, loser? Easy way out – no responsibilities, no nappies, no stress? Or are you gonna fight?" He wheeled himself further into the room. "Or do you need a timeout to think?"

"This is your way out, Alex," Becky said. "If you don't want to have a baby, if you don't want to be looking over your shoulder for Peter all the time, if you don't want to listen to Helen's disapproving parents, if you want your freedom, then here's your exit door."

For a second, listening to Pravi and Becky lay out the options felt like it was all a game, playing out like a hidden camera show. As if he'd answer, and then Helen would pop out saying, "Well done – you passed the test!" or an opposite response of enragement if he'd hesitated. Except, there was no hesitation. It could not be clearer if it were made from the purest glass and illuminated by a hundred suns.

"No. Fudging. Way." He made for the door. "I'm going to win my girlfriend back and fight for my son."

As Alex slammed the door and stepped outside, he didn't have a clear idea of what he wanted to say to Helen. Throughout the journey to his home, he didn't concoct a clear strategy or have a list of points that would guarantee things would sway his way. He had emotion, passion, and that for him would be enough, he thought. Helen would see he meant business, and that he cared enough about her and the baby. Peter would be shown as a fraud, a substitute who'd had his moment and messed it up. Alex was so pumped that when he reached the front door, he was confident that he was in control and that a new horizon was about to be reached.

All that changed when he opened the door and saw Helen at the foot of the stairs with a packed suitcase and a surprised but smug Peter.

Peter Imperfect

"If it isn't the amazing Alex!"

Peter was standing behind Helen, a satisfied smirk on his face.

Helen span round and glared at Peter, before turning back to Alex. "I … I didn't expect you back this afternoon."

Still standing on the threshold with the door open, Alex looked at the suitcase. "What's going on?"

"That? Oh no, it's not what you think, you see—"

"Not what I think? I come back unexpectedly and find you two together with a suitcase by the door and I'm expected to believe it's innocent?" He slammed the door shut behind him.

"Alex, no it's just—"

"Better be careful, H," Peter boomed, stepping forward. "I've seen what happens when Alex gets angry."

Alex breathed in sharply through his nose and stood firm.

"So, what Becky told me is true, then?" Alex said, fixing his gaze at Peter. "You're trying to steal my girlfriend and son, and you," he said, flicking back to Helen, "are happily letting him."

"No! That's not what's happening!" Helen shouted. "Whatever Becky thinks is not true. Peter is just upset about his news and came to talk to me about it."

"Steal?" Peter said, shaking his head slowly. "Helen isn't a possession, something you own, are you, H?"

Alex clenched a fist so tight he could feel his nails digging into his palm. "That's not what I meant and you know it. But I think you'll find that I am the father of the baby, so I at least have a say in that."

"Father? Hah!" Peter said. "I feel sorry for the kid having you as its dad."

Alex took a half step forward before Helen held up her hand at him.

"Let's all calm down for a moment," she said.

"Calm down?" Alex said, pointing at the suitcase. "You're packed and ready to go and you think I should be calm about it?"

"It's my hospital bag," she replied. "I've packed it early, just in case. You know how I like to be prepared."

Alex studied her expression.

"Alex, it is categorically not a weekend bag. I'm not going anywhere, trust me."

Despite the appearance of evidence to the contrary, Alex felt a bond with Helen that told him to trust her on this. There was a brief pause while he took this all in. He couldn't be sure, but there was a strong possibility that Peter hadn't shown all his cards to Helen yet. However, he could see in Peter's face that the slimeball was itching to use this scene to further his case.

"OK," he said, "I do trust you. I'm sorry I jumped to the wrong conclusion."

Helen blinked twice, but said nothing in return.

"But Peter," he said, facing him, "I would love to know why you think I wouldn't be a good father."

"Alex, don't," Helen said.

Alex knew Peter would take the bait. He had got to the line and would see this as his opportunity to step over it in order to provoke a reaction.

"You're a mess," Peter said.

Boom, thought Alex. Shot number one. He closed his lips tight and waited for the next attack. Helen bowed her head.

"Your job is in the balance. Do you even have a clue how much a baby costs to raise?"

Number two.

"Peter …" Helen faced him.

"You drink, you swear, you hang around with losers."

Getting personal now, prodding for the right buttons. Alex nodded theatrically, hoping he'd continue.

"You sit around all night and play computer games, for heaven's sake. You care more about the latest FA game – or whatever it is called – than you do about Helen."

"That's enough," Helen said, thrusting her palm towards Peter. "And it's '*FIFA*'."

Alex gave a little smirk.

"Who cares what it's called?" Peter said, now putting his hands on her shoulders. "Alex is immature, unreliable, prone to losing his temper ... and he doesn't even want the baby!"

"Peter!" Helen stepped back, sliding his hands off her. "That's enough."

But Alex could see Peter was on a roll. An unstoppable roll down the hill that had only one destination.

"But he doesn't, do you, Alex?" He stepped round Helen so that he was face to face with a still-smiling Alex. He could smell Peter's breath, he was that close.

"Deep down, you'd happily walk away if you could, wouldn't you? In your heart of hearts, you know you wouldn't make a good father, don't you?"

"And you would?" Alex said.

Bang. The trap shut. Peter's face went as red as a Manchester United home shirt.

"Yes, I bloody well would! Helen deserves better than a ... a ... waster like you. I would be the father to her child that you could never be!" He prodded a finger into Alex's chest. "You don't deserve Helen and you never have – and you certainly don't deserve to raise her child."

"Stop it!" Helen shouted.

Alex took a deep breath in preparation for his response. A Zen-like calm washed over him as he looked his rival right in the eye.

"I may not have your classy education, Peter. I don't have the background you two shared at university. I have messed up and lost control. And at the beginning, yes, the thought of having a baby petrified me to my core." He moved past him and looked directly now at Helen. "But I'm deeply in love with Helen, and that love now extends to my unborn son. I'd do anything for him, and will do everything to ensure I'm the father he needs. I may falter, I may make mistakes, but I will learn and become the much better person I need to be. Hells – you have to trust me on that."

Helen smiled the slightest of smiles, but that was all Alex needed.

Peter snorted. "Trust? Ha! I wouldn't trust him with a Barbie doll."

Helen wheeled around. "It just so happened he saved a baby's life today. Leanne called to tell me. A real, live baby who would have died if he hadn't had intervened. How many times have you done that, eh?"

Classic counterattack. Peter's breath caught in his mouth while Alex struggled to not look too smug.

"I bet he was the one who put the kid in danger in the first place," he eventually said, making a dismissive gesture.

"Oh, just piss off!"

Helen's words reverberated around the narrow hall.

"You," she pointed at a startled Peter, "are meant to be my friend, and yet you dump poor Becky, come round here to try and take advantage of my situation, and drive a wedge between Alex and me?"

"No, H—"

"What kind of man does that?" She thrust a hand on her hip. "You talk about Alex not being up to it, crumbling under the pressure and wanting to dodge responsibilities, but what about you? You find out that you can't have kids, so you turn to me as some sort of oven-ready solution?"

Alex waited with intrigue for the reply as Peter geared himself up.

"It's not like you planned to have children with him, is it?" Peter said. "You're meant to be the sensible one, and yet you allow him to suck the life out of you for years and then let him knock you up."

"You've no right—" Helen started.

"I'm offering you a way out, don't you see? I love you H, and I can learn to love your baby. I'll be the best dad it'll ever have – better than this buffoon. We can make a family – a strong family." He held out his hand to her. "Come with me for a better life."

Helen breathed heavily in and out.

Alex stood back.

Desperation filled Peter's face.

She broke the silence. "I have someone who loves me right here." She put her arm round Alex. "He may be a buffoon, but he already loves our son. I'm sorry Peter, but go find yourself another family."

The warmth of her hug matched the width of Alex's smile.

Peter's shoulders drooped. He looked from Helen to Alex and back again. His mouth opened, and a strange, breathy sound came out, as if the words had taken a diversion down his throat. He studied his shoes, before finally mumbling, "If that's your decision, then so be it." He went towards the door. "But don't come running to me when it all goes wrong."

"Peter, go home and sort your head out," Helen said.

With that, Peter walked out of the house and slammed the door. Helen turned round to face Alex.

"Thanks," Alex said.

She gazed up into his eyes. "For what?"

"For sticking with the buffoon."

She hugged him, this time a full version, or as much as she could manage, given her bump. "I must admit, I'm shocked," she said.

"At what?"

"You. I thought you were going to launch in a full-on war of words with him. Or even worse."

Although he was still unsure how he pulled it off, given the result, staying calm and letting Helen do all the talking at the end was a tactical masterclass. "Well, even three-year-old chimps grow up eventually."

Helen rubbed her bump. "Maybe there's hope for us yet, then."

"I was shocked, too, though," Alex said.

Helen grimaced. "Don't tell my parents I swore."

"I meant that you knew I play *FIFA*."

Helen gave him a gentle punch.

"On a serious note, do you think Peter might tell your parents you swore in an attempt to show my bad influence and get back in with you again?"

"No, I think he'll lie low now. He got embarrassed

tonight and will stay out of it." She gazed into his eyes. "Listen, nothing ever happened between us. He's not a bad guy and we've been close friends for so long. Before I met you, I did occasionally wonder if we'd end up together, but it wasn't right."

Alex sighed. "I thought I was losing you."

"I can't say that you haven't given me a lot to think about recently. This isn't easy for me, being eight months pregnant, and I need someone to rely on."

"Whether I'm a buffoon, moron or waster, you can rely on me from now on."

"I hope so," Helen said. "Because if you let me down again during these next two months, I shall ensure you suffer for your next two lifetimes."

Date With a Dead Woman

Saturday, 28th January 2017

Alex was preparing for two tumultuous events in his life – the final of Euro 96 and the birth of his son. Helen had gone on a massive spending spree and judging from the now bulging spare room, she had bought up enough baby supplies for octuplets until they could walk. It didn't stop her jumping at the chance on Saturday morning to help Pravi find some clothes for his forthcoming date.

"So, Pravi, tell me more about this Abby," Helen said as she walked through the menswear section of Marks & Spencer with Alex and Pravi trailing behind. "How long have you known her?"

"Well, you could that say it's taken him twenty years to get this far," Alex said, before Pravi pushed him into a clothes rack.

"Discounting the last twenty years where I hadn't seen her at all, then only a few weeks," Pravi said.

"Any baggage?" Helen asked as she examined a floral shirt.

"Not a thing, Hells," Alex said. "Aside from being in the

wrong dimension and having a recent ex-boyfriend that makes Attila the Hun look like Donny Osmond."

Helen looked up. "Huh?"

"Ignore him," Pravi said. "The ex is out of the picture and despite a few logistical challenges, she's perfect."

He was saved from any follow-up questions as Helen went to fetch an assistant to see if they had the shirt in Pravi's size, without even consulting the intended wearer first.

"So," Alex said, casually examining the shirt rack, "never mind the date – what happens after the final on Sunday? Will there *be* an after Sunday?"

"How do you mean?"

"We jumped for the first time at the very start of Euro 96 – first minute, first game. Who's to say we don't get booted back the second it's over?"

"Nah," Pravi said. "What if we don't touch the controller again? We can't just disappear, it's not magic. It needs the controller to jump timelines."

Alex handed Pravi a Hawaiian shirt on sale. "So Professor Hawking, what happens then? Life just continues in 1996?"

Pravi shrugged. "I'm only guessing. But whether we're there or not, I reckon things carry on in that timeline."

"You don't know that though," Alex said.

"Right now I don't care how it works," Pravi said, shoving the shirt back onto the rails. "We changed history. I've got another date."

Alex glanced over to see Helen still waiting for an assistant. "It's not like you were short of dates before. Remember Jasmine?"

"Jasmine was fun, but Abby's in a different league. She could be the future."

"Right now she's the past." As he said the words, he had a sudden idea. "But what about the present?"

Pravi froze, one arm in a blue jacket. "What about it?"

"The present – now, this timeline. Abby's gotta be somewhere, albeit older than what we know. Wouldn't it be strange to see how she turns out?"

Pravi bowed his head. After a few seconds, he said, "I know how she turns out."

"What? Where is she then?"

Pravi breathed deeply. "She's not in our timeline anymore." He pulled the jacket fully on. "She's dead."

Pravi turned away as Alex stared open-mouthed. The thought of someone he knew being dead and yet still alive somewhere – some *time* – else was mind-blowing.

"Who's dead?" Helen asked as she returned to the pair. She was wincing, holding her stomach.

"Are you OK, Hells?" Alex said, stroking her arm.

"Fine, fine," she replied. "Just the joys of being extremely pregnant. So, who's died?"

"Um, Carrie Fisher," Alex said. "You know – Princess Leia. I only just heard."

"That was weeks ago," Helen said as she surveyed Pravi. "That colour doesn't suit you, dear. How about one in beige? I saw a nice one over there somewhere."

As Helen went off again to find a suitable jacket for a man with a date with a dead woman, Alex said, "Are you serious, Prav? Is that true?"

"Yes," he replied. "I do tend to suit beige better."

"I meant Abby."

Pravi sighed. "Yes, it's true. I did some research the other day. Found an article about her in a local paper."

Alex scratched his stubble. "Blimey. What happened?"

"It was in '97, February. Quite soon for her. Hit and run, apparently. No one was ever caught, but they reckoned it wasn't an accident."

"Why would anyone want to kill her?"

"Don't know, but you saw the type of guy she hung around with. She could have just been in the wrong place at the wrong time."

Helen came back with both the jacket and shirt, and after a quick fitting had convinced Pravi to buy both. Alex ushered Helen into the baby section as he caught up with Pravi leaving the till.

"You want to save her, don't you?" Alex said.

Pravi looked straight at Alex. "Wouldn't you? What's the point of time travel and knowing the future but not acting on it? Look what we've achieved so far."

They picked their way through the store. "You might have saved her already though," Alex said.

"How?"

"She's not with Stabber anymore. If her association with

him caused her death and that's ended, then perhaps she'll be safe now."

"I can't take that chance. What if it's not him?"

"What do you propose?"

Pravi examined some belts. "Dunno. She could get a job round here?"

"Are you mad? How would that work? You can't say, 'Bad news – you might die soon. Good news – I'm from the future, you start down the White Lion on Monday'."

"At least she wouldn't run into her future self."

"Oh well, that'll seal it. I'm sure she'll be totally fine with it then. Might as well tell her tonight over dessert." Alex stopped, and putting on a high-pitched voice said, "Oh, Pravi, I've always wanted to see the future and miss out on twenty years of my family and friends. Take me to bed now!"

Pravi stuck up his middle finger. "It was only a thought."

"A stupid one." Alex could see Helen was busy looking at more impossibly small items. "We don't even know if we can take anyone else when jumping. Items yes, but people?"

"We take each other back. I bet the controller doesn't only work for us, so why not someone else if we hold them? And we must have around seventy jumps left."

"Well, maybe," Alex said. "But it's not really an option, is it? She has to stay there. You may have saved her or you may have to convince her to emigrate to Australia and never return."

Pravi wheeled towards the exit. "Let me have the date with her first."

Back at the flat after shopping, Alex was watching Pravi get ready to jump back and impress Abby with his modern clothes. Unfortunately for Alex, all Pravi wanted to do was chat about his forthcoming date, have the date, and then chat all afternoon about the date.

"Shouldn't you be focusing on the football?" Alex said.

"Do you mean Spurs v Wycombe today?" Pravi replied. "Should be an easy win for us."

"No," Alex said, waving the semi-final newspaper at him. "Our 1996 final tickets."

"Don't worry, I'm on it," Pravi answered, combing his hair for the seventeenth time in the last half hour. "There must be someone Abby knows who we can buy tickets from. Leave it with me."

"You've been saying that for weeks now. The size she's getting, Helen's not going to let me come round here for much longer on Saturdays. I'm only here now as I negotiated a few hours in the afternoon so I could spend the evening with her." Alex re-read the old-but-new newspaper. "And if you keep burning time in '96, we'll have no time to get anything."

"Relax, something has to turn up." A pristine Pravi finally came away from the mirror. "Right, I'm going in. Could you get me the controller? I left it in the bedroom."

Alex sighed and went and fetched it.

"So, it'll be Thursday, right?" Alex said, returning and passing him the pad. "Just make sure you don't skip to after the final on Sunday."

"Scout's honour," Pravi said, saluting with his three fingers on his right hand.

Alex suddenly saw his phone on Pravi's lap, but before he could protest, Pravi disappeared and then reappeared, this time far from immaculate but with a big grin. After making sure Pravi was OK after his jump, Alex sat back down and said, "So, what happened with Crabby Abby? And why did you take my phone?"

"We had fun," Pravi replied.

"What kind of fun?"

"*Fun* fun."

"Look, I haven't been on a date with a woman other than Helen for years now, so I have to live the whole date thing vicariously through you. So spill."

Pravi laid back on the sofa and put his hands behind his head. "We had dinner at Cody's. Nice steak and a bottle of wine. We chatted loads, her job, aspirations, family."

"Nice work. Keep it about her, make sure you don't get asked any awkward anachronistic questions."

"Big word for you. No, it was because she was interesting and I wanted to hear more about her."

Alex pretended to stick two fingers down his throat. "And after dinner?"

"Dessert. Cheesecake. Classic."

"You walk her home?"

"Of course."

Alex leaned forward. "And then?"

"We talked until two in the morning."

"And then?"

"I left."

"Oh."

"She's a classy woman, what can I say?" Pravi said.

"So, from what time on Friday did you jump back?"

Pravi shifted in his wheelchair. "Sorry about your phone. I left it there."

"What?" Alex stood up. "Great. Why did you take it?" Alex examined his friend's face. He'd had enough overnight stays with Pravi in his time to know how he usually looked the night after. "Prav, why does it look like you've got half a beard going on?"

Pravi scratched his not insubstantial stubble. "Er ... you know me, beard always grows quick, doesn't it?"

Alex leaned forward. "No, that looks like—" He took a quick intake of breath. "You stayed longer than a day, didn't you? You little ... what day did you leave?"

Pravi went towards the kitchen. "You're not my dad, Alex."

Alex hurdled the sofa, shot past him and blocked his way. "If you say that you left on Monday, I'll—"

"Chill, it wasn't Monday, OK? After Abby left, I couldn't get to sleep and then proceeded to sleep half of Friday."

"So, it's Friday?" Alex said.

"You see, I planned to come back then, but then Abby invited me to the cinema."

"Saturday! What about our final tickets? Did she get hold of some?"

"No."

"Did you manage to get any tickets while you were there?"

Pravi shook his head.

Alex stomped into the kitchen. "For flip's sake. We have one day to get the holy grail of our generation, and you're busy holding hands in the love seats in the cinema with a woman who's been dead for twenty years."

"Actually, it's Sunday morning." Pravi sat there with his hands on his lap.

Alex's jaw made a break for the floor.

"Sorry," Pravi continued. "I was so wrapped up that I couldn't face jumping back to reality, so I ended up going to the pub all day and having late drinks."

Alex's brain was overloading with this information. He marched across to the fridge, took out a two-pint carton of milk, undid it and faced Pravi. Seconds away from giving his friend a wake-up call, Pravi gave him a massive grin.

Holding up three pieces of brightly coloured paper, Pravi said, "So, it was a good thing I bought these tickets before I left."

Final Countdown

Sunday, 30th June 1996

"Prav, I admit it – you're a genius."

It was five past ten on the morning of the final and Alex had decided that this was going to be one of the best days of his life. Pravi's plan had been to obtain tickets from the present, as opposed to from the past. Since having the idea after the semi-final, he'd been scouring the eBay auctions and putting the word out for weeks for unused final tickets. A collector's item at best but worthless as an actual ticket in the present, he had been surprised at how many were out there. Not everyone had been able or even wanted to go to the final, especially as tickets had been bought many months in advance, so naturally a few unused ones were still around. The best thing was that after following up a lead from one of his contacts in the wheelchair community, he had sourced a wheelchair access seat plus helper and even a spare one close by so that he could take both Alex and Abby. Despite being immensely excited, Alex hadn't been sure about jumping back immediately. Pravi had predicted this, and had purposely left Alex's phone in 1996, knowing that he would want to be reunited with it as soon as possible. Barely two hours after Pravi had returned, they'd jumped to the day of the final.

"You're still a git for waiting a week until you told me about the ticket," Alex said as he watched a special final build-up programme on ITV. "And I'm surprised you didn't wait to jump back until kick-off. Limit me being the gooseberry."

"Get over it. Anyway, we need to sort a plan," Pravi said.

"Church or registry office?"

Pravi tutted. "The match. The pub."

Watching England captain Tony Adams on TV saying how much of an honour it would be to lead the team out to a final, it still seemed like another reality to Alex, which, when he thought about it, it was.

While Pravi fretted about the plans, Alex was glued to the coverage. Pundits were talking about a game that he'd not experienced, and for once didn't know what the score would be. Early team news was that there had been an accident in training to the back-from-suspension Gary Neville, ruling him out of the biggest match of his life.

Baddiel and Skinner were animatedly describing to an interviewer how this final was going to be the greatest event in their lives even if they were to live to a hundred and fifty.

"At least the Germans won't be singing about it coming home this time," Alex said, more to himself than Pravi who was still working out which of the many England shirts he owned that he wanted to wear.

The survivors of '66 were asked how they coped with their first final. Geoff Hurst was modest as usual, while Jack Charlton laughed and bigged up England's chances.

They interviewed youngsters with curtain haircuts in Pulp and Oasis t-shirts who were all predicting an England win in the summer of all summers. ITV also paid respect to the Czech team, going through all the main threats. There were experienced and soon-to-be discovered stars like Karel Poborský, Patrik Berger and Pavel Nedvěd. Alex had watched the original final recently, having had little memory of it the first time round, such was the abyss of despair he, Pravi and many others were still in after England's semi-final defeat. He was surprised to see that the Czechs had taken a lead, and it took a golden goal by Germany to eventually see them off.

"What happens if we lose, Prav?"

"What?" came a call from somewhere in the bedroom.

"We can't assume we're gonna win. All this time travel and changing the past, it might be for nothing."

Pravi came out sporting the 1996 home shirt in a fit of originality. "Maybe we'll get another chance to change it, who knows? I don't want to think about that. Positive thinking. We're in the final!"

By midday, they'd had enough build-up to psych themselves up for the match. A trip to the pub awaited to meet up with Abby and sink a few pints as a warm-up. They'd gone over the plan ten times, got ready, checked they'd got everything they needed, and found enough money to keep them in beers all day. Pravi stashed the controller in his pocket and got beers for the journey while Alex grabbed his phone in the hope that he'd capture Tony Adams lifting the trophy for real.

The walk to the pub was one of pure expectation, not just for them but for everyone around. Throughout the tournament there had been many flags draped from windows and cars adorned with cheap, plastic St. George's crosses, but now it was like every sports shop in town had unloaded their entire stock on the neighbourhood. Kids were out playing on grass and pavement, men and women were walking around with cans, a good proportion with painted flags on their cheeks. Occasionally, a car would roll past and beep enthusiastically at a fellow supporter. Even a sole man in a Czech shirt got a warm welcome. This day was like no other for a generation. After soaking it all in, they arrived at The Sailor.

The pub had gone even further down the football theme in light of the impending pinnacle. Football beer mats, England flags hanging down from every rafter, red and white banners everywhere. The local beers had all changed their names to England players. Behind the bar were boxes overflowing with crisps of assorted flavours. The pictures hanging up of scantily clad women were totally obscured by packets of peanuts. Posters announcing sweepstakes and raffles for the final adorned most of the pillars. If ever there was a time to cash in on one of the biggest sporting events in decades, this was it.

"We've got about an hour and a half to kill," Pravi said as they walked through the pub's entrance. "Abby should be able to finish by then, assuming her replacement arrives on time."

It was over six hours until kick-off, but the pub resembled a base camp for the uberfans who no doubt had got here as soon as it opened to stake out the best TV viewing place and claim every inch of table and chair in their reachable territory. Multiple plastic jugs meant fewer trips to the already heaving bar. Alex wondered whether some of the fans also had catheters fitted for the occasion. Pravi caused a stir as people made way for him, but as one barmaid's favourite customer, he was at least able to get served at the bar quickly.

"Hey, gorgeous!" Pravi said to Abby in a new, bold tone Alex hadn't seen for a while. "Are we still on for our romantic date later?"

She finished giving a customer his change and winked at Pravi. "Let me see ... you, me and seventy thousand others? How could a lady resist such an offer?" She got two pint glasses and proceeded to fill them. "As long as Barbara comes in to replace me, I can go at two, OK?"

Alex and Pravi squeezed themselves into the only corner of the pub that wasn't occupied by England shirt-wearing fans who look liked they'd rip your arm off if you suggested they make room for them. It had a viewing angle as such that the best you'd see of a match was of an ankle if the producer happened to zoom in on a particularly nasty tackle.

Not that they cared. By one o'clock, Alex was checking his watch every five minutes. By half past, it was down to every two. Pravi alternated his view between the four cells of TV he could see and the two centimetres of bar he would fleetingly catch a glimpse of as customers battled their way back with their drinks.

"I'll check if she's still there," Alex said, finishing his drink. "Another?"

"Nah. For a start, it'll be half an hour before you even get to the bar. Plus I don't want to get too tanked before the match."

Alex went towards the bar, stopping a good two metres behind a human wall. As he craned his neck and stood on tiptoes, he could see Abby was still working like a madwoman serving a never-ending sea of punters. He was so preoccupied watching her that he jumped when he was prodded by someone who had appeared by his side.

"You're gonna lose!"

Alex shot round to face the person, spilling some beer onto his shirt sleeve in the process. It was a face he recognised.

"Jack, er, hi." He put his pint down on a nearby table and wiped his sleeve.

"Isn't it fantastic?" Jack motioned to their surroundings. "You get to watch England lose and Gazza crying again with me right here!"

Alex glanced over to Pravi. He guessed that having another confrontation would not go down well.

"So, you're not rooting for us then, I take it?" Alex said.

"Ha!" Jack slapped a hand on Alex's shoulder. "I tell yer what – when you're sobbing in the streets afterwards, I'll give you back the fifty quid you gave me."

Alex remembered the money he'd given Jack before their drunken sing-song after the Holland game.

"Um, thanks."

"Don't mention it – I've put it all on the Czechs winning so I'll be quids in!"

For the next five minutes, Jack was a one-man show – dancing, laughing, taunting Alex and telling anyone who was passing how badly England were going to lose. Alex stood there tolerating the taunts, before beckoning Pravi to join him. When Jack finally paused, Alex said, "I'm sorry Jack – we won't be joining you here. We're off to Wembley."

Alex took out his three tickets. Jack stared at them in disbelief. Before he could respond, a woman came past Pravi, stopped and then turned back towards him.

"You must be Pravi, right?"

Pravi looked at her. "Who's asking?"

"Sorry, I'm Barbara," she said, holding out a hand. "I'm relieving Abby so you can go to Wembley. I know it's the final and everything, but I hate football and need the money. I also think that Abby really likes you, Pravi."

Pravi grinned, Jack grunted and sloped off as they watched Barbara the Saviour shove her way through to behind the bar. Another piece of the plan falls into place, Alex thought to himself.

He sat down at their table and waved the tickets. "Looks like me, you and your precious girlfriend Abby are going to Wembley."

"The hell you are," said a deep voice.

The three of them turned round as a large hand came out from behind them, plucked the tickets from Alex and held them high up. It was Stabber.

"Outside. Now."

I'll Be Back

Seeing the cup final tickets in the hands of a murderous brute who evidently thought Alex's best friend was stealing his woman, was certainly not in the plans. Alex processed the likely options and outcomes and realised none of them involved him and Pravi ending up unscathed and inside Wembley. It was now purely damage limitation.

"You," Stabber said, shoving a finger centimetres from Alex's nose, "wheel this prick outside. I'll be right behind you."

"Look," Pravi said, "you can't come in here and—"

"Who the fuck are you telling me what I can and can't do?" Stabber squatted to face him. "I ain't ever hit a man in a wheelchair before, but today I might make an exception."

"If you think I'm leaving this bar and going outside with you …" Pravi paused, "then you're more stupid than you look."

Stabber's face seemed to crumple up in anger. He rose, went to push Pravi's chair but not before Pravi had put the brakes on. Stabber had seen this and was wrestling control of the brakes from Pravi when Alex had an idea. It was a risky, short-term idea that could prove disastrous in many ways, but it was the only one he had.

"You want us to go outside?" Alex said. He barged Stabber aside and took hold of the wheelchair. "OK, deal." As he said this, he squeezed Pravi's shoulder. Pravi looked up at his friend, and a wordless communication was sent between them. Pravi let go of the brakes and allowed himself to be totally at Alex's mercy.

Stabber was now right behind and shoving Alex forward towards the exit, which was like swimming upstream as more people entered. Up on the left, just before the exit to the car park and what might be a bloody fate, was the door to the gents. Alex gripped the wheelchair's handles tightly, saw a gap and then spurted forward with a huge push, swinging into the door and bursting open into the toilets, leaving Stabber momentarily behind.

"Controller!" Alex shouted, a second before Stabber crashed into the room. Pravi handed it to Alex, who held it behind his back.

"Stupid fucks!" Stabber said, before flinging out a poor teenager who had been drying his hands. He blocked the door, leaving the three of them alone. "I can do it in here, I don't care."

Precisely what "it" was, Alex wasn't totally sure, but he wasn't about to let that happen. Stabber approached and grabbed Alex by the throat, but instead of trying to free himself, he pressed the controller's buttons … and sent himself and his assailant out of 1996.

As the usual flash penetrated his eyelids and left him temporarily blind, Alex knew he only had a few seconds. However, he had two big advantages: first, he'd been through this enough times to be used to it, and second, he knew what was going on, unlike the confused, hulking mess that had released his grip on Alex and was scrabbling around and moaning. Alex briefly considered doing something like tying him up or in some way incapacitating him, but he settled for grabbing the tickets that had dropped to the floor and launching a big kick to Stabber's testicles from behind. There was a guttural groan, and he slumped to the floor. Alex turned and was about to jump back to Wembley, but Stabber's Terminator-like instincts thrust out a hand and grabbed Alex's ankle. Alex flailed his leg to kick him off, and after the third attempt broke free. Not wishing to stay around any longer, he jumped back to Wembley.

"Alex! Alex!"

Slumped against a wall, he regained his senses to see Pravi fighting which question to ask first.

"What? Where did ... what did you do?"

Alex was panting heavily as he held up the tickets. "Let's just say that our friend had a little trip into the unknown."

They were startled when another man stumbled into the toilet, giving them a funny look. Alex half expected it to be Stabber, although he knew that would be impossible. He motioned to Pravi to get out of there, so they reconvened in the car park away from everyone else.

"You're not the only one to come up with a good plan," Alex said.

Pravi sat there for a few moments, looking very concerned. "So, you took him back to the present."

"Yep."

"That must have shocked him."

"You could say that."

"You didn't ..." Pravi gazed intently at Alex.

"What?"

"You didn't like ..." Pravi leant forward and whispered, "kill him or anything?"

"No!" Alex stepped back. "I just booted him in the knackers and left him there."

"Alone? In our timeline?"

Alex moved closer again. "Yes, but think about it. He's frozen to us right now, isn't he? Neither of us are there, so the clock's stopped. It only starts again when we return."

Pravi spun slowly around to get his head round it. "So you effectively dumped him in the present, so that he's out of the way in the past, here today."

"Yep."

"Nice plan. Although he'll be there when we return, whenever that will be," Pravi said.

They were interrupted by the arrival of a rushing Abby.

"Are you two all right?" Abby said, giving them both a visual check over. "Barbara told me she'd seen Nigel with you and that he was threatening you. What happened? Where is he?"

"Nigel?" Alex suppressed a smirk. No wonder he preferred 'Stabber', Alex thought. "I'm sure Pravi will tell you all about it on the way to Wembley." He looked back at the pub with fake worry. "Let's get out of here. Now."

* * *

It hadn't been the smoothest path to Wembley and the thought of what was waiting for him back in the present alarmed him, but Alex's delight at seeing his ticket accepted at the turnstiles and then sitting down in his seat at the final of Euro 96 two hours before kick-off more than made up for it.

"How about this?" Alex said, gesturing around him inside the stadium.

"Pretty sweet, my friend," Pravi replied.

"Just imagine," Alex said, "in another universe, England didn't make it to the final and the Czech Republic are now getting ready to play Germany. How strange would that be?"

Pravi rolled his eyes. "And maybe in that universe you aren't such a dick. But I doubt it."

Abby folded her arms. "Do you two always abuse each other, or is it just for my benefit?"

"Nah, I love him really," Pravi said, giving Alex a waist hug. "Especially after what he did with Nigel."

Abby blushed. "Alex, I'm so sorry you had to deal with him. He's an absolute arsehole and I can only apologise you had to get involved."

Alex looked down at his trainers. "Yeah, well, don't mention it. In fact, let's forget about everything else and concentrate on this." He spread his arms out wide. "I've waited my entire life for this moment – England in a final."

"What about 1966?" Abby said. "You must have been around for that as a child."

"World Cup?" Alex replied. "I wasn't even—"

Pravi loudly spluttered a cough. It took a few seconds before Alex remembered that Pravi had maintained their correct ages here and that their fake year of birth was 1957.

"I mean, yes, but … I was too young to appreciate it. My Dad wasn't into football so it wasn't such a big thing for us."

"Was it him that taught you the Vulcan death grip?" Abby asked.

Alex glared at Pravi, who had concocted the wonderful explanation on the way to the stadium of them dealing with Stabber.

"It must have been a special move to render such a lump like him unconscious," she added.

Given the possibility that they might not be in 1996 much longer, Alex thought he might as well play along. "Its proper name is the Vulcan nerve pinch. I do it on Pravi when he really annoys me. Which is quite often."

"You should try it on some of the Czechs," Pravi said as a few of the players walked round the pitch in their suits in front of them.

Karel Poborský strolled around with his long, wavy hair

next to Patrik Berger, with similarly flowing locks. Alex wondered whether anything they were doing now was different to the original final, how their mindset might have been, about to face different opponents. Unless something dramatic changed today, both were destined for big moves to England after the tournament. How much would history change if one got injured and never made it to a top club? Or Shearer could get a hat-trick and Real Madrid make an offer Blackburn couldn't refuse. Pravi and Alex had spent a few weeks watching life unfold exactly the same, and now, thanks to them, everything was an open book. Even Spurs might have more success in the next twenty years as a result.

"Those boys can certainly play," a fan said behind Alex. "I've got fifty large ones that they beat us today."

Alex turned round. "You're betting against us?"

"Why not? We win, I'm stripping off and doing cartwheels on the pitch. Lose, and at least I get enough money to drown myself in beer."

"Ignore him," said a man next to him. His face was painted with a St. George's cross, he was draped in a huge England flag and was wearing a hat covered in tiny commemorative pins. "We're going to smash 'em! Four-nil – Gazza, Shearer double and Sheringham. It's destiny!"

That about summed up England fans, thought Alex. Either pessimistic to the extent of preparing for the worst, or convinced that we had the best team in the entire history of the world.

When the England players came out later to train, there

was a massive noise in the stadium. It wasn't long before "Three Lions" was being sung earnestly by every English fan in the stadium.

"If we win, Prav, this song is going to be number one for like, ever," Alex shouted above the noise.

"I always liked 'World in Motion'," Abby said.

"Classic," Alex said. "'Vindaloo' was catchy too."

"'Vindaloo'?" Abby said. "What song was that?"

Pravi glared at Alex who quickly said, "Never mind – it was a song Pravi wrote at uni."

"You didn't tell me you write songs?"

This time it was Alex who put on a satisfied face due to a stitch-up.

Pravi threw the match programme at Alex. "Er, it was a one-off," Pravi said. "A few too many beers after a curry."

The remainder of the time was spent joining in with songs, chatting to the fans around them and soaking up the atmosphere. Alex flicked through the programme. He remembered a copy Pravi had bought on eBay for the original match. Instead of details of every Germany player, there were photos and descriptions of Gascoigne, Southgate, Ince and the team, all oblivious to their alternative fate.

"Did I miss the line-ups?" Alex said.

"He's gone for the same team as the semi," Pravi said. "Platt's in for Gary Neville again." On cue, the teams came out to a deafening roar, with England in their traditional white, and their opponents in red. The Czechs had plenty of support, no doubt a few Scottish amongst them. Alex and Pravi sung the anthem at the tops of their voices, Alex managing to get all the words right for once. As the England team huddled together a minute before kick-off, "Three Lions" once again swept round the old stadium. Alex, Pravi, Abby and even the two fans behind, all put their arms on each other's shoulders and swayed together.

A light breeze pushed white clouds lazily over the old stadium, seven years from its demolition. Shearer kicked off England's second and last final under the twin towers as another massive roar echoed around.

Perhaps understandably, given the huge expectation and also the recent Herculean effort in reaching the final, England started slowly. Southgate misplaced a pass after one minute, and Berger let fly from thirty yards with an effort that flew into the stands.

"How are your nerves, Prav?" Alex shouted to his friend.

"They were OK until I saw that. We need to settle and fast."

Gascoigne picked up the ball and went to go on a run, but was instantly tackled. England were certainly trying to build through him, but the Czechs had done their homework and were throttling him. After five minutes, Shearer and Sheringham might as well have been selling match programmes, the amount of ball they'd each seen.

Ince mistimed a tackle on the halfway line and was spoken to by the referee.

"C'mon England! Sort it out!" Abby screamed.

As the Czech player stayed on the ground, Alex leant over to her. "Hey, Abby. First time you've watched England?"

"No, I've been down a few times. Never thought I'd be here today, though."

"Thank my man Prav for that," replied Alex, as the Czechs resumed play with a short free kick. "He knows how to show a woman a good time."

Abby was about to respond, but Nedvěd had broken free on the right and wrapped his foot round the ball to whip in a cross. It was over a back-pedalling Adams, but Southgate managed to get his head on it and send it arcing to the edge of the area. A few people started clapping the clearance, but when McManaman waited for the ball to drop to his feet and start a counterattack, Poborský nipped in and struck a shot. The ball flew past everyone. Seaman saw it late and dived, getting his right hand to it but only succeeding in slowing its path towards the net.

"No!" Alex yelled.

Silence.

The ball rolled past Seaman's flailing arm and over the line. Pavel Kuka was just yards away and raised his hands in celebration as the referee looked at the linesman and blew his whistle. One part of the stadium erupted, whilst the other stayed silent.

England were 1-0 down.

Sit Down, Shut Up

"I knew it," said the super fan's pessimistic friend behind Alex. "I just knew we'd lose."

"Early days," Abby said, looking around at everyone and waving her hands to rally them.

Nine minutes in and you could hear the disbelief in the atmosphere. Was the Germany game our final? thought Alex. So many times teams had peaked in overcoming tough opponents in the semis of competitions only to not do themselves justice in the final.

"Don't worry," Pravi said. "We went 1-0 down in '66. We'll come back from this."

England kicked off again and passed it around at the back, restoring confidence. Adams gestured to his fellow defenders to calm down, while the Czechs were happy to give up possession and absorb the fact that they were winning in a final. Gascoigne was like a kid in a playground, demanding the ball whenever there was a half chance to pass to him. With the Czechs sitting back, he was clearly frustrated by the lack of good options, and so for several minutes England kept the ball around the midfield, making little progress.

The fans seemed to recover from their early shock and realise that they had a part to play, that they weren't just there to watch their team deliver the trophy they so desperately wanted. "Three Lions" began to take hold of the stadium once again, the same famous chorus being repeated over and over.

Anderton poked a ball to Sheringham's feet, and as if responding to the crowd, dropped a shoulder and made some space. The defender, Jan Suchopárek, came towards him, but Sheringham tapped it in front of Shearer, who only had one thought on his mind. He walloped it with his right foot from twenty yards out and it screamed towards Petr Kouba's goal. Alex drew breath as it stung Kouba's fingers and dropped down, the keeper pouncing on the loose ball. A collective cry of half cheer, half pain burst from the crowd, before a round of applause.

"Shearer! Shearer!" rang out.

"He'll get us back in it, Prav," Alex said.

Terry Venables and the coaching staff were encouraging the team from the sidelines, whilst their Czech counterparts were getting edgy, knowing there was still a long time left in the game. Now it was their turn to misplace passes, as Karel Rada squared one to a white shirt which led to McManaman drifting in a cross that was headed behind. Everyone seemed to channel their excitement into the goalmouth as Gascoigne lined up the corner.

"Get up there, Adams!" screamed Alex, as the captain loitered near the penalty spot. The ball was swung in but headed out of danger for an England throw-in midway inside the Czech half. England kept hold of possession, but a solid defensive unit from the team in red shirts forced Pearce to pass the ball back to Seaman.

"Plenty of time," Abby said, as if she was now the official England timekeeper. Alex looked at the scoreboard; twenty-two minutes had gone.

"C'mon England," yelled Alex, in the absence of anything more inspiring.

Seaman rolled it out to Southgate who fed Gascoigne. The blond maestro dribbled forward and rolled a pinpoint ball into the path of Anderton on the right, who took one step before whipping in a low, early ball towards the rushing pair of Shearer and Kadlec. The Blackburn striker got there first, but as he touched the ball, the Czech defender swept him off his feet with a clumsy tackle and sent Shearer down.

"Penalty!" screamed Alex, Pravi and Abby simultaneously, with about every person of England persuasion in the stadium.

The referee was running towards the linesman.

"Surely, ref?" Alex belted out. "You gotta give it, lino!"

The two officials consulted each other.

The stadium went quiet as the referee ran back from his assistant … and pointed to the penalty spot.

"Yesssss!" was the cry from Alex and everyone around him, coupled with high fives. The Czech players protested to the referee who was waving them away as Shearer set the ball onto the penalty spot.

"See?" Abby said to the boys. "Told you not to panic."

"Watch him break the net on his way to becoming Sir Alan Shearer," Pravi said.

After the Czech players gave up on their protests and the keeper had got back to his line, the stadium went quiet as Shearer walked back a few metres behind the ball. He waited, hands on hips, until the referee gave the signal to take the penalty. Shearer ran up and smacked the ball hard to the keeper's right … the crowd started to cheer … but it was fractionally too close to Kouba who got enough of a hand on it to tip it onto the post.

Alex let out a strangled cry, flinging his hands to his head. The ball ricocheted off the post and back into the area, where it sat, spinning from its encounter with the upright, two metres from the outstretched keeper but further from Shearer. David Platt was the first to react, and he sprinted in, beating the nearest opposition player. Kouba scrambled to his feet and threw himself at the ball, but Platt stuck out a leg and his toes made contact with it a fraction of a second sooner, leaving the keeper to land on nothing but Platt's leg as the ball was sent towards the goal. A few players in red rushed after it, but it was too late. The ball crossed the line.

On twenty-four minutes, England had equalised.

Alex jumped up and punched the air, screaming. He turned to hug Pravi, but he was mid-hug with Abby. Fair play, Alex thought, and instead gave him a fist bump.

"Thank … flip for that," Alex said, remembering his promise to Helen. "Can't believe Shearer missed it, but I'll take that all day."

Platt was enjoying his biggest England goal since Belgium in 1990, even cheekily taking the mickey out of Shearer by copying his trademark single-arm-in-the-air celebration.

The virtual cloud that had descended on Wembley since the opener had been lifted and suddenly everything was all right again. The obligatory "Three Lions" started up again, but this time with more oomph, as if a goal in the final had made everyone truly believe it again.

"If we can kick on now, score another one before half-time, then it really is coming home," Pravi said to Alex and Abby.

The Czech Republic kicked off, passing it around and regrouping after their setback. England looked unhurried, happy to wait for further chances now that they'd achieved parity. Venables seemed content to sit back.

The rest of the half played out with few incidents occurring in either goalmouth. England had sparked after their goal without creating any significant chances, and in the last few minutes of the half, both sides were obviously satisfied to go in level, regroup and plan for the second half. When the referee blew for the interval, Alex clapped his appreciation as the teams left the field.

Abby rose from her seat. "I need to go to the little girls' room, so I'll leave you boys to analyse the first half."

After she had disappeared into the throng of people heading to the concourse, Alex turned to Pravi. "Guess she's not so bad."

"Wow, high praise indeed," Pravi said.

Alex looked back towards the pitch. "It's going to be close, isn't it? England never do it the simple way. I wish for once we either tank in a big match or – preferably – smash it."

"You know something?" Pravi said. "It's strange, but coming down Wembley way today with Abby, to the final we made, I was content to just be here. It's like a bonus level – you don't know how it's going to turn out, but you enjoy it. But now that in forty-five minutes we could actually win this thing, I definitely want it."

Alex thought about it for a minute. "I was never satisfied just to be here. After everything we've been through and the fight for the tickets, we've got to win."

"One day we'll pick through the bones of all this and try to make sense of it," Pravi said.

"Once we do, we can sell our story. Make millions."

"Will anyone believe it?"

Alex shrugged. "Not sure even I believe it."

A short while later, they watched the subs warm up on the pitch.

Alex faced Pravi. "Do you still think we'll be here when the final whistle goes?"

"Yeah," Pravi said. "I hope so. The alternative is that we disappear in front of Abby and end up back at the flat with a psycho who's just been kicked in the balls."

Alex looked round to check Abby wasn't coming and leaned down to talk quietly to Pravi. "Even if we can control when we go back, what are we going to do with him?"

"I don't know. Let's just enjoy the game and see what happens. I'm not going to worry about the future or the past right now."

Alex wanted to do the same, but he knew the future held more than one scary thing when he returned.

"Get these down your necks, gents," Abby said, appearing beside them. "But be discreet, it's strictly forbidden here." She handed out a beer each to Pravi and Alex. She touched the arm of a tall man next to her. "This is Yohan. I met him at the bar and he helped create a diversion so I could come down with them. He's from Sweden, but supporting us today."

"Cheers Yohan," Pravi said, raising his glass. "By the way, what's your opinion of Sven-Göran Eriksson? I hear he's a good Swedish manager."

The rest of half-time was spent with the delighted Swede discussing his compatriots, some of whom had only just been discovered in 1996 but were destined for bigger things. As the second half started, they waved goodbye to him as he went back to his seat.

The crowd roared encouragement, but as some fans were still settling, Berger strode towards the England defence.

"Don't let him shoot!" yelled Pravi.

The Czech midfielder pulled his leg back.

"Don't let him—"

Berger shot.

The ball skimmed the turf, straight, with ferocious speed.

Seaman barely saw it. By the time he had dived, it was on its way past him, eventually burying itself in the bottom-right corner.

England were behind once again.

The copious amount of swearing that came from the people around Alex wasn't directed at Berger, Seaman or anyone – it was the sheer frustration of all the optimism and expectation built up during half-time that had now gone within a minute of the restart. Abby put an arm round Pravi, who had buried his head in his hands.

"I told them not to let him shoot," Pravi said into his palms.

"Better we concede now with nearly a whole half left than let one in on eighty-nine minutes," Abby said.

Alex stared ahead as the smiling players in red high-fived each other as they walked back to their half. "Do you always look on the bright side?"

"Yes," Abby replied. "Do you always look like a drab weekend in Manchester?"

The crowd took a while to respond as England kicked off again. The familiar chant of 'En-ger-lund' echoed round the famous stadium, building up speed, as if trying to create and transmit energy into the men in white. Gascoigne responded with some typical jinking runs that led to plenty of possession in their opponent's half, but with no clear chance to show for it. Shearer snatched at a shot from just outside the area which flew high and wide. Anderton had an unconvincing penalty appeal for handball with a flick that clearly hit Kadlec's chest. The Czechs threatened with counter attacks, but Adams and Southgate marshalled the back, seemingly determined not to allow another breakthrough.

"Time for a fresh pair of legs?" Alex asked Pravi.

Venables kept the subs warming up as the clock ticked on, but given his reluctance to send even one sub on the pitch for the whole of the semi-final, he didn't seem about to change things up yet.

"Well," Pravi replied, "we have the cream of English talent in Nick Barmby, Steve Stone or Phil Neville to save the day. Which would you like?"

McManaman was threatening down the left wing, who compared to those three looked like a superstar.

"There's always Sir Les. How about Fowler? Did he ever do much in an England shirt?"

"Give him a chance, he's only had a few caps so far," Pravi said, shooting a warning stare at Alex.

"I reckon we should keep faith with the eleven on the pitch," Abby said as McManaman found some space and passed it to Sheringham on the edge of the penalty area. Ince was running in from midfield, attracting the attention of the Czech defence, but Sheringham cleverly turned and fed the ball into a pocket of space into which McManaman was ghosting into. Michal Horňák reacted first and committed himself to the challenge, but the Liverpool winger had predicted this and flicked the ball to his right, sending Horňák hopelessly sliding past and out of the picture. Only the goalkeeper, Kouba, now stood in front of McManaman and the net.

Wembley held its breath.

McManaman poked out his right foot and sent the ball past the keeper at an angle towards the far post with no defender anywhere near it. The ball looked to be heading into the corner, but the ball bobbled narrowly past the post.

"You've got to be flipping kidding me!" Alex said, slumping in his seat. "Lucky so-and-so's."

As Kouba took the resulting goal kick, Abby gave Alex a funny look.

"What?" he challenged as she kept her gaze.

"Nothing. Well, it's … no, it's nothing."

Pravi turned to look at Alex. "I think she means your swearing. Or rather your total avoidance of it, even in extreme pressure."

Alex was about to explain Helen's swearing ban, but realised that might lead to a whole story that he didn't want to get into it with Abby. "Prav bet me that I couldn't stop swearing during Euro 96."

Abby looked like she was about to probe further when a few people stood up behind them to watch a Czech attack. As Poborský approached Adams, Alex waited for the tackle and what he hoped would be the start of another England move that might lead to an equaliser. But the tackle didn't appear. Instead, Poborský tried his luck with a clip of his left foot from just inside the area. It was heading wide, but Southgate went to make sure and moved to clear the ball. He succeeded in misjudging it and slicing it at a completely different angle towards the goal.

Seaman had no chance. He could only turn his head to see the ball loop into the net.

With only fifteen minutes left, England were 3-1 down.

The pockets of Czech fans in the stadium went delirious. The neutrals clapped. The England fans were motionless and silent. Alex exchanged a look with Pravi, sure that they were thinking the same thing. Was it a coincidence that Gareth Southgate – the man who missed the final penalty in the original Germany match – had now also ended their hopes in this match?

"Looks like you won't be doing naked cartwheels on the pitch then," said the man with the now-smudged St. George's cross on his face to his pessimistic friend.

"What was Southgate doing? The ball was clearly going wide," he replied.

Alex sat down. As he watched England resume and send a long ball aimlessly out for a goal kick, he considered how different it would be if they limped to a final defeat. Is that any better than a glorious but ultimately unsuccessful semi-final loss? He looked around at all the despondent faces.

How might they judge the tournament two decades later? He watched Nedvěd take down a long pass, brush past Gascoigne before being taken out by an Ince tackle so late it was in a different time zone to the ball. As Ince was getting booked, Nedvěd picked himself up and spotted the ball, some thirty-five yards out.

"If he puts this in, we may as well go home," Alex said. "Any positive words now, Abby?"

Abby gave a sympathetic smile. "It's only over when the fat lady sings?"

"I think she's touching up her makeup and finishing her scales," Alex replied.

Nedvěd curled a beauty of a kick over the wall, but Seaman was alert to it and pushed it out of harm's way. A beating by three of four might be harsh, thought Alex, and whilst getting two more goals against a resolute, organised and now buoyant Czech side might be beyond them, he at least hoped England might get a late goal to make it interesting.

Venables had seen enough to know he had to change it up, and sent on Robbie Fowler for a tiring Anderton on eighty minutes, altering the system but adding more firepower. Fowler immediately showed he understood the urgency of the situation by unleashing a shot on target with only his third touch. Whilst the ball was easily saved by Kouba, the crowd stirred and clung on to a shred of hope.

"At least he knows where the goal is," Pravi said.

The Czechs were trying to slow the game down, claiming

any small foul and then taking an age to get up and resume play. Ince was being cautious with his tackles after his yellow card, but with five minutes left, won a fifty-fifty challenge fairly in the middle of the park. The players in red threw their arms up, but the referee didn't want to know. In an instant, Gascoigne had picked it up, nutmegged a defender and did a simple side foot into space. Shearer had been following Gascoigne's move and anticipated the pass, striding onto the ball on the right-hand edge of the penalty area and letting loose a shot. It headed towards the top corner like a guided missile.

Kouba was stationary.

The net rippled.

England were back in it.

It was like someone had turned on a switch in every England fan's head. Everyone was jumping up, punching the air. The belief was back.

"C'mon! C'monnnnnnn!" Alex shouted.

"Shearer! Shearer! Shearer!" came the cry from all around. Gascoigne was asking for more volume and the fans responded, throwing everything into it for the remaining minutes. The Czechs looked panicked. One minute they must have been picturing in their minds climbing up the famous Wembley steps to claim the trophy, and now they were a goal away from being forced into extra time. England had smelled blood and were swarming over the Czechs, hustling them when their opponents had the ball and driving forward when they had it. Crosses were swung in and scrambled away. Fowler had a poke wide. Gascoigne tried to force his way through and was expertly tackled.

Alex was glancing at the clock every ten seconds. "Eighty-nine minutes," he said to Pravi. "We can't get this close and fail, can we?"

Pravi was biting his nails, transfixed at the action. Abby was jumping up and down as each chance went begging.

The referee took his first look at his watch as the match went into stoppage time. England had only a few minutes to get a goal or their dream was over.

McManaman had the ball on the left touchline and kept faking a sprint down the line, trying to get some space from Horňák, who was holding steady and watching the ball like a dog watching a rabbit.

"Go past him!"

"Help 'im out!"

"Do something!"

The impasse continued as the crowd yelled more advice and vented their frustration as time ticked on. Gascoigne ran towards his teammate and demanded the ball, which he duly received. Horňák turned his attentions to the Geordie, which was precisely what Gascoigne wanted. McManaman, now free, ran down the line as Gascoigne flicked the ball round the defender and perfectly back into the path of the winger. The crowd roared their appreciation. McManaman wasted no time and wrapped his spindly leg round the ball and sent a delightful cross into the box.

A box with Teddy Sheringham in.

Sheringham rose and powered a header towards goal, soaring towards the top corner.

From every angle, the keeper was beaten.

Until the giant right hand of Kouba stretched and steel-like fingertips flicked the ball past the post and away for a corner.

Alex made a sound like a wolf in severe pain.

Pravi almost fell out of his chair. Abby leapt up and kept both her arms aloft, as if her limbs hadn't believed that it wasn't a goal.

Alex surveyed the surrounding crowd. Most had their faces buried in their hands or were slumped forward in their seats. Everyone seemed sure it was going in.

Still lamenting the missed opportunity, Alex and Pravi didn't see Platt quickly take the resulting corner. They also hadn't seen Adams come steaming into the middle.

In the ninety-first minute, he threw himself forward to the fast, outswinging cross, defenders brushed aside.

There was no jump. There was no flick. Just pure forehead-on-ball deflection.

This time, Kouba wasn't quick enough.

This time the net bulged.

Wembley went absolutely bananas.

Alex roared until he thought his throat might catch fire. He didn't have a clue how far he was from his seat or which direction he was facing as he was engulfed in a mass of celebrating fans.

"Yesssss!" Alex was hugging a complete stranger as they bounced together, screaming. He eventually made his way back to Pravi who was also dancing in his chair with various randoms spinning him around. Alex gave him a big bear hug.

"Back in the game!" Pravi shouted.

"Ooh ooh, Tony Adams!" Alex replied.

Abby was politely and tactfully fending off enthusiastic fans who wanted to celebrate this most special moment with her.

"You can tell the fat lady to sit down and shut up," she said to Alex, with more than a glimmer in her eyes.

Alex laughed.

Somehow amongst all the celebration, play had resumed by the now deathly looking Czechs. Seconds later, the referee blew for full time.

England had pulled it back from the brink, but once again their fate now rested on a golden goal or penalties.

"After all that excitement, I'm going for a slash," Alex eloquently announced to Pravi and Abby. There would be a break of at least five minutes before the continuation of the onslaught to his nerves. As he made his way past fans smiling, laughing and composing themselves again, he decided he'd take a sneaky photo of the scene for posterity.

He carefully got out his iPhone, still over ten years away from making its debut, and shielded it from public view before taking a quick photo of the pitch and a five-second video of the crowd. "Sweet," he said. He was about to put the phone away when he saw that he had a notification telling him he had lots of unread messages and voicemail. He knew that they couldn't have come in whilst he was in 1996, so it must have been during his scuffle with Stabber when he'd briefly jumped back. He realised that this was the first time he had looked at his phone since then. Moving to the side of an aisle and turning his back to the wave of people who were passing him, he opened the message app. His heart skipped a few beats as he realised that the messages were from Helen. He looked round to see if anyone was watching, then jabbed a finger to open the messages. By the fifth message, Alex almost dropped the phone. By the tenth, his legs could barely support him.

Helen had been about to go into labour.

Hospital Pass

Alex was running.

It was the sort of running an American footballer would do, dodging and barging anyone and anything in his way. Kids with flags, men with beers, old women – they were all scattered and left behind like a wake of a ship as Alex swept past. His brain had gone into overdrive and had told him the next move was simple: get yourself into a toilet cubicle. A small part of him knew that he had all the time in the world; whatever stage Helen was at, she was frozen to Alex for as long as he was in 1996. But the rest of him was being pulled along as if he were getting sucked back into his time.

When he dashed into the toilets, a long queue greeted him for both for the urinals and the cubicles. He decided that this was unacceptable, and as one cubicle opened, he sprinted up to it and practically yanked out the exiting man. Before the bloke at the front of the queue could even complain, Alex shouted back, "So sorry! Terrible diarrhoea! Can't hold it in!"

He slammed the door and sat down on the toilet, panting. He had wanted to tell Pravi, but what would that achieve? Pravi was so wrapped up with the game and Abby that it would have only spoiled it for him. There was zero chance Alex could watch the rest of the final now, knowing what he knew. Win or lose, his mind would have been elsewhere. No, he had to sort this out himself now, and then once he was ready, he would come back to enjoy it. Once he was ready? When would that be? He sunk his head into his hands. Despite his position, he smiled as he thought about the story that he'd have to tell Pravi on his return.

He took out the controller and eyed it like a portal into a different world, not just a different world from here, but a different one to his current life back home. Then he remembered something rather important.

"Fudging hell!"

Stabber.

Whenever he jumped back, Abby's ogre of an ex-boyfriend was going to be waiting for him – no doubt thirsty for revenge, having just been kicked in the nuts.

Time for a plan, Alex thought. The trouble was, he realised, there was no time for a plan. He was in a toilet and the game was about to resume. He could only think of two options, and one of them involved murder. Instead, he decided on the other one and activated the jump back.

When Alex's hearing returned, he heard an onslaught of swearing. His eyes first focused on the fallen giant, who was obviously in some pain from their last encounter, curled up in the foetal position on the floor.

Alex's first thought was to run out of there and straight to Helen. While every muscle in his body was pulling him towards the door and away from the coiled cobra who was no doubt going to strike soon, he knew that long term that would be a disaster. Don't think – do.

Moving behind Stabber's back, Alex hooked one arm round Stabber's right leg so that he still had the use of both his hands. He went to push the buttons to send them both back to '96 when Stabber jerked, making Alex send the controller clattering across the floor. His arm was now trapped between Stabber's knees, the controller hopelessly out of reach of his other arm. He tried to yank his arm free, but Stabber tightened his grip.

"What the …?" Stabber growled at Alex with all the menace of a wounded lion who was now entangled with his assailant. Alex could only watch as Stabber screamed with rage, steadied himself with one hand, and with the other swung a big club of a fist through the air. Instinctively, Alex ducked and in the same motioned rammed down his own counter with a punch straight into the now unprotected nether regions of his opponent. Stabber's face contorted into pure agony, with his own punch passing over the head of Alex, who wrenched his trapped arm free. Alex scrambled across the room and picked up the controller again. A quick examination showed a small piece of plastic had broken off from the fall, exposing some of the electronics inside. Assuming it still worked, should he go back to 1996 again and regroup? No, that might give the brute a few vital seconds while Alex recovered from the next jump back. He had to sort this now. Stabber was howling in a way any man would after two quick assaults on his prized possessions, so Alex decided to take advantage. This time he backed up a few metres, readied his fingers on the buttons, ran towards Stabber and dived onto him. As he landed, he completed the sequence … and sent them both back to 1996.

Back in the Wembley toilet, Alex had rolled over to separate himself from Stabber, banging into the cubicle wall as he regained his eyesight from the jump. Once again, he knew he was just pushing trouble further down the road for when he returned, but right now he needed rid of the killing machine that was lying at his feet. After making sure he wasn't touching Stabber, he pressed the buttons again and returned to the present.

With three quick jumps in succession, Alex stumbled around the flat and dry-retched, before collapsing on the sofa. He listened for any noise of Stabber, but all he could hear was the quiet hum of the fridge. They were both back in their right timelines. He didn't want to think what could have happened if any of that had gone wrong. Alex breathed a sigh of relief, then immediately remembered why he had come back and whipped out his phone from his pocket, replacing it with the controller. He thought back to when they were getting ready to jump back to the final, just after they'd gone shopping with Helen. There must have been two hours in the present where he'd been without his phone due to Pravi leaving it in 1996 – two hours in which Helen had sent him a flood of text and voice messages which must have only reached his phone during his fight with Stabber here. He wanted to call her back right now, but also needed to listen to the voice messages to know what situation he was about to face. With trembling hands, he listened to each one, tears forming as the urgency increased with each message. Her waters had broken and she had been taken to the hospital by her mum, screaming that Alex would never see the child or her ever again unless he got his sorry arse down here. Taking a deep breath, he decided to make the call.

His finger hovered over the button to call her back, but then withdrew. "What do I say?" he muttered to himself. Last time he'd gone missing, he'd had Pravi to help him make up a plausible story. He tapped the phone against his head in thought, but nothing remotely useful dislodged itself in his brain. He looked at the time again. It had gone to being frozen to now racing away from him. Pressing to connect to Helen, he held his breath.

Three rings. Four rings. What if something had happened? Five rings. What if she's had the baby already? Six rings. What if—

"Hi, this is Helen. I'm probably resting right now getting fatter. Leave a message and if I remember to get back to you, I will."

As the tone screeched, Alex jabbed the button to disconnect.

"Fudge, fudge and more fudge," he said to the empty flat, ironically cursing inside at his automatic anti-swearing.

No way was he coherent enough to formulate a message that he could leave. Should he try her mum? Fortunately, his dilemma was resolved two seconds later as Helen rang him back. Heart pounding, bracing himself for the worst, he pressed the green button.

"H-hello?" Alex stuttered.

Silence.

Alex sat down. "Helen? Are you there?"

More silence. A dodgy connection? Or was something, hideously wrong? "Baby? I can't hear you if you're talking."

"Where. Have. You. Been." Helen spat out each word.

"I'll tell you later, I promise. Are you at the hospital? Is everything OK?"

"Oh, I'm totally, wonderfully fine. I should be used to having to be rushed to hospital while the father of our child has completely vanished from existence."

"I … I can explain," he said. Whatever excuse he planned to give would have to be invented on the journey.

"Just get down to the hospital, Alex. Now."

He grabbed his keys and shot out of the flat. When he got into his car, he realised that he'd still got the controller, but decided to leave it in his jeans pocket. It might be a long while before he got to return to the final, but he didn't want to lose it or risk it being stolen.

After getting lost in the labyrinth of the hospital corridors, he finally arrived at the maternity ward at half past two in the afternoon. He'd thanked the angels who must have been looking out for him and put the thought into his brain that it might be an idea to turn up with some flowers. Turning up sweating, panting and hiding behind a big bunch of multi-coloured tulips, he faced Helen and her mum at her bed.

"I'm so, so sorry baby," he said to Helen, who was sitting up and looking sweaty. "Have I missed much?"

"Almost everything!" Lynn said, arms crossed as if she'd glued them together especially for his greeting.

"So, where exactly have you been?" Helen said with a stare that made Alex step backwards.

"I think the important thing is what's happening with you and the baby," Alex said. Deflector shields on. "What's going on? It can't be happening today, it's three weeks early!"

"It is happening today, I can assure—" she didn't finish the sentence as she leaned forward with a grunt and started puffing loudly.

Alex went forward and put an arm on her shoulder. "Are those ... contraction thingies?"

"Of course they're bloody contractions!" Helen said after she'd stopped puffing. "Sorry, Mum."

Lynn looked away. "I had all three of you, no gas or anything, and I certainly didn't swear."

"Mum ..." Helen slumped back on her pillow, panting. "Now Alex is here, you can go home."

Lynn's face contorted as though someone had suggested that she go slap the pope. "You're asking me to leave? After all that I've done for you today?"

"Mum, it's just that—"

"I think you need a lot more experience and reliability than the man who can't be bothered to turn up until midway through the second quarter!" She turned away from Alex and made a fuss of Helen.

"I am the father, Lynn," Alex said.

Lynn spun round. "I hope your son has better timing than his dad, otherwise we may still be here next week."

"I came as soon as I found out, I promise," Alex said.

"What were you doing?" Lynn asked. "Asleep after a drunken game of Substitute with your silly little friends?"

"Subbuteo? No, I was at Pravi's. My phone was switched off, that's all. The battery had run out." He grabbed a water jug that was on Helen's table, plonked the tulips in and fiddled with their arrangement.

"You never let your phone die," Helen said. "Heaven forbid that you might miss a hilarious video from Moobsy or news that Spurs might be signing the next best thing from Outer Mongolia."

Time for the hastily prepared excuse. "I didn't know it had run out," Alex said with his best hard done-by face. "The Wi-Fi in the flat was down, so Pravi tethered my phone to video chat to Abby. By the time he finished, my battery was about dead and he plugged it in but he accidentally flipped the switch on his server instead." He knew he'd bamboozled Lynn, but he hoped Helen would buy it. "We then played *FIFA* for a few hours, thinking it was on charge. I had no idea I was missing calls and texts from you. I'm sorry, but I can't be blamed for that, can I?"

Helen slumped down onto her pillow. "Whatever. You're here now. Go and make yourself useful and sort out the TENS machine."

Alex blinked a few times. "How on earth can a tennis machine help?"

"No, T-E-N-S machine," Helen said, pointing at a box lying on top of a bag. "It's a bunch of electrode thingies that you wear to help with contractions."

Alex took the box and peeked inside at the strange gadget. It looked like an old iPod with a bunch of wires and pads sticking out of it. It appeared well used, with some of the wires frayed and the pads curling up at the edges.

"Is it safe?" Alex asked, putting everything back in the box.

"Yes, totally," Helen replied. "It only gives off mild electrical impulses."

"Your cousin Emily used it for each of her four labours," Lynn said. "She gave me some new pads which I've put in the box. Can't see for the life of me why you'd want to electrocute yourself voluntarily, though. Back in my day—"

"Mum, if this is a competition, let's just agree that you win. I obviously didn't inherit your pain threshold and if I want a TENS machine, gas, air, an epidural and a gallon of morphine to get through this, then I'm taking the lot."

Lynn leaned towards Helen and said, "You'll probably need all that with *him* beside you at the birth. I'm sure if it was Peter—"

"Mum!" Helen slammed her hand on the bed. "That's enough. I found out recently the sun doesn't shine out of Peter's arse."

Lynn straightened up and appeared to be about to reprimand her when Helen continued. "Alex is the father, and he'll make a good dad to our son. You had better deal with that and support both Alex and me, because he's not going anywhere."

As Helen glared at Lynn, Alex stifled a smile.

Lynn gathered her stuff. "Looks like you've got it all figured out then, so if you don't want me here, I shall scuttle off back home."

Helen sighed. "Things are different now, Mum. We don't have it all figured out, but Alex and I need to do this on our own." She took Lynn's hand. "I promise that you will be the first person we call once your grandson pops out."

They hugged, and Lynn stepped away from Helen. Turning to Alex she said, "You better take good care of her, that's all I say."

"I give you my absolute promise," Alex said.

After Lynn had waved goodbye and exited the ward, Alex said, "So, just me, you and the bump."

"Scared?" Helen asked.

Alex sat down in the chair. "Not now that your mum's left. You?"

"Now that I'm stuck with you – petrified."

She went on to bring Alex up to speed, how she'd been having funny pains when she'd first tried to contact Alex before calling her mum who'd strongly advised her to go to hospital and then ended up being the one to take her there. As he listened to the story, he imagined how frightened and alone she must have felt, and he cursed the fact that he hadn't been there with her.

"If you want to make yourself useful, you could put the new pads in the TENS machine," Helen said, pointing to the box. "I don't want to have something on my skin that's already been used for four births."

"So would you really go for an epidural?" Alex opened the box again. "I've heard some footballers have similar injections for injuries to get through matches."

"No, I draw the line there," Helen replied. "I've read too much on the risks. Even if I ask for one in the throes of labour, I give you the authority to override me, based on this conversation."

Alex gave her his best disbelieving look, but Helen put her hand on her heart. It was only a tiny piece of control in the process, but Alex decided he wouldn't question it further.

He examined the contents of the box. "Can't see any more pads in here."

"No? Mum might still have them in the car. Can you call her and go get them if she has?"

"And leave you?" Alex put on his best concerned face.

"She won't have left the car park yet. It won't take long."

"Can't a nurse get you some?" Alex looked round to see if any staff were about.

"Yeah right, you get a free set with every dilation check," Helen said.

Alex sighed. "I don't have a choice, do I?"

He phoned Lynn just as she had reached her car, who was adamant that she had included the pads in the box. He checked the box again and Helen's bag, but still nothing. After two minutes of disagreement, he told her he would come down and help her check the car.

He picked up the box and got up to leave, kissing Helen on the head. "I'm taking this down to prove to her that the pads are not in there."

Lynn blamed Helen's dad for obviously sabotaging the box and placing the spare pads in the glove compartment, which Alex had opened five seconds after being allowed to look inside the car. She sped off without further comment, which he chalked up as a victory.

Back in the main building, he waited outside the lifts to take him up to the maternity ward again. Shoving the small bag containing the new pads in one pocket with his phone, he examined the machine, turning it on. He could feel the electrical pulses through the old pads that were still connected to the spindly wires. Looking around, realising he was on his own and still waiting for a lift, he reached under his t-shirt and placed a pad under it. A light tingling worked its way around his stomach. A porter with an empty bed came round the corner as a lift door opened. Alex offered the lift to him, but as the porter swung the bed in, a folder fell onto the floor by Alex's feet. Alex shoved the TENS machine into his other pocket to free up a hand and picked up the folder to return it to the porter. The porter thanked him and indicated the lift behind Alex was now available, which he took. Throughout all this, he could feel his stomach getting the electric shocks, so he rummaged in his jeans pocket to turn off the machine.

As he entered the lift and pressed the button to ascend, he felt the bare wires connecting the pads to the machine brush against the other item in the same pocket – the controller. As the doors were closing, Alex experienced a pulsating, strobing flash before disappearing out of sight.

Getting Stuck In

Alex and Helen had once gone on a roller coaster in Busch Gardens, Florida, which was so intense in its loops, that immediately after getting off, Alex had walked round in circles before violently throwing up over a ride employee. Compared to now, that had been a pleasant experience.

Alex was still spinning. His vision was a swirl of misty white. He had a feeling that someone was talking to him, presumably a nurse, although his ears couldn't decipher what was being said over the constant whooshing noise. Had he fainted?

"… is going on?" said a deep voice in whatever room he was in, as his hearing came back. The accompanied groaning led Alex to believe that perhaps this other person wasn't a nurse. It also sounded worryingly familiar. The mist cleared and there on the floor was Stabber.

Alex moved backwards and hit his head against a wall, still staring at the man clutching his groin. How the hell was Stabber here at the hospital?

"What are you doing in there?" An unknown voice outside shook Alex enough for him to take stock of his environment. It was the toilet that only a few hours ago he had escaped from before going to the hospital. A toilet that was in 1996, a year that Alex hadn't had any intention of seeing anytime soon.

He looked down as Stabber looked up. A flicker of confusion, then recognition, and finally anger. Pure hatred emanated from the giant who was now uncurling from his foetal position less than a metre from Alex's feet.

"You!" he shouted. "You're dead!"

Alex thrust his hand into his pocket, intending to get out the controller, leaving the madman and getting back to Helen. Stabber had other ideas though, getting to his feet and grabbing Alex by the throat and slamming him against the toilet door.

"I don't know what the fuck is going on," Stabber said, "but I'm gonna hurt you real bad."

Alex was clueless to how he had jumped back into this hellhole of a situation, but he knew that even if he could activate a jump back now, he would be taking his probable would-be murderer with him once again.

"Hello?" said the same voice from outside. There was then a knock on the door that vibrated through Alex's right ear that had been pushed hard against it. "I'm not sure what you're playing at in there, but there's a queue waiting for the toilet."

Stabber pulled Alex back by the throat and then shoved him hard against the door, enough to break the lock and send him sprawling into the man outside, causing a domino effect on three of the people in the queue.

Alex was splayed out on the floor, sucking in big mouthfuls of air. Stabber stepped out of the cubicle but seemed to be confused at his surroundings, which was understandable given that a few moments ago to him he was in a pub miles away. A crowd of people were staring at him.

"Where the fuck is this?" he shouted, spinning around.

Alex used this diversion to flip on all fours before pushing himself up and forward to sprint out of the toilets. Half a second later, Stabber yelled and took off after him.

Alex didn't know where he should run to, but he figured his life might depend on it. Would Stabber try anything in front of all these people? Alex couldn't risk it. Meeting up with Pravi and Abby seemed the obvious destination, but that would be bringing trouble to them. He ran through the concourse, hearing the slap of his pursuer's feet behind him. Barging through swathes of England fans in red and white, spilling beers and apologising as he went, he saw his best option up ahead.

"Officer, there's a man trying to kill me!"

The policeman Alex was now half hiding behind looked towards where Alex was pointing at the very moment Stabber broke through a family walking past. In his desperation to reach his target, Stabber didn't clock the policeman until he had a hand shoved against his chest.

"Woah there, big guy," the policeman said. "Are you chasing this man?"

Stabber panted furiously and glowered at the policeman. Alex thought Stabber was seriously considering whether to snap the man in two and continue his quest to kill Alex. To try to sway things further, Alex moved fully behind his protector and said, "He's got a knife!" He had no idea if that was true, but figured there was a good chance. For additional impact, he added, "And he hasn't even got a ticket!"

Stabber snapped his head to Alex and clenched his fists so tight it seemed like his knuckles would explode.

"You," the policeman said firmly to Stabber, "hands on your head and come with me." Despite a crowd now gathering to see, the policeman directed him to a side wall. As much as Alex wanted to hang around and hear what possible story Stabber could come up with, he wanted to get out of there. Again. But he had to be sure – he'd had enough of ducking and diving from Abby's ex-boyfriend. Luckily, he could see the policeman holding up a knife and radioing for help as Stabber lay face down on the floor, hands on head. Alex waited until Stabber turned his head towards him, flipped him the middle finger, and quietly said, "Get out of that one, you son of a bitch."

A few fans came up to ask Alex if he was all right, possibly in the pretence of trying to find out about the second most exciting thing today to happen in the stadium. He fended off the questions and after a minute, everyone's attention went back to the game that was about to resume after its short break. Once again, Alex had the option of staying and experiencing the end of the final, but instead he headed for another set of toilets.

He'd had enough of causing scenes, so this time he waited patiently for a cubicle to become free. For the first time, he had some time to think about how he'd got here. His assumption was that somehow the TENS machine had interfered with the controller and set off a jump to here. Once he was on his own, he would check this, as he assumed that he might get some strange looks if he pulled out of his jeans a futuristic-looking game controller and a contraption for helping women in labour. Quite why he had been so much more dizzy when he arrived this time, he wasn't sure. Thankfully, the wait wasn't long, given the urgency of everyone to get back to the match. Guess that was the thing about the Golden Goal rule, Alex thought – the match could be over in seconds.

A faint whistle and a large cheer could be heard outside as extra time kicked off.

Once inside the toilet, Alex tried to calm himself, knowing that he would be reappearing in a lift that would be hurtling him back to the ward in seconds. He took out the TENS machine, noticing the damaged wires that had most likely been the culprit. He also checked the controller. The damaged section that had exposed the electronics underneath didn't appear to have got any worse. Everything seemed normal until he noticed that the display was blank.

"No!" he said, gently shaking it and hoping that it came back to life. Nothing.

Was the counter display broken? He couldn't remember the figure he last saw, but he guessed they'd done less than forty jumps. He breathed deeply and pressed the buttons to make a jump ... but nothing happened.

"You got to be flipping joking!" he shouted.

"What?" someone shouted in a nearby cubicle. "They haven't scored, have they?"

Alex ignored him. There was no other sign of life on the controller, so his only hope was that it had simply run out of battery at this unfortunate time. He slumped his head against the door. Until he could get back to the flat and recharge the controller, he was stuck with no other choice than to watch the biggest football game in his life.

"What did I miss?" Alex sat down next to Pravi as England took a throw-in halfway in their own half.

"Not much, all a bit cagey since they resumed," Pravi replied. He turned to face Alex. "You took your time. Everything OK?"

"Yeah, course. Everything's perfect, no problem. Long queue for the toilets, that's all."

A murmur in the crowd snapped their attention back to the field. Platt sent a long, fast ball up to Shearer who controlled it expertly. People around them clapped as he shielded it from a defender and then flicked it off to Fowler, who then fizzed a low ball in. Sheringham was running in and stretched out a leg.

"Go on!" Pravi shouted.

Sheringham connected and diverted it upwards towards the goal and away from the keeper. Half of Wembley leapt up. The ball continued its high trajectory, missing the top of the bar by inches and bouncing harmlessly behind.

"Nooooo! That was it!" Pravi yelled.

Abby had her hand over her mouth, as if in shock.

Alex said nothing.

"Teddy could've won it for us right there!" Pravi said, looking at Alex who was straight-faced.

"Still plenty of time for us to do it," Abby said, sitting back down.

For the rest of the first period in extra time, Alex sat still, not even bothering applauding when a shot from Vladimír Šmicer, who had come on for Poborský at full time, was palmed away by Seaman. When the referee blew to end the first fifteen minutes, at least five players collapsed to the ground and got treatment for cramp. Alex sat back and closed his eyes.

"Looks like it might take a while for changeover, so I'm going to the loo," announced Abby. She gently patted Pravi on the shoulder and sped off.

"Tell me what happened and tell me quick," Pravi said to Alex, moving closer.

"What? Nothing happened." Alex replied, pretending to be interested in the physio techniques on the pitch.

"You jumped. I can tell. Don't even begin to deny it."

Alex faced his friend, but paused.

"What happened? Did you see Stabber again? Have you seen Helen?"

Alex looked towards the exit to check Abby hadn't come back and lowered his voice. "Nothing happened … aside from discovering a series of missed texts to say Hells was in labour, pretending I had diarrhoea, fighting with Stabber, sending him back here, jumping back to see her in hospital, accidentally returning here again, another fight with Stabber, getting him arrested and finding the battery is dead which has stranded me here."

Pravi stared at him, open-mouthed. "Seriously?"

"Yep."

"Whilst I'd love to hear the full story, we need to get you back to Helen. Otherwise you won't be able to fully appreciate all this." Pravi moved his chair. "Come with me."

Alex started to protest but eventually followed Pravi out towards the concourse again.

"Push me to the disabled loos," Pravi said, pointing.

They zipped into the toilet, which was larger than a normal one.

"This isn't going to get me back, and now we're going to miss the game," Alex said.

Pravi fiddled around with the underside of an arm on his wheelchair. "Shut up and use this." He shoved a black object towards Alex.

Alex took it and spun it in his hand. "Is this …?"

"Yep – a battery pack," Pravi said. "Supposed to give you an extra twenty hours."

"You little beauty!" Alex let out a small laugh. "You carried this with you?"

"Of course. A good time traveller needs to be prepared when in the past, just in case."

"And the security check here wasn't suspicious?"

"Nah. Even if they did see it, I taped it up and made it look part of the chair."

Alex struggled to work out how it plugged into the controller.

"Here, let me," Pravi said, taking it and snapping into the micro-USB port on the back of the controller. "Got it from China a few weeks back. Seems to work. The pad should take power from that, so hopefully it'll be fine for jumps." The light came on and he was about to chuck it back to Alex when he noticed something and said, "Uh oh."

"What? Isn't it working?" Alex said.

"It seems to be on, but that's not the problem," Pravi said. "Look." He held it up so Alex could see the count that displayed the number of jumps they had left.

"You're kidding me?" Alex said.

"That's what it says."

"Three? We only have three jumps left? That can't be right."

Pravi shook it a few times. "Last time I saw it, it was sixty something. What have you been doing since then?"

"I told you," Alex said. "I went back and forth a few times but definitely not—" He stopped to think. "Wait a minute, no, surely not …"

Outside, they heard another whistle and the roar of the crowd.

"What?" Pravi said. "We've kicked off again so talk!"

"Helen had this electronic impulse device and the wires

must have touched the insides of the controller, sending me back here without me pressing any buttons, but the weird thing was the jump was super intense and I felt very sick afterwards. Almost as if—"

"You'd gone back and forth several times in succession?"

"Yeah, possibly."

"Perhaps around sixty times in rapid succession?" Pravi asked.

Alex yanked at his hair. "Christ, now what? Three? That's next to nothing."

"Hmm, let me think," Pravi said. "OK, it's simple then – we only need three. You go back now, the baby is born, you jump back sometime later, finish the final with me and we both go home."

Alex chuckled. "You've distilled the most momentous moments of my life into one sentence." He took the controller and hugged his friend before backing away. "See you in a second – I'm about to become a dad."

Painful Challenge

Saturday, 28th January 2017

Alex wasn't sure if Helen was screaming in pain or calling a horde of demons from the underworld. Whichever she was doing in the delivery room as she writhed about on the bed, it was clear that the gas and air pain relief was having as much effect as if Alex had been stroking her arm with a feather.

"Do you want some Lucozade? It'll keep your strength up," Alex said, waving an orange bottle near her.

"What I want," Helen replied, grabbing his arm, "is for your son to come out now and stop tearing up my uterus!"

Alex put the bottle back in Helen's bag on the floor, making sure it was kept away from the controller that he'd stashed there after jumping back to the hospital. He looked to the midwife for help.

"Toby – any sign?"

The tall, skinny midwife pushed his glasses backwards on his nose and squatted down to check the progress, hands on his knees in front of Helen, like Peter Crouch about to commence a sumo contest.

"I'm sorry Helen, but there's still some way to go," Toby said. "You're doing very well, though. Did you want to consider further pain relief?"

Alex straightened up and said, "No thanks we—"

"Yes!" Helen shouted, gripping the bed sides, matted hair draped across her face. "We would very much like further pain relief!"

"Hang on, Hells, I thought—"

"I've changed my mind!" She was heading into full-on banshee mode.

Alex swallowed. "But earlier you said that I could happily go against—"

"I don't care what I bloody well said earlier!" she said with a volume close to ten, grabbing his arm. "Earlier was when my entire lower half of my body didn't feel on fire! Get. Me. An. Epidural."

Alex was desperately trying to weigh up the options before her grip on his arm led to some permanent scarring. The easiest choice would be to give in, get the paperwork sorted, get her the relief she yearned for and needed, and for them both to have an easier rest of the birth for a few hours. For some reason, the evaluative part of his brain presented his mouth with the alternative.

"No, Helen," Alex said, clasping his own hand on hers and trying to prise the vice from his arm, "you don't want this. I'm overriding you."

Toby let out a little cough, turned away, and proceeded to check his notes.

Alex's heart was racing. He tensed his whole body, vision blurring on the edges as he held his stare into her desperate eyes, waiting for her response.

Chest heaving, crimson cheeks puffed out, Helen leaned over and moved her face to within an inch of Alex's. "Give me an epidural," she whispered calmly, "or when I get home, I will destroy every damn football thing that you've ever owned."

She's bluffing, thought Alex.

"Your special 1982 England Subbuteo team?" She squeezed his arm even tighter. "Crushed."

Surely she wouldn't?

"England 1982 home shirt? Slashed to ribbons."

It's a big risk …

"That signed Spurs championship-winning photo you paid a grand for that you think I don't know about?"

Alex gasped.

"Ripped to pieces!"

She was now full-on, demon-possessed Sigourney Weaver in *Ghostbusters*.

Alex turned to Toby, who was opening a folder and pulling out a form and two pens. "Would you like to sign the consent form with a black pen or a blue one?"

12:00 a.m.

After being told she wasn't far enough gone to push yet, for the last ten minutes Helen had been making everyone's life a misery during contractions and had violated her no swearing rule on at least twenty occasions.

Alex was slumped in the chair, fingernail marks on his arm, a crushed hand and battle defeated. The anaesthetist and the midwife were discussing the epidural while Helen rode the next wave, chugging down on gas and air.

"What's taking you guys so bloody long?" she shouted at them. "I've signed the forms so give me the good stuff!"

"We're almost ready, Helen," said the anaesthetist, a slender woman with a French accent. "But we need to check you to see if it's still OK."

Toby examined Helen, staring intently. Alex resisted an urge to join him to see what was happening. From the midwife's face, something wasn't what he'd been expecting.

"Is everything all right?" Alex asked.

Toby glanced at the anaesthetist, then Alex, before addressing Helen directly. "Helen, you're doing great, just great. But … a little too great, unfortunately."

Somewhere under the mop of hair over her face, Helen frowned. "What do you mean?"

"The baby is progressing and you're now in the next stage of labour. Which means, I'm afraid, that it's too late to give you an epidural."

"What. The. F—"

"Are you sure?" Alex said, interrupting Helen.

"Yes, I'm sorry," Toby said. He then gave a big, toothy smile. "But the super-duper good news is that you can now push!"

12:05 a.m.

The anaesthetist had scurried out of the room, having now been made surplus to requirements, no doubt glad not to be subjected to any further outbursts emanating from Helen. It was as if she was making up for half a lifetime of bottling it up. For the start of pushing, there were no words, just primeval screams that Alex had never thought he'd heard in any David Attenborough documentary, let alone from his girlfriend.

"Good, good, Helen," Toby said, checking the progress like he was checking a cake in the oven. "It's still going to take a while, but push when you feel you can."

"You're doing fantastic, baby," Alex said, stroking her sweaty arm. "Anything I can do?"

She shuffled up the bed, panting. "More gas. More drink."

He helped her take in some more gas and she sank back on to her pillows once more.

She knocked back another half bottle of drink and gave it back to him. Alex couldn't remember how many hours he'd been awake, having already had a long day in 1996 before jumping to the hospital, so finished the bottle off.

"Why do you need Lucozade Sport?" Helen spat. "Going out for a marathon?"

"I'm sure we have other bottles, don't worry. Relax." As soon as he said that last word, he realised it was a monumental mistake.

"Did you just say relax?"

"I meant—"

"Do you think I can shitting well relax while trying to squeeze out a baby for hours on end?"

"Actually, Helen," Toby said, "if you can try to relax after each push, that might help."

"Whose side are you on?" she retorted.

"There are no sides, Helen. I only want what's best for you, Alex and the baby."

12:30 a.m.

As much as she'd hate to admit it, Helen was calming down between pushes. However, that was probably more down to the gas and air she was regularly inhaling. When she wasn't pushing and sounding like she was summoning Beelzebub from the depths of hell, she seemed to be spaced out.

Toby was crouched down, performing another inspection. "Good news – we're not too far away now."

"Really?" Alex said, wiping Helen's head with a cold compress.

"Yes. I might be wrong, but if Helen keeps pushing like this, then your son won't be too far away."

"Wow." Alex sat back and tried to imagine what might be about to happen. It was definitely getting real now. "See? You're doing great, babes." Alex leaned over and gave Helen a kiss on her head, dropping the compress onto her chest. "Do you need anything?"

"Drink."

Alex bent down to rummage in the large bag that was by the bed. Helen, being the organised one, had packed a bag even in advance of the early birth. There were several pockets, each containing various items of clothes, snacks, baby stuff – but no more drink.

"Sorry Hells, but looks like we are out." He stood up. "I'll go get something."

"No, stay," she said, flopping an arm over the side of the bed. "Pass the bag up."

"I've checked and I can't find any drink."

"Bag!"

Alex held up the bag for her and allowed her to feel inside.

"What's this?" Helen took out the controller and held it up like she'd pulled out a dog turd.

"Er, I must've accidentally dropped it in there." He reached to take it, but she moved it away out of his reach.

"You brought this here with you?"

"No ... well, yes but—"

"Hoping to sneak out and play a game whilst I was in labour? Bloody typical!"

"What? No! How would that even work? It's just a controller."

Toby stood up. "Can we concentrate on the pushing, please?"

"When this," Helen pointed to her crotch, "baby comes out, you'll be too busy for this," she waved the controller. "So you might as well say goodbye to it, Alex."

With that, she drew back her arm and went to throw it across the room. Alex stuck out a hand and blocked the throw, before yanking his arm backwards and up away from Helen ... and succeeding in smashing Toby in the face. His glasses clattered to the floor.

"Sorry!" Alex blurted out as Toby stumbled, sweeping the floor with his hands.

"No worries," Toby said. "I've lost count of the number of times I've been smashed in the face with a game controller in the middle of labour." He put his glasses back on and glared at Alex through cracked lenses. "So, that's not ideal. I'll have to get my spare pair." He marched off and called back to Helen, "I'll be thirty seconds – don't go anywhere!"

As soon as he left, Helen shouted at Alex, "You bloody idiot!" She grabbed the controller again, but this time Alex didn't let go.

"You don't understand!" Alex said, trying to wrestle it back from her. "Let go!"

"Give it up!" Helen spat, now with two hands on it and sitting up.

The controller was yanked back and forth between them, Alex desperately trying to claim it back to prevent any damage from occurring.

Helen screamed and said, "You stupid, childish—"

And then they were gone.

Game Over

Sunday, 30th June 1996

Alex immediately knew he had jumped back to 1996. In a second, when his senses returned, he knew he'd be facing Pravi once again in a disabled toilet in Wembley Stadium and that he had to return that instant. What he didn't initially realise was that he hadn't come back alone.

"Alex! Alex!" Pravi's voice burst into Alex's ears. "What the hell is going on? Why is she here?"

When Alex's sight recovered, he could see a very worried Pravi staring behind Alex. "What? Who?" He looked round and almost had a heart attack. There, lying on the floor of the toilet, was Helen.

"This is bad, Prav, real bad." Alex squatted next to Helen. "It was an accident. We've got to get back!"

Perhaps due to all the gas and air in her system, combined with the fact that she had just made her debut time travel, Helen was barely conscious. Her head had flopped to one side and she was murmuring.

Alex snatched the controller up from the floor, checking the battery pack was still in place.

"Wait!" Pravi said, grabbing Alex's wrist. "Look how many jumps we have left now."

A red "1" appeared in the display.

"So ... you mean I can't come back here?" Alex said.

"And unless I come with you, I can't get home."

They stared at each other, both desperately trying to think of a solution. Helen was still groaning behind them.

"You can't have the baby here," Pravi said.

"I know!"

"Nor can you leave her here and finish watching the match."

Alex shut his eyes tight and cursed the predicament. "I'm sorry, so sorry, Prav. I've messed it up for both of us."

"W-what's happening?" They spun round to see Helen reaching her hands out in front of her face.

"We'd better go," Alex said. "I'll make sure you, me and Helen all have a hand on the controller so we all get back safely."

He crouched back down next to Helen. "It's OK, baby, it was a ... power surge or something. Nothing to worry about. Hold this for a sec." He made sure both he and Helen were holding the controller before beckoning Pravi.

But Pravi didn't come.

Alex waved with more urgency, trying to ensure there wasn't a chance Helen would see or hear Pravi.

Pravi shook his head.

"What are you doing?" he whispered to Pravi.

"I'm staying," Pravi said.

Alex frowned. "I don't understand. You can't stay. We've only one jump, remember?"

"I know. You take it. Leave me here."

"What?" Alex steadied himself. "But ... how will you get back?"

"I won't." Pravi glanced at the door. "I'm staying."

"Who's that?" Helen said behind Alex. "What's going on? Where's my bed?"

Alex could see Helen was about to regain her sight, so he found the cold compress and placed it on her eyes. "Er, temporary switchover of beds, that's all. And Pravi stuck his head round the door to say hi."

"Prav, you can't stay here," Alex said. "Where's your brain?"

"I have my survival kit," Pravi said. "I'll work something out."

"Tell him he's not allowed in here," Helen said.

Ignoring her, Alex whispered, "Just grab the controller."

"I'm sorry, Alex," Pravi said solemnly. "If I can never come back here again, then I'd rather take my chances here, now."

"But you're not meant to be here!" Alex said.

"That's what I—" Helen started, before groaning in pain again. "More gas!"

Alex spun round to Helen and then back at Pravi. "Jesus, Prav. If we go without you ... I'll never see you again, will I?"

Pravi looked at his feet. "I know. That sucks and all, but

after everything we've done here, I want to stay to see this." He gestured to the door, which filtered through some of the crowd noise outside. "And me and Abby ... you never know."

"You're giving up your entire home life solely for the chance of a girl and seeing England lift a trophy?"

Pravi sighed. "For once, I don't want to think 'what if?'."

Alex stared at Pravi, before turning to see Helen beginning another push. His future was there.

"Are you sure?"

"No." Pravi smiled. "But it means I'll remain the King of *FIFA* forever."

Helen started screaming.

"You mother ... fudger. Look, I have to go before she pops." He gave Pravi the biggest of bear hugs, slapping him on the back until his palms hurt.

"You've got some balls," Alex shouted over Helen.

"Good luck with fatherhood."

"Cheers." They moved apart and Alex added, "I'm gonna miss you, mate."

"Twat."

"Don't mess it up with Abby. She's OK, even if she thinks I'm an arse."

"You are an arse."

"An arse who's outta here." Not knowing the protocol in this situation, he saluted Pravi. "Been a pleasure knowing you."

"Pleasure was all yours," Pravi said, saluting back.

With a screaming, confused girlfriend, Alex made sure they both had a tight grip on the controller before activating the final jump back to the hospital, leaving Pravi alone in a Wembley toilet cubicle with ten minutes left of Euro 1996.

Coming Home

```
3 months later
```

Legs up. Bum wiped. Old nappy in sack. New nappy installed. Spurs sleepsuit on. Job done.

Alex held up his son in his hands so that their eyes were level. "Superb defence skills there. Demonstrating lightning speed and agility, he cleaned up at the back and gave the attack no chance to strike again. What a performance!"

With Arthur now dozing in his arms and Helen at work, he felt it was safe to turn on the TV and mute the sound. It was only his first week of shared parental leave, but so far he had watched seven *Marvel* films, got a photo of him and Arthur outside White Hart Lane and had successfully trained him to vomit over Helen's mum twice. Unfortunately, another earlier victim of his vomit had been Alex's PlayStation, which had refused to work since. Alex did have an alternative though, which had sat unused under his TV for the past week. Alex looked at Pravi's console, which he had collected from the empty flat.

"We had some good times on that thing," Alex said to Arthur, looking down on him.

"One day I'll tell you all about Pravi. Of course, you'll only get to hear the official version, the one where he had to go into hiding with his Russian internet girlfriend, running from the mob, never to be seen again."

He stroked Arthur's hair. "I know, it was all I could come up with. I think he'd like it. Seemed too risky to fake his death."

Without disturbing the baby, Alex turned on the console with his foot.

"Perhaps one day I'll tell you the whole story. I'm sure you won't believe me, though. Sometimes even I don't believe it."

The console burst into life.

"Almost had to tell your mummy, but luckily the effect of the hospital drugs covered it up. If she had found out that I was close to stranding us all in 1996 … well, let's just say I wouldn't be fathering any siblings for you."

He picked up a controller and accessed a few menus to see what was on the machine. It was a standard controller that had come with the console with no modifications. Alex had locked away the special one, content to never see it again. Sure, there had been times when he'd thought about seeing if there was any way he could jump back. Perhaps the counter would reset and activate again one day, maybe allowing one last leap to watch the final, but would he risk leaving what he had here? From the second Arthur had been passed to him and he'd laid him on his chest, he knew where his priorities were.

Alex noticed there was an unread message for Pravi and clicked on it. He could see it was from the Kickstarter guy they'd originally got the game and controller from, in what seemed now to be another lifetime. Alex opened the message.

Congratulations on winning Euro 96 with England

He was about to close it, thinking it was just a copy of their original message telling them about activating the retro controller, when he noticed the rest of the text underneath.

Please access the special edition, Euro 96: Extra Time, by downloading at the link below

"That's weird," Alex said to Arthur, who kept his eyes shut and yawned. "Maybe he's got a new version. Let's have a look." Alex clicked the link, and once it had downloaded from the online store, started the game.

At first, all he could see was a black screen, so he turned up the volume one notch, keeping an eye on Arthur. There was a crowd singing. A little more volume confirmed it was a repeating chorus of "Three Lions". Then there was footage of Shearer scoring against Switzerland in their first match, running away with his arm raised in celebration. This was followed by his strike against Scotland, then Seaman's penalty save in the same match before a slow motion of Gascoigne flicking the ball over Colin Hendry and stroking it in. "Pure genius."

On to the Holland match, where Alex nearly woke Arthur up just so he could witness the sheer glory of England's victory. What a night that had been, he thought, reminiscing about the time with Jack.

The England show continued. A close-up of Spain hitting the post. Zooming in to see Pearce's primal scream. The elation of Seaman with his last penalty save.

The song faded out and the commentary from the Germany game kicked in.

"We were there!" Alex whispered. "Well, only outside the stadium and not this actual match that you're going to see. It's kind of complicated."

The camera panned over a proud Adams singing the national anthem, the Shearer goal that had Alex and Pravi dreaming all those years ago, before Kuntz celebrating his equaliser. There were multiple views of Anderton hitting the post, and close-ups of disbelieving fans.

"If you think that was close, bubba, wait until you see the next one."

As Sheringham laid it on to Shearer, Alex gently angled Arthur to the screen, even if he still had his eyes shut.

Shearer crossed.

Gascoigne started his run.

He stretched out his leg.

He was going to be so, so close ...

And he scored.

Alex held Arthur tightly and leaned forward on the sofa. "Hang on ... this isn't right."

While he and Pravi had seen the footage and had replayed it countless times, that had all been in 1996. As Gascoigne and the rest of the England team were jumping around on the pitch, Alex snatched his phone out of his pocket. With his heart beating, he realised he was still in 2017. This was still the present. Alex had checked the history after he'd jumped back for the last time and nothing had changed here. Which could only mean one thing ... this match was the one from the other timeline.

The screen went dark again.

A rhythmic heartbeat boomed out of the speakers, at about a third of the speed of Alex's heart right now.

The silver European Championship trophy appeared on the screen, reflecting the sky above. Two huge flags split the screen in two – England and the Czech Republic.

"This is our final," he whispered.

There was no explanation as to how it was possible that he was watching the alternative past, but there was no doubt that what he was seeing didn't happen in this timeline. Close ups of England players faded in and out with each beat, before the same with the Czech players. Alex moved closer to inspect the TV. These were real images he realised, not computer graphics.

The camera swept around the stadium, flashing past supporters with painted faces, flags, and multi-coloured costumes. A sharp blow of the referee's whistle, then rock music. Tackles flying in. The Czechs scoring, Shearer's penalty miss and then Platt's rebound for the equaliser.

"Bubba, we were here! This is our game! Me and Prav – we were at this game. We made this happen."

Another slow motion of Berger's rocket shot and then the agony of Southgate's looping own goal to make it 3-1 to the Czechs.

"Don't worry, son, we come back. I know we do."

Shearer pulled one back. The Sheringham header that was tipped round the post before the Platt corner.

"Get up there, Big Tone!" Alex said loudly, waking Arthur, still in his arms. The pair of them watching as the ball was crossed in and met with a thundering Adams header, replayed from multiple angles.

And then a realisation struck Alex that caused him to stop breathing. One simple fact: this was the only Euro 96 match that he didn't know the ending of.

Alex moved closer to the screen as he watched the first half of extra time that he'd witnessed in the stadium.

And then it continued.

There was no pause at the moment Alex would have jumped out. There was no frozen time Alex could jump back to even if he knew how. The game … Pravi … life continued to roll on.

Alex and Arthur's eyes were wide open as Nedvěd strolled forward and shot. Alex held his breath as the shot rebounded off the inside of the post and safely away. The music was building to a climax, guitar riffs getting faster.

Gascoigne played it to Sheringham, who knocked it on to Shearer.

Shearer turned and made space for himself, before shooting.

An outstretched leg of a Czech player deflected it clear, but only back to Gascoigne, who calmly collected it.

He went past one player.

Dropped a shoulder.

Past a second.

Lined up a shot.

It was heading towards the goal.

Alex and Arthur had their mouths wide open.

The speakers went silent.

The camera panned to behind the goal.

And with a crescendo of guitar, drum and screaming vocals, the ball hit the net.

Alex cradled his son and leapt to his feet. "Yeeeeesssss! Yesssss! We did it! We won! We won Euro 96! Get in!"

Through blurry eyes, they watched the England players celebrate, Pearce screaming at the crowd, Terry Venables sporting a grin bigger than the Wembley arch that was to come. Tony Adams lifting the trophy, as proud as any Englishman in thirty years.

Alex danced round the room, still holding a bemused Arthur. As they turned back to the screen, the camera swept through the crowd, showing the joyous England fans who'd finally witnessed football coming home.

And celebrating in front of one fan encased in a huge England flag, shown for less than half a second, was a man in a wheelchair being kissed passionately by a woman.

"You beauty!"

Acknowledgements

This book has been a long time coming, proving the "difficult second book" syndrome. A lot of people have helped me along the way …

A huge thanks to the ever-helpful Peter Finney for not only being a beta reader, but for all the football knowledge and advice shared over several plot discussions throughout the story's journey. This book would be in a much worse state without you.

Chris Smeeton is not only a fellow Parkrunner who I can swap back injury advice with, but someone whose enthusiasm for the book kept me going through the times of self-doubt.

Steve Pocock – always there on the other side of the Atlantic to encourage and keep me positive. You helped validate my initial ideas and get the story started. We lived through the pain of Euro 96, Italia 90 and many fruitless England adventures. Hope you enjoy reliving the Scotland match.

Massive credit goes to my cousin and supremely talented designer Claire Yeo for the book cover.

My editor, Lizzy Duffield-Fuller, who gave me plenty to think about, as well as hundreds of hyphens to fix.

Iain King and David Green – two work colleagues who provided such great feedback late on in the process. Thanks also to Iain's friend, John Mower, for his valuable comments.

Thom Sutcliffe for culinary advice, Claire Doherty for PlayStation guidance.

Rachel Martin and Gary Parker, who sent me their memories of Euro 96 matches they attended.

Pete Haine for putting me in touch with Rachel and Gary, sending me some used Euro 96 tickets and for general encouragement. I hope they show the Spurs games wherever you are.

Jamie Jones for feedback on my initial synopsis all those years ago which helped get me going on the story.

Alex Muscella and Greg Rose for offering to read early versions.

Last and certainly by no means least, enormous thanks go to my family. Michelle – thanks for putting up with me writing this for so many years. I know football isn't your thing, but you supported me throughout, even when I disappeared every night to edit it.

Amber – I'm sorry this book took almost as long to write as you've been alive, and that it delayed your "Pinky Bear" picture book. I promise – pinky promise – that I will get that out, too!

About the Author

Andrew Males lives in Stevenage, south-east England, with his wife who tolerates his football mood swings, his daughter who loves his bedtime adventure stories, and a cat who would happily traverse forward in the space-time continuum if it meant he would get to his next meal quicker.

England's agonising defeat in Euro 96 devastated him for many years after. He hopes that having written this book, he can finally watch the Gazza chance and not scream out in pain.

Extra Time is Andrew's second novel, having published *26 Miles to the Moon* in 2015.

X (Twitter): @andrewdmales
www.andrewmales.com

10 HOPEFULS. 26 MILES. 1 TARGET: THE MOON.
THE GREAT SPACE RACE IS ON!

26 MILES TO THE MOON

ANDREW MALES

From London to the New York City Marathon, Jon and nine other going-nowheres risk everything to compete for the most exciting prize the world has ever seen.

THE GREAT SPACE RACE IS ON!